W9-ABD-150

Early Praise for *Tita*

"Marie Houzelle is a master of the first-person narrative. In Tita she has created a strange, utterly original child whose deadpan certainties are a beguiling invitation to readers of all ages. Like Louise Fitzhugh's classic *Harriet the Spy,* the story is powered by a precocious and independent loner whose observations and reports are both charming and moving. *Tita* is a remarkable debut."
 - **Katharine Weber, author of *Triangle and True Confections***

"Like opening the door to a secret garden, Tita transports the reader straight into life in a small town in southern France during the 1950s, as seen through the eyes of a precocious seven-year-old heroine not soon to be forgotten. Houzelle's prose is unfailingly deft and refreshing. This book is a delight!"
 - **Anne Korkeakivi, author of *An Unexpected Guest***

"The best book I read this year. Witty, wry, and clever, Tita's young voice captivated me from the first page. *Tita* poignantly portrays small-town life as well as the end of the Catholic church's grip on France, revealing cracks in society that a decade later become the riots of 1968. A rare novel written in English that gives a real taste of French culture. I cannot recommend it enough!"
 - **Janet Skeslien Charles, author of *Moonlight in Odessa***

"This book has a charm so unique and powerful, it pulls you in simply, effortlessly, like following a tree-lined path on a summery day. The language is utterly original and quietly moving and very very funny and it makes you want to follow Tita onward past the last pages and into the years beyond. I loved it."
- **Nicola Keegan, author of *Swimming***

"We're laughing, but we're also intrigued by this child whose understanding can be razor sharp or dense as a thicket. Where will this odd combination take her? (...) There's nothing simplistic about this novel. Tita is not an exercise in blind nostalgia for a lost past. It is a rich and warm, yet open-eyed portrait of a place and time just beyond our current reach. It's a book worth savoring."
- **Judith Starkston, *New York Journal of Books***

"Tita is precocious and clever, but in some ways painfully inept. She is thoughtful but frail—obsessed with rules and rituals, and determined to understand the nuances. Through Houzelle's sharp, straightforward prose (which captures Tita's perspective), the story of how Tita grows takes center stage. (...) At the novel's end, Tita is still a little girl, but her brilliance, potential, and unusual way of looking at the world will have won readers over."
- ***Publishers Weekly***

TITA

by

Marie Houzelle

Summertime Publications

TITA

American paperback edition first published
by Summertime Publications Inc (USA) in 2014

copyright © Marie Houzelle 2014
Summertime Publications

cover design by Joëlle Jolivet

This book is a work of fiction, and any resemblance to persons
living or dead is purely coincidental.

Library of Congress Cataloging-in-Publication Data
Houzelle, Marie
Tita / Marie Houzelle 1st edition
Library of Congress Control Number: 2013944782

Summertime Publications Inc.
7502 E. Berridge Lane, Scottsdale, AZ 85250
All Rights Reserved
ISBN 9781940333014

For Olga Zilberbourg

Table of Contents

Stick

I'd like to be a nun. Or a saint. In the classroom today, after we finish reading the mass like every morning, fast, one paragraph each, round and round, in Latin, mademoiselle Pélican asks, "Do any of you feel called to the consecrated life? Put up your hands!" My hand is the only one, and she looks at me with blatant misgiving. Although I'm keen on everything religious, know all my prayers perfectly, and go to mass on weekdays as often as Mother lets me, Pélican doesn't seem to like the idea of me as a nun. Because I'm not meek enough, I guess. Because I don't leave her alone, don't accept everything that comes out of her mouth as the absolute truth. Who says she's got the absolute truth?

The *Pope* is infallible, okay. Only in religious matters, though, I forced her to make that clear. She tried to equivocate, but my brother Etienne had read up on this. She had to admit it in the end: if Pius XII himself told me I'd made a spelling mistake and I had the Robert, my favorite dictionary, on my side, Robert would win. The Pope can decide that the Assumption of the Virgin Mary will be dogma, but he is not infallible as far as spelling is concerned.

Neither is mademoiselle Pélican. When she made an obvious mistake correcting one of my dictations, she refused to admit it. Making a mistake is human, but persevering is despicable. She asseverated (my sister Justine will like this word) that I should never question her corrections. Gave me three hundred lines for insolence. *Insolence* comes from a Latin word that means "unusual". I looked it up in the Robert, which always starts with a word's etymology — the most interesting part.

Now Group One — the youngest girls — is set to copy a paragraph about saint Agatha, a virgin martyr whose breasts were cut off before she was rolled naked on a bed of live coals; Group Three gets a math problem; and we, Group Two, are given a chapter in our history books to read and summarize: Joan of Arc's early life and vocation. Nothing new there. Downstairs in the nursery class we learned all about Joan of Arc and her Voices.

Break. I sit on a bench and watch the others buying and selling various kinds of candy. They use holy pictures for money. I have a pocketful of holy pictures, but no interest in candy. Maryvonne, at the other end of the bench, her back pressed against the wall, is looking at her feet.

"What's wrong?" I ask. She has two younger brothers who often catch colds and flu. Her mother is a widow, and works as a waitress at the Café du Stade. Sometimes Maryvonne stays home when one of the boys is really ill, sometimes she comes to school and worries. Now she's biting her lower lip. She turns just a bit, to let me see her back. There's a sign hanging from her neck saying, in bold capitals, "Ignoramus".

"What's that?" I ask.

Maryvonne raises her chin towards mademoiselle Pélican's house, at the other end of the yard from the school building.

"Do you mean Pélican made you wear this?"

She nods.

"What a beast!"

My friend Eléonore's mother told me that when she was in school, the kids who spoke Occitan were made to wear dunce caps and signs. But I'd never seen any of these.

Maryvonne laughs. A few tears come out of her eyes at the same time. "That's because I made eleven spelling mistakes. But I don't care," she says, vaguely wiping her tears with inky fingers; "I'll be out of here in less than three months, as soon as I turn fourteen on June twenty-eighth. My God, I can't wait!"

Anne-Claude runs out of Pélican's house, her black ponytail half undone, and yells: "Tita, your turn!" My turn to join Sister Germaine.

"May Pélican roast in hell!" I say to Maryvonne.

"And Sister Germaine too!" she answers. Which is generous of her, because she doesn't have to put up with Sister Germaine. But she knows. Sister Germaine comes at every break to coach those of us who take piano lessons. And most of us do — most of the paying students. For there are two kinds of students at Sainte-Blandine: the ones whose parents pay, and a few, like Maryvonne, whose families are

11

helped by the parish. The rich (or formerly rich, like us), and the very poor. Nothing in between. I wonder how Pélican makes a living, actually. Upstairs, at the moment, there are only twelve of us; downstairs with madame Riu, about fifteen kids. Everybody else goes to the *école laïque*, the state school.

I enter the musty room filled with dark furniture and heavy drapes, with the smell of beef stew, cabbage soup and homemade yogurt wafting from the kitchen on the other side of the narrow passage, and I start playing my Beethoven sonatina. Every time my finger slips, every time I hit the wrong note or am slightly late or early, Sister Germaine hits my hand with a long stick, the one she also uses to point at the place where she wants me to start again. Down comes the stick on my hands, every other second, and I'm not allowed to stop playing until the bell rings. We're supposed to stay for fifteen minutes, but it feels like hours. I press the keys, I make a mistake, down comes the stick.

Back in class, Group Three is called to the blackboard, one by one, to correct their math. We're supposed to go over our verbs, but I'd rather listen: a grocer buys ten twelve-kilo sacks of potatoes for a hundred and thirty francs each, then sells them by the kilo. At twelve francs a kilo, what will his profit be? Maryvonne, at the blackboard, doesn't remember that the sacks are twelve kilos, she makes them ten. Pélican sends her back in disgust and calls Elisabeth, who gets it right.

When Pélican gives us back our corrected Joan of Arc summaries, she simpers in my direction and says, "Euphémie is *not* as knowledgeable as she thinks, and this should be a lesson for all of you." She gave me only 9 out of 10 because I wrote, Jeanne was *tout émerveillée* (all amazed), when she recognized the Voices of Saint Catherine and Saint Michel. Pélican added an e at the end of my "tout". I'll have to check, but I'm practically certain she's wrong. *Tout* is an adverb here, so it's invariable except if followed by an adjective that starts with a consonant, as in toute *contente*.

I learned a lot with mademoiselle Pélican at first. Now, not much. I've been in her class for nearly four years. I "went upstairs" when I was not quite four, much earlier than you're supposed to. In my group, the other girls are ten or eleven, and most of us are destined to go to boarding school next October. The ones who don't do well enough will stay in Group Two one more year or, if they're twelve, go into Group Three. Group Three is for the girls who want to leave school when they're fourteen instead of going on to boarding school. They'll help their mothers at home, or they'll work for a while in their parents' store or restaurant. Until they get married. For the rest of us, the choice is between Assomption, twenty kilometers away, and Sainte-Trinité, which is still farther. We'll be shut in all week, only allowed home from Saturday after class to Sunday evening. Not something we're exactly looking forward to.

But Sainte-Blandine isn't much fun either. Mademoiselle Pélican sits behind her desk in a tight blue cardigan, her face pasty, her eyes suspicious behind her gold-rimmed glasses, her sandy wig sporting inflexible coils. I get restless, cooped up in a room all morning, all afternoon, and mostly doing what I already know how to do. I'd like to study Latin. I'm utterly familiar with the Order of Mass and all the Propers in our missal, and I need to read something different. My brothers do Latin and Greek translations; I too want to learn conjugations and declensions. And why not speak Latin, write it?

Father went to a school where they wrote poems and gave speeches in Latin and in Greek. The school was in the Montagne Noire, between here and Toulouse. There were horses, bicycles, boats, and the boys were allowed to roam the forest, row on the lake. They also put on plays, and sometimes Father acted a woman's part, because there were no girls in the school. Even now, it's still a boys' school.

There doesn't seem to be anything of the kind for girls. Justine has been in several boarding schools, and she hated all of them. She's fed up with schools, she'd like to get a job as soon as possible. Legally she could do that: she turned fourteen last January. But I have nearly seven years to wait. Seven.

Misfortunes

Tuesday. *Mardi*, day of Mars, god of war. In a war, I could get killed and then I wouldn't have this calamitous day ahead of me. The sun, behind the maroon curtains, is harsh already. The Paris-Portbou night train has just entered the station across the avenue: it must be ten to eight. I can hear Mother in the bathroom next door, warbling *Rossignol, rossignol de mes amours*. "A king's daughter was locked in a tower and she cried all the time; but a nightingale flew by, bringing her hope."

Every day, three loathsome meals to get through. Chunks of dead animals, eggs out of a hen's belly, milk stolen from a cow's udder for béchamel sauce, rice pudding or flan. I recite in my head La Fontaine's fable "The Wolf and the Dog", which I learned last night. I want to be the wolf, live in the forest, run where I please, and never have to eat, like the dog, "cold pullets, pigeons, savoury messes".

And Mother is going out this evening. Out, like every Tuesday and Friday, with Father. There are cinemas, parties, concerts, here in Cugnac, in Narbonne, Carcassonne, Béziers or Perpignan. All through the day I fret, try to find out where exactly they'll be, how far from here. If it's in town, or at least in a house I know, I'll feel a little better. But they sometimes decide at the last minute. I try to concentrate on Wednesday, one of the two good days when Mother, in the evening, stays

15

at home with us while Father goes to his club; but gloomy, endless Tuesday stretches before me.

Loli, our maid, trips into the room. "Good morning, girls." Her full voice flutters up and down, enthusiastically. Her *r*s are long and rolled, she pronounces every letter, and the last syllable of each word resonates. That's because she grew up in a village, speaking what she calls *patues*, "patois" (my brother Etienne says we'd better use its real name, Occitan). She still speaks it with her family and friends — with me too, when Mother isn't listening. Mother hopes that Dolores (Loli's official name) will learn "better French" by living with us, but I love the way she speaks now. In the still room, I let her sounds slip into my mouth; silently, I try to reproduce her inflections.

Loli opens the curtains, takes clean underwear from a drawer. She's small and bouncy, with curly black hair in a ponytail. Coralie jumps out of bed, kisses her, and gets dressed. She's only five, and she hardly needs any help. Just for her shoelaces, and buttons once in a while. I'm seven but slow, clumsy, likely to put on my sweater back to front, my socks inside out; so Loli helps me dress.

When we're ready, Loli washes our faces with a flannel in our *cabinet de toilette*, takes us across the landing, through the music room and the library, and knocks on our parents' bedroom door. We could have gone directly through the large bathroom that separates our parents' bedroom from ours. Not with Loli, though.

Our parents are sitting in armchairs on each side of a round coffee table. Father looks up from *L'Indépendant* to greet us. Loli gathers their breakfast plates, cups and knives on a tray and takes them away. Mother sits me on a low stool in front of her to untangle my hair and do my plaits. She starts with the brush, slowly, then goes on to the comb. It's torture when she hits a knot, but it doesn't last. She does her best not to hurt me. I keep very still. The two plaits have to be tightly braided, or they'll come undone before the end of the day. She ties them with red ribbons. Red is supposed to be my color. Coralie's ribbons are blue, like her eyes.

Coralie's turn. She ducks, yells, tries to shield her head with her hands. Her hair is finer still than mine, it tangles up more dreadfully. She'd like it short, like Sophie's in the comtesse de Ségur's novels. It's a very light yellow, an unusual color around here. They say she inherited it from Father's mother Clara, a Parisian. Our mother is enormously proud of it.

Downstairs in the kitchen, while Coralie gobbles her bread and butter, her bread and jam, her hot chocolate, Loli takes me in her lap to feed me my porridge. God knows, I'm too old to be spoon-fed, but I can't make myself bring the sticky paste to my mouth. I could eat bread, but bread on its own is not considered sustaining enough. And butter is out of the question, the mere smell of it makes me sick. When I'm angry with Coralie, I call her "Butter Baby" because of the slimy traces on her fingers, around her mouth, in her hair.

Loli shouldn't have to coax me, so I let her get on with it. I try to forget about my body and what it's undergoing. I think of *Les Petites Filles modèles*, where Sophie, because her parents have died, lives with her stepmother, madame Fichini, who pulls her hair and whips her. Sophie is much more like Coralie than like me: she loves to eat, to experiment, and she keeps getting into trouble. She cuts up goldfish and salts them, steals a hunk of bread from the horses, makes herself sick by eating a big jar of *crème fraîche*. When she wants something (candied fruit, a sewing basket), she just takes it.

Coralie can't read yet, so I read the comtesse de Ségur books to her. But what she likes best is when I make up new stories for Sophie, from what's just happened to us and our friends. She's always begging for "stories about little girls good and bad."

As I hurry to school behind Loli, who holds Coralie's hand, I wonder what's wrong with me. Why do I fret so much about the idea of Mother going out? This evening, I'll tell Coralie a story, we'll scratch each other's backs, maybe slip out of our beds to explore some of the attics. I'll forget about Mother and where she might be.

Why do I spend whole days tormenting myself about something that, when it happens, doesn't really bother me that much? And why do I hate most foods? Other children don't. I have every reason to be happy. Nobody beats me or even yells at me. I don't live with madame Fichini. My parents are handsome, elegant, sweet-smelling. They never shout, scowl, whimper, groan, or use bad language. They are so splendid, so perfect, I wonder how other children can bear to have parents who are not them.

Gravel

On Thursday, as Mother serves coffee after lunch, I ask Grandmother, "Does a consecrated host, when it's inside you, actually feel like the body of Jesus?" Grandmother shakes her head. Father raises his eyebrows.

"First communion on April seventh," Mother says.

"Don't they have it when they're around twelve or thirteen?" he asks.

"That's the *solemn* communion," Mother explains. "With the long dress and veil and vows. At Sainte-Blandine they also have a private communion for the seven-year-olds." Her words are a bit blurred, because she's set a sugar lump under her tongue, which every sip of coffee infiltrates and slowly melts into her mouth.

"Two first communions!" Father says. "That doesn't make sense. You'll have to choose, Tita. If you have it now, that'll be it."

"Impossible," Mother says, swallowing the last of her caffeinated sugar. "The solemn communion is the important one. It's absolutely indispensable."

"Then you'll have to do without this one," Father says. "One first communion is trouble enough."

"But all the other girls..." I'm near to crying now. Which won't help with Father. At all.

"You don't have to do what the other girls do," Father says.

"But... I've been so looking forward to it. I can't wait five more years! We've learned all the hymns. Please."

"I don't think so," Father says. Which for him is a pretty definitive statement.

If Mother chose to declare herself on my side she'd probably win, because Father always tries to please her. And this is not crucial for him. It just shocks his sense of logic: two first communions. In the eyes of God, I know the only one that counts is the private one, where you receive communion for the first time and celebrate this event with your family. The solemn one is just a social occasion, but nobody in town can do without it. Not even the communists. It's one of the... stages. For my older sister Justine's I went to the flower shop with Father. The florist said, "Solemn communion, eh? Wedding next time."

You are born, baptized. You have your private communion, your solemn communion. You get married, you have kids, they get baptized, they have their private communion, their solemn communion. Then you die. More flowers.

If I don't make my private communion, my teacher, mademoiselle Pélican, will be outraged. Not to mention the other parents and the *Dames de charité*. Every time I go to mass, I'll stay in the pew with the younger kids while my schoolmates walk to the altar in a procession, with the grown-ups, to receive communion. I'll be a martyr, my father a persecutor. He's already a divorcé, so he's barred from the sacraments.

In fact, most men in Cugnac don't go to church anyway. There's monsieur Lacrose, who owns the electrical store (his tenor voice resonates all over the nave), and monsieur Nourrigat, the undertaker. Those two come to mass every Sunday, but the other men turn up only on special occasions, and seldom bother to receive communion. So in spite of his divorce Father doesn't draw much attention to himself.

But he will, if he doesn't let me make my private communion. I need to act. He's in his tasting room clearing away some bottles. I go and tell him again that it's really important for me, and that it won't cost any money — I already have a white dress from last year.

"What about you?" I ask. "Didn't you have a private communion?"

He's looking out the window, not moving at all. Trying to remember? He was born so long ago, in 1897. The nineteenth century! When he was seven, he was already in boarding school, with Dominican monks.

He shakes his head. "We had only one first communion," he says. Quietly, as if to himself.

"But for us it's different! Please, may I? You don't even need to come to church if you don't want to!"

He sighs, and I can see he's irritated, but not at me exactly: at Sainte-Blandine, Cugnac, the whole world maybe. He opens the glass door and goes into the garden.

I run after him and catch the hem of his jacket from behind. "Please, please." And I don't know where the inspiration comes from, but I actually kneel on the gravel. It hurts, this layer of tiny stones my mother spread all over our garden because she so dislikes dirt and weeds. There I am, kneeling in front of Father, my face bathed in tears (the stones help), embarrassingly like the bad girl in the comtesse de Ségur's *Caprices de Giselle*, who always cries and carries on to make her parents do what she wants. Father takes one tired look at me. "Do what you like," he says, and strides away into the back street.

I run to tell Mother, who's sitting at the kitchen table with a fork in her hand. She holds a petit four, spreads a spoonful of almondy-smelling paste over it, puts it down on a rack and goes on to the next one. "Good," she says. "You were a baby at the time, but I remember your father having to pay for Justine's private communion party at her mother's in Paris. So there's no reason..." She finishes her frosting, washes her hands, takes off her glasses, wipes them with the special beige cloth she keeps in a small box above the sink, puts the glasses back on.

Upstairs she makes me try on my white dress, decides that it won't do, and drives to town to buy organdy for a new one. We'll borrow a crown of tiny flowers from my friend Anne-Claude Espeluque, who made her private communion three years ago.

"Maxime, Etienne and Justine will be here for Easter vacation," Mother says as she marks and cuts the organdy on the dining-room table. "We'll have a party at the Cabarrou, in the sun." My older sister and brothers are not her children, but they're all fond of her and she's proud of being nothing like the classic stepmother. They spend all the school vacations with us, but their mother and their schools are in Paris.

We're careful not to mention any of our preparations in front of Father: we don't want to aggravate him.

Cucumber

Mother isn't at home when we come back from school. Where is she? Father doesn't know. When will she be back? Grandmother shrugs. Coralie couldn't care less; she's just wolfed down her third hunk of *gros pain* and, with her mouth full, is asking for another chocolate bar. Mother is shopping in Narbonne, or having tea with friends. She'll be back for dinner. No need to worry. I don't worry, I'd just like to *know*.

Our friends join us, our neighbors. Eléonore's house is just across the back street, Roseline's father runs the garage next to the railway station, Monique and her little sister Nicole live at the top of the townhouse around the corner on the avenue. We play together every evening after school. Not the same school. They all go to the state school (*école laïque),* whereas we go to what's called the free school (*école libre)*, which is a joke because at the state school the students are about twenty times freer than we are at our private "free" school. Father explained that our Catholic school is *free* insofar as it doesn't have to follow the national curricula and schedules. But our teacher is also free, every time we forget a book or open our mouths, to make us write a hundred lines for the next day. A kind of punishment they haven't even heard of at the other school.

Eléonore has brought a collection of old tutus, two pink, one white, one yellow, and our friends slip into them while Coralie pulls on a leotard and I look at my play. "Let's work on Act II, Scene 2," I say.

Coralie cries, "Yay! That's where I fight with the ghost! Let me get my sword!"

Roseline is moaning, "This is too tight for me! What shall I do?"

"You don't need a tutu, you're the baker's daughter," I say. Actually, nobody needs a tutu, but Eléonore brings them, and they're happy to wear them. "Let's find you a dress in the trunk," I say. That's where we keep the treasures we bring back from our explorations into the attics. One of them has mostly magazines, papers and broken filing cabinets, but the other two are full of sideboards, chests of drawers, wardrobes, with inexhaustible stores of clothes, fabrics and knickknacks. "Do you like this one, with the purple flowers?"

But I hear the front door shutting. Could it be Mother? I have to go and see. No, it's Loli, coming back from the corner grocery with lemons and bananas in her basket.

In the playroom (which we call "the pantry" because that's what it used to be) my friends are all in costume now. Monique, who is tall and thin, plays the ghost, in a white tutu, with a white sheet over her head. Little Nicole, in the pink tutu (much too large for her), is lying under the ping-pong table on a blanket. She's an orphan, dying of consumption.

I didn't give her much to say, for she is shy. Eléonore never wants to learn a part: she dances around, changing tutus between scenes.

As we start rehearsal, I can hear Mother's high, mellow voice; she's talking on the telephone in the hall. She must have come in through the front door. Normally she uses the back door after leaving her car in our garage. Did she park it in the railway station's forecourt? This would mean she's going out tonight. But she *can't* be going out tonight, on a Wednesday.

Roseline, in her flowery gown, singing softly, is looking out the window, knitting her brows. Her fiancé is late. Actually, he's fighting with the ghost under the bridge, but she can't see him. End of scene. Maybe I should add dialogue before the ghost and the lover start their fight. But first I'll work on the song with Roseline, while Coralie and Monique practise fighting.

Mother calls us for our bath. Eléonore decides to leave the tutus in our closet. We say good-bye, *à demain*.

In the bathtub Coralie and I play with our boats and stones. Our brother Maxime used to have what he called a rock collection, but now he's taken up photography so he's lost interest in the stones and said we could have them. We throw Maxime's beautiful stones at the boats to sink them. Coralie is good at this, I am not.

That's when Mother puts on a plastic apron and attacks us with a flannel. Coralie wants to go on playing. Mother says, "Don't wiggle like an eel!" I don't resist: I like the rose-scented soap, and to be clean. Mother holds out a large white towel, warm from the radiator, and takes me in her lap to dry me off. Coralie doesn't want to get out of the water, but as soon as I'm dry, she has to.

While she runs around the bathroom, Mother cleans my ears with cotton wool she's rolled around the tail end of a match. When the match scrapes my left ear, I cough. "Your coughing ear," Mother says. She pours cologne on a ball of cotton wool and dabs the skin around my hair. She helps me with my nightgown and robe, then tries to get Coralie into her lap, which is never easy.

Mother's not taking a bath now, which means she'll have it later. Which means she's not going out. Then why did she come in through the front door?

On Wednesdays we never have guests, and we dine early, around half past seven. After dinner, Father gets ready to drive to his club. The club, where he plays bridge twice a week, is on the upper floor of the Café du Commerce, on the promenade. "Will you give me the keys to the 4CV?" he asks Mother. That's it then. He's taking Mother's car. That's why she parked it outside.

"Is there anything wrong with the 402?" I ask Father as he puts on his overcoat.

He tousles my hair. "I hope not. I left it at the Peugeot garage for an oil change. And your mother had mentioned a noise, so I asked Perez to take a look at the engine. I'm sure it'll be fine."

The 402 is fifteen years old, older than my sister Justine. Father says it's in good condition. It's light brown, stable and strong, big enough for the whole family, reassuring. It's the only one of its kind around here, but it doesn't stand out.

Mother says it's too old. Eléonore's parents have just bought a Vedette, and they're all excited about it. Mother thinks we should get one too. I'm glad for Eléonore, but I don't like the Vedette. It's light blue, and ridiculously long, like an American car. Kind of flashy. I like the 402, I hope it lives for ever.

Every Wednesday and Saturday, as soon as Father is gone, we all retire to Mother's bedroom and bathroom. These are Mother's beauty evenings, and we're allowed to spend them with her. Mother gets into her bubble bath (tonight, gardenia) and I scrub her back with a sponge. Then I peel the cucumber she's left in a bowl on the table near the basin and cut it up into tiny pieces. I add almond oil and crush the mixture into a paste with a fork. When Mother comes out of the bath, she puts on her light-green bathrobe; she sits in a wicker chair in the middle of the bathroom, and I dry her hair with a towel. I comb it, shake the bottle of Pétrole Hahn and sprinkle the lotion onto Mother's hair then massage it into every part of her scalp until she says it's enough. I have mixed feelings about Pétrole Hahn, the way it smells: nice and fresh on the surface, bergamot, I think, and lemon; but a pungent fetor underneath, which Mother says is what makes it effective. Against dandruff, and for sparkle.

I hold the hair dryer with one hand while, with the other, I comb Mother's hair. It's auburn, shoulder-length, and slightly curly. I have to brush it from underneath, to give it what Mother calls "volume". Mother's hair is completely different from ours. It never tangles up, and lends itself painlessly to comb and brush. A beautiful, docile possession, which changes color with the light, and shape with her movements or the wind.

When I'm done, Mother covers her hair with a pink scarf. She moves to the easy chair near the window, and I spread the cucumber cream on her face and neck. There's some left, and Mother wants me to smear it on my face, but I won't. I rub my hands with it, then rinse them.

Time to join Coralie, who all this time has been sitting in the bedroom in Father's armchair, with her feet on the coffee table next to a heap of *Pieds Nickelés*. She loves these comic books about three lazy crooks who play tricks on the pompous and the rich. But we need to go on with our little soirée. In the alcove, Mother settles against a large pillow on the outside of the bed, next to the lamp, with a few issues of *Jardin des Modes*. I climb into the middle to share the magazines, and Coralie joins us on the inside with her *Pieds Nickelés*.

Once in a while, she has a question for me. "What is Ribouldingue saying to the lady with the hat?" "Why does the policeman have to let Filochard go?" There's a lot of text in these stories, a whole narrative, not just dialogue. Mostly she can make it out for herself, from the drawings. I find this amazing. I'm exactly the opposite: I read only the text, forgetting that these are comics, and after a while I don't understand what's happening. Sometimes I try to go back and look at the drawings, but usually I just give up.

Mother studies the latest fashions and critiques the models as well as the dresses and coats. One has horrifyingly thick ankles, another practically no waist, yet another a microscopic nose. "Just look at this!" she says. I look. But I can't get too interested in these women's physiques, or their outlandish costumes. Amid the fragrance of cucumber and almond, I read the descriptions: *alpaga, zibeline, dentelle rebrodée de ruche, mousseline de soie, georgette de laine.* Mysterious words, which I'll look up tomorrow.

By the time Mother gets up from the bed and goes to the bathroom to take off the cucumber paste, Coralie is asleep. Mother, when she comes back, takes her in her arms and carries her to our room, but I'm allowed to stay. And stay. Mother critiques, I read, it could go on for ever. She won't need to carry me to my bed, because I won't fall asleep.

When she decides to turn off the light, I kiss her and go to our room, black and filled with Coralie's rhythmic breathing. In my bed, I try to hang on to the bergamot, the cucumber, the quiet of the alcove. But I can't help looking towards the future: the days to come, the weeks, their arcs of relief and disquiet.

Tomorrow evening, at least, our parents will play Pharaoh with the Pujols. In our house.

Champagne

Today I'm tasting the host. Anne-Claude compares it to paper, Justine says it feels more like cotton wool. Intriguing.

I get to church half an hour before the ten o'clock mass because we have to rehearse our hymns and movements one last time. When the congregation comes in, we stand at the back of the church; then we all walk very slowly in procession from side chapel to side chapel, between the parts of the mass, and we sing. In front of saint Régis, I do my solo, *Au ciel dans ma patrie*, about the bliss of joining the Virgin Mary in heaven. I'd love to die and be forever ecstatic, but I don't feel any special attraction to the Virgin. Except I'd like to give birth in a stable, like her. Not to the son of God, though. I want daughters. Four, like in *Les Quatre Filles du docteur March*.

Mother is pleased because I look good in my new white dress, white ankle socks, white patent-leather shoes, crown of tiny white roses on my dark ringlets (her work of the morning, with a curling iron). Father has come too, and he doesn't look disgruntled. The host is fine. You feel something smooth and quiet on your tongue, but solid, not slippery. It sticks a bit, and after a while it dissolves. Hardly any taste at all. I wish I could live on hosts.

After mass, we all drive to the Cabarrou with Grandmother, my two brothers and two sisters, a few friends of my parents', and my friend Eléonore. The Cabarrou is our park, but it isn't attached to our townhouse, or even very near. To get there, you have to walk for ten minutes to the other side of the railway tracks, into the vineyards.

Today, as soon as we open the gate, a foul smell attacks me. Barbecue. I run all the way to the other end of the park, but I can't find a cranny that's free of the reek. Behind the pine trees it isn't so bad, but once in a while you get hit by a wave of burning flesh. My brothers are the ones who instigated the barbecue. They said they'd take care of it.

The only good thing about a barbecue, especially when there are people coming, going and jostling around, is that nobody pays any attention to what I eat. Or don't eat. Except for my brother Etienne, but he's not going to rat on me. "You should taste this lamb chop," he says. "It's perfect."

"No, thanks."

"If you had a choice between eating this and having your eyes gouged out," he asks, "what would you do?"

"Try to find a quicker way to die?"

Etienne shakes his head. "You know, you must be a Cathar."

"A Cathar?"

"From the Middle Ages. Simon de Montfort massacred them. They didn't eat any meat or cheese. For them, Matter was a prison. They were vanquished, but they survive in you!" He takes my waist between his large hands, throws me up, catches me and sets me back on the ground. Then he runs to tend the barbecue.

I try a tiny radish, and it hurts the whole inside of my mouth. People seem to gobble them as if they were figs, or cherries. Many are sticking wedges of butter on them. I ask Justine why anybody would want to do this, and she says, hoping her vocabulary will dazzle me, "It assuages the pungency." As if people had to eat something that stings their taste buds in the first place.

At the end of the meal Father starts pouring Champagne. Eléonore drinks hers in one gulp, and shivers. I taste mine slowly. After every sip, my tongue keeps on tingling. Then someone gives us more, and I drink it up although I already feel dizzy. I'm not sure what happens after that. I climb some trees with Eléonore and Coralie. A branch snaps. Coralie slides into the pond and gets her blue dress all muddy. Justine rescues her. "You're lucky I happened to be around. I wonder how you all manage to stay alive when I'm in Paris." Right, Coralie was going to drown in two feet of slime.

Eléonore wants to play ballerinas, and my sisters agree. Justine suggests a corny choreography inspired by the film *Violettes Impériales*, and Coralie says she'll provide acrobatics. I roll my eyes, and leave — they're so busy plotting their entrechats, they don't even notice. As I walk about the park trying to think of something to do, I bump into my oldest brother Maxime, hard at work taking photos of lilac blossoms. I can only see his back, all bent and awry as he concentrates on his task. Next to playing ballerinas, taking photos of lilac blossoms must be the most stupid occupation in the whole universe.

Maxime got a state-of-the-art camera for his twenty-first birthday in February, and he's been obsessed ever since. He used to take lots of photos before, but normal ones: of the family, friends, some neighbor's new car, his rugby team, the cats. Now, with this new equipment, he's become an artist, so he's no longer interested in the kinds of photos anybody could take. If you see a human being in a photo of his, it'll only be their wrist. Or a bit of their ankle. An earhole, a strand of hair. That's what artists do; he's explained it all to me.

"Please, Maxime," I say. "When you're done with this, could you please take a photo of me with the parents." I have a very clear idea in mind: me in the middle, with a parent on each side. A Jesus-in-the-crib configuration.

"No, I can't," he says, pressing buttons and turning knobs as he peers into his camera. "I'm not even sure I'll have enough film for what I want to do."

"Maxime!" I wail. I sound like a baby. "This is my private communion, there should be a photo of it, don't you think?"

He's still busy with his focus and his flowers. Can't even spare me a glance. "There must have been a photographer at the church door, when you came out," he says.

"It will be everybody coming out of the church, a jumble of people. What I'd like is a photo of just the parents and me. Please."

I want this very much all of a sudden. I don't know why, but I can't do without it. Who needs all these lilacs? I hate him. I decide to look for Father. Perhaps he could ask Maxime in a way that would make him do it.

But when I finally find Father, Maxime says he's used up his roll of film, there's nothing left, sorry. Father is here, I can hear Mother nearby, and this dolt had to take thirty-six shots of lilac blossoms. I want to kill him. Instead, I start crying, which makes me angrier still.

A few days later, in the family album, there's a square black-and-white photo of a skinny girl in a longish white dress and a rosebud crown. She's stamping her foot, her face distorted with rage, tears flowing down her cheeks, her arms raised toward the torpid skies. Maxime wrote the caption: "Tita on the day of her private communion."

Names

Tita is what most people call me. Nobody but mademoiselle Pélican, the nuns and the priest use Euphémie, my baptismal name — I had to get a new name when I was baptized because my legal name, the one on my passport, wasn't a saint's name. Last week Justine asked me, "When you are my age, and you meet a boy, if he wants to know what your name is, what will you say?"

This was not an idle question; it was a test question. "Tita," I said. To keep her happy, and even though Euphémie might sound better when I stop being a child.

"Right. Tita is so much sweeter, isn't it? You should always be called Tita, even when you're older. Even as a married woman. It's so charming. It's *you*."

Well, I thought, there's at least someone in the world who thinks she knows what "me" is. I wasn't at all convinced, though. Justine is extremely interesting to watch and listen to; but I don't think she has all the answers.

In the music room Ginette, our cleaning lady, is dusting the window frames. I sit on the piano stool with my back to the instrument and look at the portrait, high on the wall, of a girl who must be about my age: my aunt Marta. There are portraits of great-uncles and forefathers all over the house, most of them in military uniform, but aunt Marta is the only female who rates one. Is it because she died in boarding school (Father says "convent") when she was twelve? In the painting, she wears a thin white animal around her neck, with the head and tail clearly visible, and a white pillbox hat. She is pale, and looks serious. A bit timid, perhaps.

Ginette is now rubbing the piano keys with something sour-smelling from a bottle. She lives across the back street with her husband and daughter, and she's been working in this house for ever, every day but Sunday. "Did you know my aunt Marta?" I ask her.

"Of course I did. My mother used to work for your grandmother, and I sometimes came along. Marta was three years older than me, but she was nice. She read books all the time, and she lent me quite a few good ones."

"Did she ever do forbidden things? Did she climb roofs?"

Ginette laughs. "I never heard about that. But she was lively enough. When she went out with the maid, she always wanted to take some of her dolls with her. Said they needed the fresh air."

"I have this porcelain doll, Jacqueline, that used to be hers. Do you remember her playing with it?"

"Yes, and she broke both Jacqueline's legs trying to get her to do somersaults. Her mother, your grandmother Clara, said the doll would have to remain legless — that would teach Marta. Then, after what happened... your grandmother gave me some of Marta's toys, and put away the rest. But just before your second birthday she went to the linen garret, found this broken doll, and took it to the repair shop in Narbonne, in the rue Droite. She wanted you to have it. From the beginning, she said you were very much like your aunt Marta, and I guess that's why she called you Tita."

"Was Tita her...?"

"Yes, Tita is what we called your aunt Marta. I think Marta made it up herself when she was little. People called her 'Martita' sometimes, so... Then, not long after you came here, your grandmother took a fancy to you and started calling you Tita. After a while, everybody followed suit. Do you remember your grandmother Clara? Probably not, you weren't even three when she died."

My grandmother Clara. People, when they mention her, say things like, "She was such an amazing lady, walking tall in her long black dresses and her high white chignon. So refined, so imposing."

I do remember her, but not like that. "She always stayed in her room," I tell Ginette. "She read me fairy tales. She let me play with her fans, she had a whole drawer of them. With her scarves too, and her embroidered handkerchiefs."

Two tears slide down my cheeks. Ginette puts down her duster, pulls me up from the stool, takes me in her lap, and kisses me a few times. I kiss her back then go downstairs, across the garden and out through the back door into the street. The dirt road on the left leads down to La Fourcade, our rambling orchard. I sit on a wood bench under a fig tree, thinking about my name. If I were Marta, if I were dead, would I like someone else to get my nickname, the name I made up for myself?

There are worse things in the world than feeling uneasy about your name. There are enormously worse things than I and my friends are ever likely to experience, as mademoiselle Pélican reminds us every other minute with her stories of miscellaneous martyrs and Chinese children who not only go hungry but haven't been baptized, so they will be sent to limbo at best when they die.

I don't intend to fall into self-pity. I should be grateful to Grandmother Clara: if she hadn't thought of calling me Tita, I might be stuck with my legal name, the one Mother chose for me: Lakmé. Mother says that she looked forward to having a daughter just for the sake of naming her Lakmé, which is the title of her favorite opera and the name of its heroine, an Indian girl who falls in love with an Englishman who abandons her so she kills herself at the end, with poison. I can't imagine a more ridiculous thing to do than killing yourself over some man. Mother said that she had a lot of trouble with the registry officer at the clinic, Lakmé was so unusual. But she told him about the opera, sang the beginning of *Sous le ciel tout étoilé*, and he couldn't resist. I wish he had.

I make a decision: I'll give each of my children three names, all as unobtrusive as possible, and they'll choose between these when they're seven. Seven, because it's the age of reason.

Now I can relax in the smell of fig leaves. Behind the tree there's a hut with quinces, apples, nuts, some tools and, on a low shelf, a heap of books. I start reading *Léonie veut aller à la fête*. Léonie, the heroine, is invited to a dance for the first time. Her father, who is a sailor, is away in Africa. She's excited about the party and would like to wear the dress her father sent her for her birthday, but there are a few snags. Her stepmother, madame Mercier, thinks she's too young. Then Dora, the stepmother's daughter, wants to borrow Léonie's dress. As Dora is much larger than Léonie, the dress might not survive.

The story is good, but I've read it before. What catches my attention is the way Léonie addresses her stepmother. Léonie calls madame Mercier *Belle-mère*. Which is the French word for both *mother-in-law* and *stepmother*, and literally means "beautiful mother". This sounds like a solution.

Because Coralie and I have a problem: we don't know how to address our mother. She *is* a *belle-mère* to our older brothers and sister, but they just call her Odette. Justine even coined a pet name for her: Dette (which actually means "debt"). Coralie and I are supposed to say *Maman*, but we don't. Ever. We don't call her anything. At all. Which might get us into trouble. Because it's not polite to just say "yes", or

41

"thanks", or "please"; you should go on with the name or title of the person. As in "Thanks, Loli", or "Please, Grand-Mère". We can't do it with our mother, we just can't bring ourselves to pronounce the word *maman*, it sounds so babyish; so we try to avoid situations where we'd have to.

Now why not call our mother *Belle-mère*? She *is* beautiful.

I can't wait. I run back to the house with the book. I find Coralie in the coal shed, grinding chunks of coal onto her hair with both hands.

"Hi," she says. "Where have you been? I'd like to be a gypsy. Can you *become* a gypsy?"

"I guess. Shall I read you *Léonie veut aller à la fête?*"

Coralie wipes her hands on her dress and follows me outside. On the green bench under the wisteria I read aloud, practicing my *Belle-mère* responses. I notice that Léonie hardly ever says anything to her stepmother. Most of their exchanges consist in madame Mercier's giving orders and Léonie's answering "Oui, Belle-mère".

Then our mother calls from inside, "Tita, Coralie! Lunch!" Normally, we'd just go. Silently.

But I answer, "Oui, Belle-mère."

Coralie echoes, "Oui, Belle-mère."

Our mother doesn't seem to notice. She never pays much attention to words.

Currency

This morning when I wake up my nose is so clogged I can only breathe through my mouth, but my throat is swollen, so not much air gets in. When I try to say good morning to Loli no sound comes out, not even a whisper. Mother decides that I'll stay home from school. Dr Barral drops by, and Loli goes to the pharmacy for the usual lozenges and tablets. Meanwhile I follow Mother up into the bathroom. She takes a long twisted metal stick out of the medicine cabinet, disinfects it, winds a cotton swab around one end, takes me in her lap, dips the stick in a bottle of tart-smelling red liquid and thrusts it into the back of my throat. I should be used to this. Every time, though, I'm sure the stick is going to pierce my vocal cords.

Some gagging is going on in my throat, but the rest of my body stays very still as Mother dips and paints, dips and paints. I'm trying to stop my mind, pretend I'm already dead so nothing can hurt me. When she's done, Mother closes the bottle, lays the stick in the washbasin, and gives me a long cuddle because I've been so quiet. "My sweet little sick girl," she says. Then she carries me to my bed, where I leaf through a bunch of old *Lisettes* and *Fillettes* from the night table, because I'm too tired to go and look for a book.

After a while I fall asleep. When I wake up, the gold clock on the mantelpiece, held up by three curly-haired naked boys with outstretched arms, says twenty past five, and I feel like getting up. I walk slowly downstairs (I'm still dizzy) and into Father's study. I can vaguely hear Father's voice coming from the office, in conversation with Simone (the secretary) and Berthe (the accountant), while on the other side, in the sitting room, Mother is having tea with her friends.

I slide into the sitting room, as noiselessly as I can, and sit on a low stool between the wall and a wide armchair that has a full square back and straight legs. The women are all at the other end of the room near the windows, in flimsier chairs with curved legs, with their teacups on small painted tables, all of slightly different sizes so you can stack them if you like. Nobody notices me. I often try this, and succeed about half the time. I do it as an experiment, to find out how invisible I can be, but today I also have a practical reason: if Mother saw me she might, instead of asking me to pass the cakes and then forgetting about me, send me back to bed.

Cami Espeluque, my friend Anne-Claude's mother, plump and blooming in a low-cut yellow dress, is telling the others about her two-year-old twin boys, who have colds. "Can you believe those rascals? They get a kick out of sneezing into each other's faces!" Mother often says that Cami "has no conversation" because she tends to go on about the twins, but the twins are a pretty good topic, I think. More entertaining than hats. Mother talks about her children too, but she never tries to be amusing. Or maybe she doesn't know how.

But *I* am the topic right now. "Tita too has a cold." Mother announces. "She's in bed! Again! Throat infection, cough, the works. She's so delicate, and such a bad eater. I don't think this climate is good for her — all this dry wind, it's enervating. I do everything I can to make her stronger, I never stop. Every morning I give her cod liver oil, nose drops three times a day, enemas every evening. I wonder what would happen if I didn't. I guess she wouldn't be alive by now."

I've often wondered why Mother lies so much. Thank God she doesn't wield cod liver oil every day. Or enemas! She does inflict those torments on me, but not very often. So why "every morning, every evening"? A lot of what she says is like that. For instance, last week, the owner of the fabric store in Narbonne said, "This ochre silk is perfect for you, you have such a beautiful complexion!" Mother looked delighted. "Thank you!" she said. "And you know, it's absolutely natural. I never do anything to my skin other than wash it with savon de Marseille, never use any kind of cream or lotion. Ever!"

When actually she keeps a whole array of pots and bottles on her dressing table — she brings them back from Lyon, a big city far away near the Alps, where she used to live before she married Father. She often visits there because that's where all her real girlfriends are, from the time when she had her own beauty salon. Through her friends, she can still get the wholesale price for serums, oils, masks, toners, moisturizers, foundations, powders. She uses a few of them evening and morning, over and above the concoctions she creates from fruit and vegetables.

I can't imagine why her words are so at odds with the facts. I tried to discuss this once with Justine. She rolled her eyes at my instances of Mother's mendacity: "You can't call this lying! It's *hyperbole*."

"I'm not sure Dr Barral is up to scratch," Mother goes on, "so I called a specialist in Béziers, Dr Viala. Have you heard of him? He was written up in *Le Midi Libre*, sounds like he's the best. Very handsome too, at least according to their photo. I was lucky to get an appointment for tomorrow afternoon, at three thirty. Oh, and there's a sale at the Galeries Modernes. They're going to remodel the store. I think I'll take a look at it after the specialist. I need beach towels, and a bathing suit. Would you be interested?"

Estelle shrugs. "Why not? I haven't been to Béziers for quite a while. Let's go and see what's going on."

"Good idea," Cami says. "What about you, Denise? Let's all go, shall we? In my car?" Because of her four children, Cami has the largest car.

Denise Pujol, our next-door neighbor, hesitates. "I'd like to take a look at their tea towels," she finally says, "but I'll have to talk to Roger."

The other women try not to look at each other, but I know what they're thinking: "Poor Denise!"

Not that the Pujols are poor, financially. Quite the opposite. They live next door to us in a bigger and more ornate house (ours is neater, though, with its plain façade and slender roof balustrade). Roger Pujol is one of Father's oldest friends. He's a *notaire*, and his offices take up the whole ground floor of their house. Their daughter lives in Toulouse (she married a surgeon), and their son is studying economics in Germany. They have a cook, two maids and a gardener. Every summer they go to the spa in Luchon, checking into the Grand Hotel. But Denise doesn't have her own car. She doesn't even drive. Also, the way the Pujols deal with money is peculiar. Roger gives Denise, every morning, the cash needed for grocery shopping. If she wants more than usual, she has to *ask*. He's not actually stingy, he'll give her what she wants, but she has to ask.

Mother finds this humiliating. "Every month, I get sixty thousand francs in my bank account," she likes to say. "Which isn't a lot, but at least it's mine. Henri trusts me to spend it as I see fit." What about Cami? Does her husband, too, put money into her account? He's a *propriétaire*, he manages his vineyards with *his* father and my impression is, they're in trouble. But Cami's parents own a few houses around town. Her father has a real-estate business, and her mother a perfume store.

Estelle "has her own money", people say. Is this the same as a dowry? My throat starts tingling, my chest is burning, I think I'm going to cough, so I slide back into Father's study, which is empty. I sit at Father's desk, forget about coughing, look up *dot* in the Robert. A dowry, *biens dotaux*, is what a woman brings to the marriage, to be managed by her husband. What she actually owns personally is called *biens paraphernaux*.

Crocodile

At noon Loli is waiting for us in front of Sainte-Blandine. On our way back, we meet two friends of hers near the *école laïque*. Coralie, followed by the other maids' little boys, climbs onto the benches along the avenue, jumps down, runs around the trees, hops on one foot, waves to acquaintances, while I listen to the maids discussing dances and boyfriends in Occitan. They exclaim, disagree, make fun of the men. They're not going to be maids all their lives, and they don't want to go back to their parents' farms: they all came to town to find a husband.

Loli says to her friends, "There's no hurry, is there? As long as you don't have to wear Saint Catherine's bonnet..." Nobody wants to be a *Catherinette*, which is what you become if you're still unmarried when you turn twenty-five. For Saint Catherine's Day all the *Catherinettes* make elaborate headdresses and walk in a procession wearing them. Loli is sixteen; in November for Saint Catherine's day she'll be seventeen, so she still has eight years left to find a fiancé. I hope it takes her a while, because I like her. She's so cheerful. It's not easy to be a maid: even though you are a grown-up, you have to do as you're told, all day long. Our previous maid, Jeanine, who got married last spring, was often in a bad mood; she yelled at Coralie, and quarrelled with Justine.

As soon as we come through the garden door, I feel queasy. Veal blanquette. The smell of the sauce, creamy, vealy, makes me want to run away. Instead, I wash my hands and enter the dining room, where my parents are kissing against the central-heating radiator. The radiator is cold and if they wanted heat, which they probably don't on this warm day, they could stand in the sun at the other end of the room, near the windows. But they always hold each other and kiss in front of the radiator. It's a large radiator, as tall as Mother's shoulders. Its top part is a cabinet that's supposed to hold plates and dishes to keep them warm but it's now full of old newspapers for the stove. For we also have a small wood stove, which is needed when it gets really cold. Eléonore's grandmother told me that our house was the first one in town to get central heating, which is why our ancient radiators don't produce much warmth. Mother says it's also because the house is too big and too drafty.

"Where's Coralie?" Mother asks. But I can hear Grandmother in the next room urging my sister to dry her hands more thoroughly.

After the asparagus, which I don't mind, Loli brings the main dish and sets it in the middle of the table. When mother takes the lid off, I stop breathing. She lays two pieces of veal on my plate. "It's very lean," she says.

I examine the stringy fibers, the gelatinous texture. "Please, no sauce," I whisper. I'll eat the rice, at least the side of it that hasn't touched the meat or the sauce.

"Just a little meat," Mother says, cutting it up for me. "You know how important it is to eat meat. If you don't, you'll catch another ear infection. Or throat infection. You don't want to be ill and miss school again, do you?"

Luckily she forgets about me as she starts telling Father about the wonderful crocodile handbag André gave Cami for her birthday. This is hardly news: Cami turned thirty-one more than a month ago, and I thought her friends were done with the oohs and aahs by now. Not to mention the fact that Father has never shown any interest in handbags. "André got it in Montpellier," Mother goes on, "at Maxence & Fils, avenue de Pézenas. That's where Estelle got her beautiful suitcase too."

This must be the beginning of a campaign. Mother's birthday is April twenty-sixth, in hardly more than a week, and she wants her own crocodile. But I don't think her approach is going to work. Father has been different for a while. Preoccupied. Everybody says that our local wines don't sell as well as they used to. Eléonore's parents are even talking about bottling theirs instead of dealing wholesale. It's the sensible thing to do, they say. They wouldn't need their two tank trucks, then. Father has three. Sometimes, for short errands, I'm allowed to sit next to one of the drivers, high above the netherworld of the streets. But when I happen

51

to see one of these trucks in town, I cringe at my name out there on the back and sides of the tanks, green on yellow, bold and huge.

"Maxence & Fils, avenue de Pézenas, just after the Crédit Lyonnais," Mother repeats.

Heedless of crocodiles, Father slowly savours a new wine and considers. For him, Mother is babbling; he has no idea what's at stake. Every lunchtime, he brings three or four small bottles to the table. All morning, in the tasting room, he's been sampling a dozen or two that various brokers came to submit, each with a handwritten label (grower's name, broker's name, date). Here are the ones he's interested in — he's written his opinion of them on index cards. Before buying a wine, he likes to taste it with food.

Coralie's plate is empty. She points towards mine — I've dealt with the rice but haven't grappled the veal at all. I nod, and she deftly picks up the bits of meat with her fork while Grandmother concentrates on tossing the salad. Mother is still expatiating on the glories of Maxence & Fils. Father asks her if she wants to taste a fruity Minervois, which might be a bit on the heavy side. She swills nearly half a glass and says, "Yes, too sweet." She's irritated because Father hasn't caught on to Maxence & Fils. I think he has other problems on his mind. Mother doesn't like problems, except the ones she can solve immediately and brilliantly, like a drain to unstop, a room to paint, a child's dress to make. She is proud that she managed to marry a man who has vineyards, a business, many friends, a great reputation. A good-looking man. Very tall, which is essential for her: she is tall, and needs taller. All her girlfriends from Lyon envy her. She's made it, that's all she wants to know.

Cheese time, and Mother makes sure Loli puts two petits-suisses on my dessert plate. "Please, just one!" I beg. But Mother is adamant. "Remember, without calcium, your bones will crumble, your body will be crippled, and you'll never grow tall. Is that what you want?"

What I want? A life without food. To go to heaven as soon as possible, or hell, or limbo, or any place provided there's no food in it.

Petits-suisses are less offensive than Camembert, and less slimy than yogurt, but anything made from milk has this sour smell. Grandmother peels an apple and cuts it up for me. She urges me to hide spoonfuls of petits-suisses between slices of apple. I try; the chalky paste ruins the cool purity of the fruit. Two spoonfuls, and I give up. Thank God Mother is busy again, pronouncing on the last two wines while eating her Roquefort. How can she put that ancient curdled milk into her mouth, so rotten it's covered with blue spots, so putrid that, if she didn't know it was Roquefort, she'd look for a dead rat behind the furniture?

She professes that wines are always best tasted with cheese. She doesn't use her nose, as Father always does before his lips touch the liquid. She swallows fast, and empties her glass. "Excellent, this one," she says with complete self-assurance. Father tries to explain its pros and cons, but she isn't listening.

On school days, as soon as we're done with lunch, I have to go and practice the piano for half an hour before we go back to school. Loli brings coffee, Mother takes her cup and saucer and leads me up into the music room, where she sits in an armchair and waits. Not that she enjoys listening to my mindless exercises, but she wants to make sure I never stop. She never had to play the piano, by the way. Why do I have to suffer what she didn't? Because. *Parce que c'est comme ça.*

Cartwheel

Again we're getting ready for a show. "We" means madame Robichon and her ballet students, of whom Coralie and I are the most unwilling. There are nine of us, eight girls and one boy, Jordi Puch. He won't come back next fall, he told me. He'd rather play rugby, but his mother wants him to finish the year. He says it's okay, he likes our company. I like him. He is six, and in the downstairs class at Sainte-Blandine. Slender, with pale curly hair. Nimble, energetic. His gestures never look contrived. His feet stretch easily even though he never practices apart from the classes.

The classes! Who ever got the idea of standing on their toes must have been demented. Justine has friends in Paris who take ballet lessons, and she says they don't start pointe work until they are ten or eleven, because it can hurt your feet if they're not "ossified". Since the Easter vacation I've been calling Justine every Sunday morning, around eleven. Father wouldn't allow it at first, but Justine explained that I'm her confidante. Father said, "All right, six minutes maximum, you'll have to use the egg timer."

The show is next Wednesday, and today we rehearse at the theater. Madame Robichon decided that the way it will start is we'll all walk onto the stage, one after the other, very fast, and do a cartwheel. Zip zip zip, the nine of us, across the stage. After which most of us will stand at the back and let the stars do their stuff. Eléonore will wear six different tutus, all kinds of lengths and colors. Her mother and aunt will be in the wings to help her change. Coralie and I hate tutus. Anyway, according to Justine, you shouldn't cartwheel in a tutu. She discussed it with her ballerina friends, who called it "sacrilege".

"Can't we wear our leotards?" I ask madame Robichon.

"What a ridiculous question!" she answers, rolling her globulous eyes, whose eyelashes are always congealed by a thick layer of mascara. "This is a show we're putting on! The whole point of a show is dressing up." There's something uncanny about madame Robichon: she wears her hair rather short, in a pageboy, and it's always exactly the same length. It doesn't grow.

"Jordi will wear his leotard," I say. "Why couldn't we?"

"You are not boys, are you? Please, we have a lot to do, there's no time for silly talk."

"I'd like to be a boy," Coralie says. "I'd wear a leotard. No, I'd play rugby."

Madame Robichon makes us rehearse our cartwheels. On a beach, it's fun to turn a cartwheel. Or two, or three. What I don't like is doing it on a small stage. Anyway a cartwheel, according to Justine, is gymnastics, not ballet, and shouldn't be part of a ballet performance.

While Eléonore capers and pirouettes, Coralie turns to me and makes a pig face with her nose and lips turned up. I'm so tired of the whole thing, I squat for a while. "Stand up, please!" madame Robichon cries. "Think of your parents, how proud they'll be to see you on stage in your beautiful tutus next Wednesday!"

"I'm so looking forward to this show!" Eléonore exclaims in the changing room. We're all ready to go, but she's still busy with her many layers of undershirts, blouses and cardigans. "She's always as covered up as a honeypot," Mother likes to say. Which doesn't make any sense to me, but is certainly derogatory.

Mother is waiting for us outside, with Cami Espeluque and Estelle Vié who, like her, take classes with madame Robichon, twice a week. Not ballet: *culture physique*, to enhance their figures. Estelle is lean and brisk, she says she'd like to become more flexible. Cami wants to lose the weight she put on when she was pregnant with the twins and breastfed them for more than a year, but I don't think she should: she's beautiful as she is, all chubby and sparkling. Mother's aim is to remain as slim and perfect as she's always been. For ever.

Eléonore comes with us in the car. "How's it going?" Mother asks. Eléonore explains how hard it is to remember all her moves, in the right order. After we drop her in front of her house, Mother says, "That girl shouldn't do ballet. Not with those thick ankles."

"She has strong legs," I say. "She's a good dancer." Actually, I don't think she's so great — she tries too hard, and worries too much about how she looks. But I won't let anyone disparage my friends.

"Don't talk nonsense," Mother says. "She's a nice enough girl, but her mother shouldn't put it into her head that she's pretty. It won't help her. With her heavy limbs, her pasty skin, her mousy hair, she should realize her prospects are very limited."

Mother pays huge attention to appearance. As if she'd never heard of souls. According to school, church, and the comtesse de Ségur, *being* good is what matters, not *looking* good. Of course madame Fichini is cruel when she makes Sophie wear a coarse cotton dress with a dirty spot on it to visit her friends. That's rude. You need to be clean, to dress in a way that suits the occasion, your social situation and your age, neither too coarse nor too elaborate. But having an attractive body is just luck, there's no reason to gloat about it.

At home, I look for Father. He's in the music room playing the piano, trying out some composition of his. The same tune in various keys, with a few variations. I wait on the landing, because I know that if he sees me he'll stop. Then when I haven't heard anything for three minutes I go in.

"Hi, Tita, how's life? Do you want the piano?" How can he be my father, live in the same house with me, and not know I *never* want the piano!

"Have you met madame Robichon?" I ask.

"Who?"

"Madame Robichon, our ballet teacher."

"I don't think so. Why?"

"She's the stupidest person I've ever met," I say. "I just wondered if someone more stupid could exist. You know so many people."

"How would you define stupid?"

Now. This is difficult. You can *see* that madame Robichon is stupid. If he'd seen her he'd know. But define it? "She's like wood," I say. "Her face never moves."

"Is she paralysed?"

"No. She's normal. But you always know what she's going to say."

"Our words are often pretty predictable," Father says.

That's not it. How can I explain? "She's *more* stupid," I say. "Most people, they mouth the usual phrases, but you can feel something else going on, underneath. They're alive. With madame Robichon that's all there is, and it's... contagious. You end up feeling stupid too." I'm not making my point. "Try to talk to her on Wednesday after the show."

"Oh," Father says, "a show? Your mother didn't tell me. I'll have to call my bridge friends."

"You don't have to come," I say. "Honest, don't come for me, or for Coralie. We're no good."

"But I want to come!" he says. "You must have worked hard for this show!"

"We haven't," I say. "We hate it. We'd like not to do it. I guess it's too late for this year, but could we please not take ballet after the summer?" I hadn't thought about this, it just comes out. And as soon as I hear myself, I know I should have kept quiet. Father looks at the piano stand, at the notes he's been making for his song, in lead pencil, and the revision, in green.

"You'll have to see about it with your mother," he says.

Time for the show. Coralie and I squeeze into the back seat of Eléonore's car between Eléonore's large father and her larger grandmother, under a mountain of tutus. Coralie hugs me and whispers in my ear, "If we suffocate, let's be buried in the same tomb." Eléonore is in front next to her mother, with a few more tutus in her lap, including a rainbow one with, her mother says, seventeen layers of tulle. When we arrive at the theater, Coralie grins. "I think I forgot my demi-pointe shoes," she says, looking into her bag. But madame Robichon sends Eléonore's mother to the office to call our parents. Coralie should have waited. It's no use anyway. We're doomed. What can we do? Grow up, but it takes for ever.

Mother arrives in time to re-braid my hair and stick in some flowers. Then it's Coralie's turn. She yells. Madame Robichon is giving a speech on the other side of the curtain. Thanks, art, support, Mr Mayor. Now it starts! Coralie goes, then Jordi… "Your turn!" Madame Robichon whispers loudly behind me. I throw my hands onto the wooden floor, but my legs don't stick up in the usual way. I don't know what they do, but my feet are back on the floor on the wrong side. "Hurry, try again!" madame Robichon urges. But I don't feel like trying again. I just step to the other side of the stage. I don't run away, but behave as if nothing had happened, looking straight at the audience. I bungled my cartwheel, and I want to laugh.

We're done. It's been amazingly fast, and almost painless. Now there's clapping and stomping. The room is full. We bow and re-bow, and come back onstage twice. That's the most strenuous part.

Father doesn't talk to madame Robichon after the show. Everybody presses in to congratulate and exclaim. In the car, Mother says, "You have good muscles, Coralie, but you need to exert yourself."

"I want to play rugby," Coralie says.

"If you work hard," Mother says, "I'll make a new tutu just for you."

"I could go to La Patriote." Coralie says. "With Nicole, and Roseline."

"What is La Patriote?" Father asks.

"An athletic club," Mother says. "On the place du Marché."

Coralie bounces up and down. "They do asymmetric bars, springboard, vaulting horse!"

"Isn't this a good idea?" Father says.

Something has happened. Father has spoken up for once. And Mother is a sportswoman. It must be obvious to her that Coralie will be good at this, will be able to make her proud, for a change. Coralie might be freed!

"Coralie is enough of a tomboy already," Mother says. "And the children at La Patriote are a mixed lot."

So we all know there's no hope.

Lyon

Mother likes to talk about me. I might even be one of her favorite topics. Along with dresses, coats, hats, shoes, rings and handbags. There isn't much difference, for her, between me and a scarf. That's because I'm quiet.

"This one?" she says, when people ask how I'm doing — tradesmen, visitors, neighbors. "This one is a dream! She never makes a sound." Unlike Coralie, noisy Coralie who clamors for candy, juice, toys, playing outside on the street.

My impression is, I was born a listener. I only speak up when there's a reasonable chance of achieving a result, while many people keep flaunting their feelings and opinions, and seem to enjoy expression for expression's sake. I am odd, in quite a few ways.

But how odd? This afternoon (Thursday, so no school) Mother is having tea in the sitting room with her friends, and I've just finished passing the petits fours. The women are admiring my smocked dress (Mother's latest masterpiece) and exclaiming over the fact that I always look so neat, spotless and wrinkle free. I stop listening, as this is the kind of prattle I find embarrassing, not to mention terminally dull. But something in the air warns me that they must have moved on to another topic.

"Two months!" Mother has just proclaimed in her clear, buoyant voice.

63

Everybody's staring. At her, not me — I'm sitting on a low stool now, pretty much out of sight.

Estelle Vié smacks her cup down on the enamel table. "My God," she says. "That child must have been a total prodigy." I can hear, in her placid, slightly raspy voice, a hint of irony. "None of mine," she goes on, "were out of diapers before their third year. I thought it was because the first two were boys, but Mireille was no different. She sat on the potty quite happily, but nothing much happened until she was two."

Among Mother's friends, Estelle is one of my favorites. She always wears interesting little scarves on her head that she ties at the nape of her neck. She keeps them on all the time, even inside, even in her own house. Mother says it's because her hair is so thin she'd rather hide it. "She's not quite bald, but nearly," I've heard her say quite a few times. I wonder how she knows.

"Yes," Mother goes on breezily, "with some children, it takes a lot of time and effort." (She should know: Coralie still has accidents pretty often.) "But this one was marvellous. From two months old she never dirtied a diaper again. Not once! All I had to do was hold her above the toilet once in a while. I never needed to use a potty. She immediately knew what a lavatory was for."

Probably just another lie, I reflect as I retreat to our bedroom, where Coralie is lying on her bed face down, hands between her legs, doing what Mother and Grandmother don't want her to do.

I sit at my desk and remember Mother saying, "I was back at work just a week after I gave birth. The salon couldn't do without me. Obviously. All the clients were asking for me. So I had to go back. I couldn't keep them waiting for ever." I've never thought about it, but I start wondering. Who was taking care of me when Mother was in her beauty salon all day? I was born in Lyon, four hundred kilometers from here. And I don't think Father ever left Cugnac. Why did we stay in Lyon? How long did we go on living there?

Lyon, according to Mother, is a wonderful city with a lot of stores, chic restaurants and cafés where she has all these friends from the time when she was young and single, with her own booming business. She loves staying there at her goddaughter's, a niece who married the owner of a large sewing-machine store. She often says that Cugnac is a one-horse town where people don't even speak proper French.

Cugnac has only seven thousand inhabitants, but every Wednesday lots of villagers come from far away to our open-air market. We have three cinemas, a busy promenade, many cafés. And our accent is different from hers, but she only knows French, whereas here we also speak or at least understand Occitan, Catalan, and some Spanish too, because we're not far from the border. For Mother, the only real language is French. She looks down on all the rest.

According to my brother Etienne, the Greeks (a long time ago) were like her: they called all foreigners "barbarians".

Downstairs, in the dining room, Grandmother is sitting near her favorite window, the one with the best view of the railway station forecourt and the avenue. I wait until she's done with the Cugnac page of *L'Indépendant*. When she resumes her knitting (a brown sock), I ask, "Did Mother go back to work after I was born?"

"As soon as she was out of the clinic. She stayed there five days, because the doctor made her, but she couldn't wait to get out."

"Who took care of me then?"

"I did. We stayed in the apartment. I cleaned, I cooked, and we went to the park in the afternoon."

"Was that in Lyon?"

"Yes, up on the Croix Rousse."

"So I wasn't with Mother much."

"Only on Sundays. On Sundays your father came to visit, and they sometimes took you out with them. When they didn't go to the cinema. On Mondays she didn't work but she had to check out new products, go to the stores." She adjusts her glasses, looks at her knitting. "You always wanted your mother," she goes on. "You howled when she left, and in the evening you never went to sleep before she was back."

"So you fed me, you changed my diapers?"

"Yes. I prepared your bottle early in the morning while she got ready for work. But you never wanted it until she was gone. When she was around, you were too excited."

"How old was I when I stopped wearing diapers?" I ask.

Grandmother frowns. "You started walking when you were eleven months old, and you still had them then. But after that... I'm not sure. When you and your mother moved to Cugnac, I went to stay with my sister Julie for a while. Your father had a maid who looked after you, what was her name? The one before Jeanine."

So I was not a complete freak. "How old was I when I came to Cugnac?" I ask.

Even before I finish my sentence, I know I shouldn't have asked. Grandmother stands up, puts her knitting back into her work table. "I'll go and see about dinner," she says.

In the evening, I decide to try Mother. As she runs our bath, I ask again, "How old was I when we came to live in this house?"

"Oh," she says. "We came here... just after you were born."

This can't be. We were still in Lyon when I was *walking*. And what about the clients she went back to? But I won't badger her about these incongruities. I wonder why. In school, when there's something I want to know, I ask. When the answer doesn't satisfy me, I insist. If mademoiselle Pélican doesn't like it, too bad.

Going to school for the first time was such a treat. I couldn't wait. People opened books and looked entranced: I wanted to know what that was all about. Mother often boasts that I learned to read in three weeks, as soon as I got to Sainte-Blandine, when I was two years old. Probably another exaggeration.

I was happy in the nursery class downstairs. Relaxed, and utterly comfortable. Learning to tell time with the big clock on the blackboard, listening to stories of saints. Writing. Away from food. We all brought a *goûter* for the afternoon break, but nobody cared what we did with it. So I ate it, easily. Two slices of bread, a bar of chocolate. Safe.

But before I started school, before I came here, I lived in Lyon. I have clear memories of being in a walker, and moving from the front door, through a passage, into a room with a lot of light. I remember enjoying the movement, to and fro, from the door, through the passage, into the room, around the room, back to the passage. The large windows, their square metal frames. Hiding behind the front door, waiting. My mother opening the door, and not seeing me behind it.

Poppies

Today is Mother's birthday, and I'm expecting trouble. For weeks she's been obsessed with crocodile handbags, stopping entranced when she sees one in a shop window, fondling them in stores, asking everybody around (especially her husband) which ones they like best, indicating her own preferences. Last Christmas it was mouton. She didn't see or talk about anything but mouton coats, and Father finally caught her drift. Not quickly, though: two weeks at least after it had become obvious even to Coralie.

This time, I'm pretty sure Father hasn't been paying attention. He's distracted. Even when reading a Série Noire thriller in his study, he stops every other minute, holds his cheeks in his hands and looks into the distance as if afraid of what's coming. Yesterday, over *apéritifs* in the garden, while Estelle Vié admired Mother's tulips, her husband Bertrand was telling Father about a storm off Cap de Creus last week, when he was sailing back from Spain with Laurent, his older son. Usually Father likes to hear every last detail of his friends' adventures, but he wasn't listening. Bertrand noticed, after a while. "Is anything wrong?" he asked.

"No, no," Father said. "Just the usual. You know. The business."

"I'm sorry about that," Bertrand said. "Tell me if there's anything I can do."

"Thanks," Father said, "but it's all right. I'll just have to find a way."

I was sitting in Bertrand's lap. I'm getting a bit old for this, but I can't resist: it's so comfortable up there. Bertrand's skin, his hair, smell of lavender and wood smoke. His voice is deep and light at the same time, his ruddy face always looks contented. I'd have liked Father to tell him more about his troubles, and I thought he might, since they've been friends for ever. Maybe Father felt Bertrand wouldn't understand. The Viés are so rich, they have so many *propriétés* with olive groves and apricots and cherries, that it doesn't matter if their wine doesn't sell. Or maybe they couldn't talk because the women were near, and you don't discuss business in front of your wives.

This morning, with breakfast, Loli brought three cards for Mother, two of them in the same envelope from my brothers who attend the same boarding school, Saint-Ignace-de-Montreuil, and one from Justine. Mother read Justine's aloud: "To my beloved beautiful Dette who, unlike most inhabitants of this planet, becomes younger with each birthday." We didn't get to hear my brothers' prose, but Mother pored over their cards with a wide smile. "Isn't it incredible how much your children love me?" she said to Father. "What stepmother gets this kind of tribute, I wonder. I'm so fortunate!"

At lunchtime, after Mother has blown out the candles and we've all eaten cake (except I discreetly give most of mine to Coralie), we get out our presents. Grandmother's is a bottle of lavender oil, I embroidered a handkerchief, and Coralie made a clay pot for Mother's dressing table. Mother looks her usual amiable self. Then Father gives her a flat, floppy parcel. Can't be a handbag. It takes Mother so long to undo the ribbons, Coralie gets scissors from Grandmother's worktable.

It's a scarf. Light-brown silk with yellow poppies. Mother's face collapses into a sulk and, as the gorgeous fabric unfurls in her lap, she starts breathing slowly, angrily. Leaving her presents on the table, she walks into the hall. I follow her, but when she goes on towards the kitchen I decide to stay put. I can still see her, though, at the end of the passage beyond the pantry. She says something to Loli, then puts on her garden apron and gets busy with her box hedges.

Coralie goes into the garden too, the other end of it, and for a while I watch her from the hall, through the tasting room windows. She's making ragout in her bucket with soil from Mother's hydrangea beds and water from the hose. She hasn't noticed anything but the scarf's beautiful colors. When I go back to the dining room, Loli is clearing the table and Grandmother sitting near her window with *L'Indépendant*. All as usual, except Father is still standing in front of the gifts with questions on his face. When he sees

71

me, he starts and walks across the hall into his study. As he leaves the door half open, I follow him.

He's sitting at his desk, with an open book in front of him. I stand beside him, and read, "May 10. I am no longer here. I've stopped existing long ago. I just occupy the place of someone other people think is me."

The sentences, the tone, feel familiar. "Who wrote this book?" I ask.

Father closes the small white volume, and I can see the front page: André Gide, *Journal 1942-1949*, Gallimard.

"So it's a journal?" I ask. "Like Anne Frank's?"

"Yes," he says. "It's a detailed account of Gide's daily life and thoughts in Tunis then Algiers. He was there during the war, and not writing much else."

"Because of the war?"

"Maybe. Or maybe he was just tired of fiction, and politics. Or just tired. In 1942, he was seventy-three."

"Is he still alive?"

"He died last year."

"Do you like his books?"

"A lot." He smiles. "But they're not for you. Not yet. Maybe *Isabelle* in a year or two."

In Father's opinion, practically nothing is for me. Books, films. I don't understand this. I love the comtesse de Ségur, but I know all her books practically by heart. I've read all the children's books we have here, many times, even the dreary ones about brave wolf dogs or endearing wild horses. So

I *have* to check out the adult shelves. As Justine *has* to lie when she wants to go out with boys. Justine says Father is old-fashioned. Last time she was here, for Easter vacation, he told us once again how sorry he was that he won't be able to give us dowries. "Dowries!" Justine said as soon as Father was gone. "Why would we need dowries? My mother had one, but that was ages ago. I'm pretty sure Odette didn't."

It does sound like a word from the past. I've read several novels that belonged to my grandmother Clara (she wrote her name on the title page), which take place at a time when dowries were essential. If you didn't have one, nobody would marry you. Which meant you had to become a governess, or starve.

Father is inspecting the surface of his desk, vaguely pushing around pens, ashtrays, paperweights, a newspaper open at the crossword puzzle. His shoulders are stooped, his face confused.

"I love the scarf," I say. "I've never seen one like that."

"Maybe it's too… different for your mother?"

"No," I say. "I'm sure she likes it."

He stops moving, his chin on his fist. "Then why…? Was there something else she wanted?"

I shrug.

"Didn't she mention a crocodile handbag? But she has so many handbags. Didn't she get a lizard skin one in September?"

"If she wants a crocodile one," I say, "she'll get it for herself."

"Maybe," he says. "Maybe not."

He looks so sad. I kiss him, and go out to get my bike. I don't feel like calling Coralie or Eléonore. I pedal to the end of the back street, down the slope along Eléonore's parents' orchard, across the outer boulevard, into the vineyards. I'm pushing against the north wind, which is wild today. My plaits are undone, my hair flies. I decide that I'll never want a gift. Or anything, from anybody.

Communist

Our friends Monique and Nicole live at the top of the Maison Bousquet on the avenue. It's a large townhouse, higher than the rest and divided into apartments. Monique and Nicole are on the top floor. Usually, when we go to fetch them, we run up the four flights of stairs, and our footsteps resonate all through the staircase. Before we get to the top, under the glass roof, Monique and Nicole have come out and we can all barrel down the stairs immediately.

But this Thursday morning, when Coralie and I get to the fourth floor, only Monique is out on the landing. "Can you wait?" she says. "Nicole isn't dressed. Two buttons are missing from her blouse, Mother needs to sew them on. Or tell me where you're going, we'll join you soon."

Now her mother comes out too, holding a needle and thread. Her eyes look tired behind thick round glasses. "Come in," she says, "I won't be a moment, come into the kitchen and sit down. Would you like some coffee?"

Coffee? For *us*? Monique has been loitering on the landing, but now she follows us into the kitchen, takes out three glasses, fills them with water from the tap, and sets them on the table. She leaves the door open, and I soon realize why: there are no windows in this room, no windows that open. Just a square piece of translucent glass through which a little light comes in, so the room is not completely dark but

75

nearly. The air doesn't move at all. Monique's mother goes on with her sewing. There's only one bulb hanging from a wire above the table, and it doesn't give off much light either. Coralie has drunk all her water and is fidgeting in her chair. "Where's Nicole?" she asks.

"In the bedroom," Monique says. "I'll get her."

Outside the kitchen door, beyond a narrow passage, there's another door. Monique opens it, and Coralie follows her. "Don't!" I say. But she's quick, and to stop her I have to follow her into the passage, from which I get a glimpse of the bedroom: a double bed on one side, where the father is asleep, and another where Nicole is feeding her teddy bear with a tiny bottle. The bedroom is exactly like the kitchen, but without any window. I pull Coralie back into the kitchen.

"Why can't I?" she cries.

"Hush!" I say. "We need to wait here. Can't you see that monsieur Delpech is asleep?"

"He's resting," madame Delpech says, cutting the thread with her teeth. "He hasn't been well. It's his chest."

Nicole and Monique are back in the kitchen. Monique helps her sister put on her blouse. "Okay, let's go," she says. They both kiss their mother, we say goodbye, and as we walk down the stairs I wonder: Monique and Nicole have been my friends for ever and until today I had *no* idea how they lived when we weren't playing together. There must be so much more I don't know. It makes me dizzy.

Roseline and Eléonore are waiting for us in the back street, playing hopscotch, and we all walk to an abandoned stone hut in the middle of the vineyards that we've decided to clean out and set up as our new base. It's beautiful, a perfect square with a tile roof, but full of chaff, dung, and broken tools. We all work steadily, and manage to clear about a quarter of the space. When we get home at the end of the morning, Mother is appalled. "Have you been rolling in garbage? Whose idea was this?" Actually, I think it was mine. She sends us up with Loli to shower and change.

After lunch Father asks us if we want to go to La Fourcade with him to see the new chicks. Of course we do. Ginette told me that, a long time ago, we had hens in our back garden. When Grandmother Clara died, Mother had them moved to La Fourcade because they did too much damage to her flowers.

Coralie runs ahead of us on the dirt road, but I walk with Father, holding his hand. "Do you know where the Delpechs live?" I ask him.

"Yes, they have an apartment in the Bousquet building, don't they?"

"Have you ever been to their place?"

"No, why?"

"It's... not an apartment. Just two rooms, with windows that don't..." As I explain, I feel I'm going to cry, so I breathe deeply before I start again. "There's no air, no light from outside, it's... like a prison. And they look so weary, so... The parents. As if they've been... forgotten. They live in the dark! Why can't they have a house, or at least windows? And we have so many rooms, it can't be right."

"Would you like them to come and live with us?" Father asks.

"Would I? I don't particularly want to live with them, I don't think they want to live with us, but why do we have all this, and they're shut up in those two murky rooms!" My voice is horribly shrill and teary.

"Yes," Father says. "It isn't fair at all, and thank you for telling me about it. I'll talk to Rigaill."

Talk to Rigaill? I have no idea what Father means, but the chicks are all around us, not at all shy. Coralie wants to feed them, to hold them; I have to show her how to do it without hurting them. Father is discussing something with Achille, the gardener. Rigaill plays bridge with Father twice a week, and he is the headmaster of the boys' primary school. What can he do about the Delpechs?

Five days later, Father tells me that a social worker went to look at the Delpechs' place and signed them up as an emergency case. They'll have a house near the stadium in three or four months. "Before the end of September at the latest," he says.

What is this? Magic? "Can they afford to buy a house?" I ask.

"They'll rent it. Rigaill had been telling us about a bunch of houses the town council is building on the other side of the stadium, precisely for families like the Delpechs. But you have to apply, and apparently your friends' parents hadn't. So, it was lucky you happened to find out about their circumstances."

"And that you play bridge with Rigaill!" I say. I'm so happy for my friends. Even though they will live at the other end of town and we won't play together all the time as we do now.

"Yes," Father says. "Thank God for our Communist mayor!"

Rigaill is also our mayor, how did I forget? "What exactly is a Communist?" I ask.

"Well, it sounds like you're one! You are against social injustice, aren't you? You don't think people should live in two airless rooms when others have a large house."

"What about you? Do you think that's *right*?"

"Right, probably not, but what should be done about it isn't obvious. Some people think that one can help poor people individually, as the *Dames de charité* do, but that the state or the town shouldn't meddle. Our town council has Communists, Socialists, and a few Radicals. If the Communists didn't have a majority, I'm not sure those houses would have been built. It was Rigaill's idea. Some councils aren't very interested in public housing."

"What about you? Are you a Communist?"

"No, I'm not. I'm not anything much, actually."

"Don't you vote for your friend Rigaill?"

"No, I usually vote for the Radicals. I like Mendès France. I think he's right, as a whole. About Indochina, Tunisia, Morocco. And about the need for a European Union."

"But what's the difference?" I ask. "Between Radicals, Communists, and... the other kind?"

"Socialists," Father says. "In my opinion, they're too stagnant; and I don't agree with what the Communists are doing in Russia, in Hungary. But in the council here, they work well together."

"What do you care what they're doing in Russia if they build houses for people who need one here?"

"Well, you might be right," Father says. "Maybe next time I'll vote for Rigaill."

Petals

May first, lily-of-the-valley day. Mother came back last night from a few days in Lyon. While she was unpacking, Father showed me the sprigs he brought from La Fourcade and hid in the tasting room. This morning Coralie and I, as soon as we open our eyes, run down in our nightgowns to find them and present a few to Grandmother and to Loli. We get kisses in return. Then we run up to our parents' room and give Mother her little bouquet. "It smells wonderful," she says, and kisses us too.

Back in our bedroom, Loli helps us get dressed before we join our parents again. Father is reading *La Revue Nautique*. Mother plaits my hair and Coralie's, then helps herself to more coffee. When she pours milk into it, I run to the window and hide behind Father's chair. I rather like the way coffee smells on its own (especially when it's roasting and not yet soaked in water), but mixed with milk it's mephitic.

Coralie is already tripping back towards our room but Mother, gulping her coffee, calls her. "Come here, let's make you presentable." Coralie, her feet wide apart, stops but doesn't turn round; I alone, from my hiding place, can see her pouting lips and ferocious eyes. Mother pulls down the skirt of Coralie's blue-and-white smocked dress. She also tries to straighten up the short puff sleeves, but she can't get hold: they are too tight around Coralie's plump arms.

"Coralie has grown so much this year," she says. "And she's put on so much weight, there's not a chance Tita's dresses from last summer will fit her. I'll have to get some fabric and make at least two new dresses for each of them. I found amazing patterns in Lyon, the kind nobody in Cugnac has ever heard of. Wait and see."

Father looks up from his magazine. "Of course," he says. "Poor Coralie, you can hardly breathe! But maybe you'll choose another color this time? Isn't there anything you like apart from blue?"

"I — don't — like — blue," Coralie articulates. "And I don't like dresses. Can I have shorts and shirts instead?"

"Nonsense," Mother says. "Do you want to go to school in shorts? To church, and to birthday parties?" She breathes in slowly, then out through her nose, and says, looking in Father's direction but not at him, "What's wrong with blue? It's her color. It looks perfect with her eyes."

Father smiles, and shrugs. "I know it's silly, but blue always reminds me of Children of Mary. I find it a sad color. So, if Coralie doesn't particularly..."

How can he imagine that Coralie's tastes, or mine, have any influence on what we wear? "What's a Child of Mary?" I ask.

Father shakes his head. "I don't even know exactly, but there were lots of them when I was growing up. I think it started with a nun in the nineteenth century, who had seen some apparitions. The Children of Mary wear a miraculous medal on a blue ribbon. They also wear blue capes. Everything must be blue."

"Medals are so gruesome," I say. "Not to mention miraculous ones." Actually, I despise all ornaments.

Father nods slowly. Coralie has settled in his lap and is drawing a horse on a discarded envelope. Father makes me laugh sometimes, the way he recoils from religion. It's almost like me with cheese. No-good Children of Mary! But that reminds me of the *Month* of Mary (nothing to do with the Children), which starts today. Tonight. And for which we need to get ready.

"Can we have our baskets, please?" I ask Mother, who is studying the fashion pages in *Modes et Travaux*.

She doesn't even look up.

"Our Month of Mary baskets!"

"Oh. Of course. They're in the main attic. I'll get them for you later."

She's totally engrossed in the beach outfits. "Can I go and get them now?"

She doesn't answer, and I decide it means yes.

Downstairs in the kitchen, Loli is amazed at how fast I eat my porridge, on my own. "Hey, you're making progress!" she says. "Soon you might even get hungry like the rest of us." While Coralie goes on with her breakfast I run up to the main attic, look around, and finally make out the baskets in the top of the white cupboard, above the Christmas

83

decorations. I climb on a chair to reach them, and the chair is wobbly, but I hold on to the shelf and reach for one, then the other. Mine is oval, larger and slightly deeper than Coralie's round one. Both are covered with white muslin and have ribbons that will go around our necks.

Tonight, like every Friday, our parents are going out, probably to the cinema. For once I don't care. Every evening of this month we too will be away from home. In church, with our friends. May is the Month of Mary, and the hymn says it all: it's the most beautiful month, *le mois le plus beau.*

In the afternoon we join our friends in the back street, but we're all so excited about tonight we can hardly concentrate on our games. We try cops and robbers, hopscotch, Mother May I, but every time neighbors walk by we stop them to ask what time it is. When the sun finally sets, I appeal to Eléonore's grandmother, who is sitting outside the cellar in her garden, reading a book of poems. She tells me it's five past seven. "Are you going?" I ask her in Catalan. She and her husband are famous for coming to France on foot before the war. From Ripoll, over the Pyrenees, pushing a wheelbarrow with their belongings. She shakes her head, and grins. "I'm an atheist, remember? Have a good time!"

We dine at quarter past seven, in the kitchen with Loli. At ten past eight, Coralie and I hang our baskets around our necks and go to the garden to choose our flowers. Peonies, dahlias, sweet peas, narcissi. Mother said we can take only those that are completely open, and where at least one or two petals have started shrivelling. I snip off the whole blossom (Coralie is not allowed to use the clippers), and we pull the petals off into our baskets. Then, intoxicated by the surfeit of scents, the sharp red ones, the acid yellow, the many shades of pink, the quiet white, we stand among the rose bushes, fingering the supple membranes, the soft shallow cups, warm from the afternoon sun.

Eléonore is at the back door. Roseline, Monique, Nicole are waiting for us around the corner, and we all walk up the avenue with our full, fragrant baskets hanging from our necks. Further on, we pass friends from both our schools, all hurrying to church while the bells break out in fancy chimes. In the church, Coralie and I go and sit with Sainte-Blandine on the left; our friends from the state school are across the aisle with their catechism classes.

Soon the organ starts and we're all on the move again, for the procession. In front, four choirboys carry a statue of the Virgin Mary, and we follow, first Sainte-Blandine then the rest of the children, reciting the rosary as we walk, one Our Father, ten Hail Marys, and again, five times, while the organ punctuates our prayers with crisp, cheerful chords. After each decade of the rosary, the bearers stop in front of a different side chapel, where incense burns and lights shine on the statue. Then, as the rest of us pass the chapel, singing, we throw our petals to the Virgin. I so love to sing, I tend to get carried away and not pay attention to what I'm doing.

But we need to be careful: there are five decades, five stops in front of chapels, and it doesn't look good if we spend all our petals too soon and then have nothing to throw but air.

For each stop there's a different hymn but in between chapels we go back to *C'est le mois de Marie*, where Mary is compared to the spring, to a lily (pure), a violet (humble) and a rose (loving). During the last decade, the Virgin is taken to the middle of the chancel, and everybody faces her to recite her litany. In Latin, not in French like at school in the Sacred Heart room. The Latin invocations sound so much more thrilling: *Rosa mystica, Turris eburnea, Domus aurea, Stella matutina.* As if ivory, gold, morning were burned into the Virgin's substance, had become part of her body. The Latin, the sweet scents, the songs waft me above the ground, and I seem to swing there, light and swift. Giddy.

The organ, silent during the litany, booms again in full glory to tell us it's time to go. In the aisle the two schools mix again as we stroll out of the church. Our baskets are empty now, so we can skip and romp through the narrow winding streets around the church and into the avenue, greeted as we pass by the many older people who sit in cafés, or on benches and chairs outside their houses, enjoying the fresh air and the action. Among the adults, all but a few devout women eschew the *Mois de Marie* ceremonies, which take place around the usual dinner time. But at nine thirty, when we children walk home, the whole population of the town is out.

Artichokes

As we sit down to lunch, Father announces that he's managed to sell Le Cabarrou, our park. He sounds relieved, and wretched. He enunciates cautiously, as if his voice couldn't proceed without a walking stick. Mother's face is rigid, her eyes on the Pyrenees behind the railway station. I think she knew already.

Father keeps selling bits of property, that's what we live on. I don't think his vineyards or his business really make a profit. When he sells a piece of land, he usually says it's "for peanuts". Not this time, though. Maybe we're going to be fine for a while? Maybe he got a lot of money for Le Cabarrou. It's huge and beautiful. There's a chalet, a pond, a tennis court, lots of almond trees, lilacs, irises. Also, at the back, beyond the laurel bushes, an old railway car.

The people who bought the park aren't exactly friends of our family, but we've known them for a while because their daughter, Noëlle, is in my class, and her father is our dentist. They have an apartment in town, above the dental practice, with a puppet theater where we sometimes put on shows. Noëlle makes all the puppets, and she paints all the sets. She has a younger brother, and her mother is pregnant again. Now they're going to build a house on the tennis court. No more tennis. I'm happy for them, because their apartment is so small, and in the new house Noëlle will have her own room; I'm happy for myself too, because there are few things I hate more than tennis, and as long as the court was there I had to play every Thursday and Sunday (except when it rained, but it hardly ever does). Mother likes tennis, though, she's good at it. And she'll miss being the hostess, the owner of an attraction that fostered so much social activity.

The sale creates a link between Noëlle's family and ours, even though people here, adults, tend to be wary of newcomers — Noëlle's parents came to Cugnac just after Noëlle was born, but they're still outsiders. Mother says that at least Le Cabarrou won't go to the kind of people who already have too much and never needed to work for it. I think she's more sympathetic than most to those who haven't been here for ever, like Noëlle's parents.

With Father's friends, even though the women invite her and the men compliment her, she tends to be wary. When they allude to something that's foreign to her, like troubadour poetry or existentialism, her shoulders and her feet contract for a second or two. In her place, I'd ask a question, or at least try to pick up some information from the conversation. She doesn't. And she doesn't completely withdraw either, as she does when they reminisce about sailing adventures. She tries to saunter through the problem, brushing it aside as if she knew all about the topic but it didn't deserve her full attention. She pulls it off mostly, but it can't be easy.

This afternoon she takes us to what is no longer our park, and she sits with Noëlle's mother, drinking tea and knitting in our old deckchairs in front of the chalet. The younger children are playing hide and seek, but Noëlle wants to draw the artichokes that border the wide path, all the way from the chalet to the front gate. She says they are extraordinary, all in bloom. She gives me paper and crayons, and I'm about to say that I can't draw, but I change my mind. I don't feel like hide and seek, or anything else. And artichokes are one of the few foods I like. Coralie loves them too. When we were small, people said we must have been born, instead of in cabbages, in artichokes.

We sit cross-legged on the dry earth, and as Noëlle concentrates on her artwork I vaguely listen to our mothers, who are talking on the other side of the lilac bushes. About headaches. Mother says hers can last for days; but sometimes they go away when she smokes a cigarette. Noëlle's mother never gets any, thank God and touch wood. Noëlle shows me her first drawing, which I sincerely admire. She hasn't gone into details, but her purple flowers inside the spiked leaves look so alive. I have nothing to show; as usual the lines on my piece of paper don't make any sense. Noëlle says she'll get some watercolors from the chalet. Meanwhile, the women have gone on to another topic.

Noëlle's mother is laughing. "I was already five months pregnant with Noëlle when we got married," she says. "We'd been thinking about it for a while, but our families were far away, we had to decide where it would take place, organize it... We were both busy at the time, with our final exams.

Then of course we could no longer wait. My mother was upset. She couldn't believe I really liked René. She thought I was marrying him because I had to!"

"You won't believe it," Mother reciprocates, "but *I* didn't get married until Tita was more than a year old. When I met my husband, he was getting a divorce. Then his wife heard about me, and suddenly she no longer wanted the divorce. She set impossible conditions: she claimed everything he had. This took for ever to sort out and meanwhile, I got pregnant."

This is all news to me, and probably "not for children". But the lilac bushes are thick.

"It must have been hard," Noëlle's mother says.

"It was all right. And something really funny happened. When Tita was born, I didn't give my name at the clinic. The doctor told me there was a new law: the mother doesn't have to register if she doesn't want to. So I didn't."

"Why?" Noëlle's mother asks.

"Because Tita's father wasn't divorced yet, so he couldn't recognize Tita legally. If I didn't give my name, when we got married she'd have her father's name right away. There'd be no trace of her being born out of wedlock."

Wedlock? Noëlle's mother doesn't react in words. Noëlle is back, with new implements. She offers me some, I choose haphazardly, and she settles down with her easel further up the walk.

"I forgot about this," Mother goes on, "until one day my mother, who was taking care of Tita, said that a social worker had called and wanted to see me. Two women visited us at home. They said, 'We have good news for you: we've found a very nice family to adopt your daughter.' I couldn't believe my ears. Then they explained that when a child was born to unknown parents, it was automatically put up for adoption. I was so happy to tell these women that my baby didn't need to be adopted, I was marrying her father next month. Then they were all congratulations and so on. We had such a laugh. Adopted!"

Again, no reaction from Noëlle's mother. "There I was," Mother insists, her voice overflowing with rare delight, "there I was, telling them, 'I'm getting married next month.' They hadn't expected to hear this. They wished me luck, again and again. They were so happy for me, they said."

Coralie is sure that *she* was adopted: her real parents were gypsies, who were killed in a horse-drawn cart accident of the kind that happens at the beginning of *Les Petites Filles modèles*. Only a baby survived; Mother, who happened to drive by, took her in because of her blond hair. It's a good story, except everybody says that Coralie looks a lot like Father's mother, so I don't think she could have been adopted. And now it turns out *I* am the one who almost was. I could have been raised by... that "nice family". I wonder what those parents would have been like. But I have zero imagination.

Noëlle is back. She shows me her varicolored artichokes. "Great," I say. Her colors blend into each other, sharp and delicate; you can feel how thrilled she was when she looked at the plants.

Now that she's started, Mother can't stop. She must like this story, which allows her to present herself as knowledgeable (the new law) and adventurous, modern, different from the Cugnac *bourgeoises*. A few days later, she recounts my near-adoption to Eléonore's mother's secretary, who has come to take cuttings from some geraniums. The next Thursday I hear the tale again, in the exact same words, while I'm passing the cakes. I have a question and I decide to ask it. In public (the public consisting in Estelle Vié, Denise Pujol and Cami Espeluque). On purpose. Because I've noticed that when you ask her a question in front of her friends, Mother can't afford to be absolutely deaf.

"What was my surname before you married Father?" I ask. It couldn't be hers: the whole point was that she remained anonymous.

She starts, and spills some tea on her off-white skirt.

I'm waiting. Everybody is. She hesitates, her eyes on the wet spot, her right hand playing the piano on her thigh. She could say something about the chocolate cake. No, she can't. She raises her head, inhales, gives a loud sigh.

"You didn't need a name," she finally says. "You were just a little baby."

"But nobody can go without a name," I insist. "Not in France."

Something is happening to Mother's face. It's drawn and grey, her big eyes wan behind her glasses, all the sparkle gone. "Don't be tiresome," she says. "Ask Dolores if she can bring some more hot water. Then go play with your sister."

I'm dismissed. I stand in front of Mother and her friends, holding the empty plate in front of me as if it were full. Mother has already turned her back on me, but the other women are not ready to resume their conversation. They're not eating or drinking either, but watching me sideways. Cami's hands are joined against her mouth, as if she were praying, and Estelle's lips are trying to stop themselves from smiling. I want to ask again, to make a scene, but I don't know how.

Mink

This morning, for once, Mother doesn't pounce on my hair or Coralie's when Loli takes us to our parents' room. She hardly seems to notice us. She's reading a letter.

"Good news?" Father asks.

Mother nods, munching her bread and butter, and goes on reading. "Michel is opening a new store in Villeurbanne," she finally says. "He's there all the time, and Yvette is very bored. But she shouldn't complain, she got a mink coat for her birthday!"

So the letter is from Yvette, Mother's niece and goddaughter, who lives in Lyon.

"Maybe minks aren't the best possible company?" Father says.

Mother doesn't even smile. Has she changed her mind about mink coats? I've often heard her say to her friends, "Mink is not as indispensable as people think. Anyway I'm too young, and I'm perfectly happy with my three-quarter-length mouton coat. More my style. It's a bit too sporty for Paris, but Caroline, my sister-in-law, has so many fur coats, I can always borrow one."

I'm sitting behind Father on Mother's dressing-table stool. Coralie has sneaked into the bathroom, from which various rolling and tumbling noises emanate. But mother doesn't seem to hear, she's so absorbed in Yvette's letter.

"Yvette loves me so much!" she exclaims. "Listen to this: *I've met some people down here but I don't think I'll make any friends. Why did I let Michel persuade me to abandon my dear hill of Fourvière? Do I need a ten-room house, a pool, a garden, far from the city and everything I like? Every time I see these suburban women I wish you were with me. We'd have such a great time making fun of their frumpy outfits and their quenelle recipes. And we'd go to the opera! Michel is always too tired. Please come soon, I literally can't live without you!*"

"She doesn't sound very happy," Father says. "Or very patient with her new neighbors."

"She misses me too much," Mother says. "But I can't go right now. Maybe she could join me when I stay in Paris with Caroline. It would take her mind off her husband! Lucky for him he makes so much money, else he wouldn't stand a chance of keeping her."

Father frowns, and goes back to his newspaper. He doesn't like Michel very much either, and I can see why — the man is such a show-off, always going on about how well his business is doing, and what a clever deal he just made, and his new house, and the fancy car he's going to buy for Yvette. He keeps checking his appearance in mirrors, straightening his tie and his hair, simpering to himself. But Father never disparages anybody.

When Yvette brought Michel here last summer before they got married, Mother was thrilled because he had a sewing-machine store in the center of Lyon. Yvette's first husband, whom she'd married when she was sixteen (and he eighteen) had been a construction worker. We liked him very much, all of us except Mother. He and Yvette looked like they were in love, they had a beautiful baby daughter, and they took me around on their motorbike. But she divorced him last year to marry Michel. Now the little girl lives with her father and her father's parents, so we never see her.

When we met Michel, Mother wanted Father to share her enthusiasm. He said, "Not exactly my type, and I wouldn't have thought Yvette's type either, but what do I know?" That's about as far as he'll go when he objects to someone.

Father is *good* — everyone says so, even people who hardly know him. It's his reputation, and I often hear the same kind of praise for my grandfather, *his* father, who died long before I was born. I think Coralie takes after them. Mother wouldn't agree about that. She often says, "What a terrible child!" and "I don't know what to do with her!" Father will answer, "Well, she's full of life!" And yes, Coralie doesn't always do as she's told, but that's because she knows what she likes, and wants to be left alone to pursue her projects. She can be fierce, but only if crossed. Like the comtesse de Ségur's Sophie, she misbehaves, but deep down in her heart she's good.

Do I know any children who are bad? Mother says that Eléonore is spoiled, because she has so many dresses and such a large collection of dolls from the French provinces. And it's true that her mother spends many evenings making clothes for her after working all day in her office downstairs. But Eléonore is the opposite of demanding. Her mother just loves sewing. Once I asked her, "Do you ever make dresses for yourself?" and she laughed. "Look at me!" she said. So, I did. And I blushed.

Eléonore's mother is fat, and her dresses are like sacks, but I hadn't noticed this before, because she always wears large colorful shawls over her shoulders. "It's so much fun to dress Eléonore," she said. "And so easy. Anything you put on her will look good!" Which is not exactly true, and sounds silly, but who cares? I don't agree that Eléonore is spoiled. She's exceptionally obedient, and she loves her parents. We make fun of her because she's obsessed with ballet, and it takes her a while to get our jokes, but she's not *bad*.

Father puts down *L'Indépendant*, looks around, and fetches Coralie from the bathroom. "You're going to be late for school!" he says. "Run down to Loli, and ask her to do your hair."

So we both go down, and Coralie's hair is perfect in three seconds — she keeps very quiet today, because it's time for her bread and butter *tartines*. Who is bad? I wonder as I pretend to bring spoonfuls of porridge to my mouth while Loli does my plaits. Not even Michel, probably. I don't know him well, and I don't feel like knowing him better, but that

97

doesn't mean he's bad. I still have to meet someone who's bad, in real life. Someone who's sure to go to hell. But if parents are responsible for their children being bad, shouldn't they be the ones who go to hell? The comtesse doesn't say.

What about me? I don't think anybody (except maybe, at times, mademoiselle Pélican) would call me *bad*. At home, I'm supposed to be extremely good. But I don't *feel* good. It's just an appearance. I'm certainly not like Sophie — I'm not sure I *have* a heart. There is no "deep down" in me. I wonder if I even exist.

Idéal

Friday. Our parents are going to the cinema: the Idéal, hardly a ten-minute walk from our house. Coralie and I are in bed in our nightgowns, waiting for Mother to come and kiss us good night.

But I can hear her and Father in the hall, putting on their coats. I call. The wooden door to the vestibule creaks open. Soon they will be gone. And we haven't been kissed.

I run to the landing. Lean out over the balustrade. Call again. The front door rumbles open, metal and glass resonate into my body. I call. Call again, as loud as I can. Listen, on tiptoe, my head thrust forward over the bannister, my shoulders. Call. Listen. Call.

I'm hanging on the other side of the balustrade, in the void. How did I get here? I stop calling, try to send all my strength into my hands. The front door bangs shut.

When I wake up, my whole left side is black: foot, leg, thigh, hip, arm, back. They say I was lucky: I fell onto the wicker table before hitting the stone floor of the hall. I don't remember falling, and they say of course not: I fainted, then was out for more than thirty hours. Father brings me a book, *Petite Princesse*, but I'm too stunned to read. I look at my skin slowly becoming blue, purple, red. Bruises. Nothing is broken. I wonder if our parents ever went to the Idéal.

2

Le Bon Usage

Back at Sainte-Blandine after nine days in bed. As usual, first thing in the morning, we're reading the mass aloud in our classroom, one verse for each of us, round and round. When it's my turn, we've got to *Quare tristis es, anima mea, et quare conturbas me*? "My soul, why are you sad, and why do you trouble me?" Exactly what I often ask myself. What's wrong with you, why can't you be like everybody else?

When I'm done reading, I look back at verse 3: *Emitte lucem tuam*, "Send me your light and your truth: they will lead me to your holy mountain, and to your tabernacle." But do I want to be led to some mountain? And what's a tabernacle doing there? Isn't that the box on the altar, where the hosts are kept?

Meanwhile I've lost my place, but I hear Elisabeth in the *Confiteor*: she confesses to almighty God, to Mary ever virgin, to Michael the archangel, John the Baptist, Peter and Paul, etc. that she has sinned exceedingly in thought, word, deed, and omission. It's her fault, her fault, her most grievous fault. And it goes on: have mercy on me, grant us pardon, take away our iniquities. I often wonder what this is all about. All this sin, fault, and iniquity.

Could falling over the banister count as a sin? I didn't deliberately throw myself onto the stone floor, so I didn't sin *cogitatione*. But *opere*? And *omissione*, too — I could have been more careful, could have kept from leaning forward. Actually, I should have stayed in my room, in bed, as Coralie did. And I shouldn't have called out: I sinned *verbo*.

But I'm not going to discuss this with monsieur le curé. Our priest is a gracious, respectable man, but I can't imagine having an actual conversation with him. He's very old, and he has the whole parish to take care of. He's on a different plane, but on our side, somehow; so we children, among ourselves, call him by his first name, Olivier.

When my friends and I prepare for confession every week, we look at the list of sins in our catechism and select a few: I didn't say my prayers, I disobeyed my parents, I lied, I swore, I cheated, I hit my sister. Practically all of mine are fiction. I don't even mention my "insolence" to Pélican, because I'm proud of it. I guess it's a sin to invent sins for confession, but what can we do? We have to say *something*.

Once I was kneeling in the chapel in front of the confessional awaiting my turn when I heard a girl from the *école laïque* address the priest in a loud, vehement voice. She seemed to have so much to tell, I assumed she was a great sinner, which made me envious. But when I listened more closely I realised she was just describing in detail her quarrels with her brothers, then giving elaborate explanations for a few perfunctory lies to her teacher. She was making it all sound intensely dramatic and rather fun, which I hadn't imagined you were supposed to do in confession. Such a contrast to my bland lists.

Careful: it's my turn again, and I am the *indignus famulus*, the unworthy servant, with *innumerabilibus peccatis, et offensionibus, et negligentiis*. But in the Sanctus I get to say *Sabaoth* and *Hosanna*!

Now we have to copy a map of the Garonne and its tributaries. I look at the shape of the river in my geography book and try to understand its twists and turns. Coming down from the Pyrenees, a right angle of nearly 90°, then left at... 120°? The river I draw is totally different from the model, but Noëlle's looks perfect. Anne-Claude is already writing the names of towns along the Gers, the Tarn and the Lot: Auch, Cahors, Albi. I have to erase everything and start again, knowing that I won't do much better.

After the break (hopscotch), Group One is at the blackboard to recite their lesson on the plural of nouns ending in *ou*, while our group gets a conjugation test. *Choir, gésir, coudre, falloir, faillir, mourir*, in the past anterior, future perfect, past subjunctive, pluperfect subjunctive, and the two forms of conditional perfect. After a while I hear Anne-Claude, flushed and dishevelled, whispering on my left. "Tita! Your feet!" Between our desks lies a folded piece of paper. I pick it up while Pélican corrects the first set of exercises. It says, "Noëlle and I are stumped on *gésir*. Save us and you can choose one each of our pictures."

104

Pictures are the main currency at Sainte-Blandine. There are several ways of getting them. Pélican gives you one for ten *bons points* (small pieces of cardboard with the Sainte-Blandine stamp on them that you get for good marks or good conduct). You also get pictures for your friends' or siblings' solemn communion, to commemorate the event. All these are holy pictures, but we also collect scented perfume ads. Anne-Claude has quite a few because her grandmother owns a perfume store.

"*Gésir* has no past participle," I answer on the other side of Anne-Claude's note in my best handwriting (which is still pretty bad). "So no compound tenses." I fold the paper, drop it on the floor when Pélican isn't looking, and give it a push with my foot. Everything's fine so far: I'm trying to choose mentally among Anne-Claude's sweet-smelling pictures. I know! I want *Soir de Paris*, with a couple sitting in the back of a cab. The woman wears a long pinkish dress, a fur stole, and dark-red gloves. She looks dreamily into the distance while the man, in a top hat, white gloves and a white scarf, concentrates on her face, as if waiting for an answer.

And from Noëlle's collection? I'll have the one where Jesus, outside the stable, naked in a wicker basket, lifts his arms to his kneeling mother. Her keen eye, in profile, is intent on the child, her whole body straining towards him while her arms remain crossed on her chest in gratitude and amazement. Joseph has a white beard and a red robe; he too bends toward the child with his palms pressed together in prayer. Three naked angels fly above the family, with something in their hands that looks like sheet music. There's a crucifix on the left and, in the background, a clear sky with trees and hills. I already have quite a few Holy Family pictures.

Pélican has been busy writing on the blackboard: *chou, caillou, fou, pou, sou, genou*. All of a sudden, as if she had eyes in the back of her head, she turns around and says in a creaky voice, "Anne-Claude, give me that immediately."

Pélican is coming towards us, and Anne-Claude hands her the piece of paper that tells the whole story. "Zero for both of you!" Pélican announces. "Shame on you! You'll spend the rest of the afternoon kneeling in front of the Sacred Heart, and if I hear another word out of you, you'll also be there all day tomorrow. Now go." She hasn't looked at the other side of the paper, so Noëlle has escaped. Pélican turns to me: "You especially, Euphémie, should know better. The more gifts God has bestowed upon us, the more careful we should be in using them properly. You will write a hundred lines for tomorrow morning: "I won't connive with dunces and betray my teacher's trust."

When I get home I write those stupid lines in the dining room, listening on the phonograph to *La Belle de Cadix* — a Luis Mariano song about a woman who has many suitors but doesn't love any of them. She finally enters a convent. Then I go to Father's study to look up *tabernacula* in the Gaffiot. I only find *tabernaculum*. Oh, *tabernacula* is the plural. And the word means "hut", or "tent". Do I want to be led to God's hut? I already have a hard time sharing a room with Coralie. I'd like to live in a hut, but I'd rather have it all to myself.

I reach up for another book, *Le Bon Usage*. It's about the French language, and all that can be done with its words and phrases. Every time Pélican makes a dubious assertion about French, that's where I go for clarification. I also use it when I read something in a book that doesn't feel right.

Pélican counted as an error my "Les rois qui se sont succédé sur le trône," which is the only solution according to *Le Bon Usage*, since there's no direct object. Pélican used the general rule about "être", which doesn't apply to pronominal verbs. I'll keep quiet about this. You can't just say, "But there's a special rule about pronominal verbs". You have to wait. Until the right time comes for an innocent-sounding question that won't sound like an objection but will bring her whole house down.

Now I'm checking the plural of compound nouns, and here's a surprise: I hadn't realised that the "nouveau" in "nouveau-né" (newborn) is an adverb, not an adjective. Therefore invariable. So you should write "des nouveau-nés", not "des nouveaux-nés". Nice. But what about the feminine? "Une nouveau-née"?

I'm trying to remember what it felt like being a *nouveau-née* when Father walks into the room. I'm sitting in his chair, so I stand up. He takes me in his arms, seats me on the desk in front of him and gently strokes the long smudge on my right shoulder and arm, which is now yellow mostly, and light brown at the edges. Whereas my hip is dark green, with some blue. "Does it still hurt?" he asks.

"No," I say. "But this side of my body feels different. Lighter."

Father sees *Le Bon Usage* next to me. He frowns. "What do you want with that book?"

"I just... like it," I say.

"You do? It's a very good book, but you probably have something simpler, written for children."

"Our grammar book is much too vague," I say. "For instance, about the agreement of past participles, it only gives the main rules, but there are lots of exceptions."

Father is shaking his head. "Why on earth do you care so much about past participles?" he finally says.

"Don't you care about words? This book looks like it has been used a lot."

"Too much, maybe. You can have it."

I jump up to kiss him. "Oh, thank you! But are you sure you won't need it?"

He smiles. "If I need it, I'll tell you. But I haven't used it in years."

I like rules, and I like to catch Pélican's blunders, but what I like best is just to think about words. *Le Bon Usage* is special: it doesn't tell you, "Do this, do that," like our grammar book at school. In each case, it describes what many writers do, and others don't; what various grammarians think, what was more usual in the seventeenth century, what's happening to the language now. You can see that the author, monsieur Grevisse, would like precision and common sense to prevail, but he never says, "This is right, that is wrong". He gives quotations that illustrate one usage, and quotations for a different usage, and he tells you what he thinks. Then you can make up your own mind. I'm in love with him.

"Enjoy yourself," Father goes on. "And if you have trouble finding something, ask me. The index is so detailed you might not always know where to look."

Early Mass

Mother is going to stay in Paris with Aunt Caroline, Father's sister, who lives in a fancy house with columns and turrets next to the bois de Vincennes. Aunt Caroline's husband is a politician with a long white beard. Sometimes he is *ministre des Finances*, then he becomes *ministre de la Marine* and then it's his friend monsieur Morel-Basset who's *ministre des Finances*. At other times neither is a minister, but never for long.

Aunt Caroline invites about twenty people to every meal. Mother always has great times with my two cousins, aunt Caroline's daughters from a previous marriage, who are nineteen and twenty-two. Operas, plays, parties, nightclubs. "When we go out together," Mother says, "people always think we're sisters." Being mistaken for someone much younger is one of her great pleasures in life. She's in heaven when people assume that my brothers are *her* brothers, and you hear of nothing else for days. Justine's ambition is just the opposite: she wants to look like she's at least sixteen. As for me, I just wish people would refrain, when Coralie and I are introduced, from asking who is older. But Coralie is almost as tall as I am, and much bigger, so strangers get confused.

Usually, as soon as Mother starts making plans and I overhear her on the phone giggling and planning frolics with my cousins, the air becomes so thick around me I have trouble breathing. She's going away, soon she will be gone: the thought insists, pressing on me night and day. I try to stand still in the overcast limbo, to close my eyes, shrink my skin, empty my head, forget that I am *there*, with nothing before me but the abyss.

But somehow this time it isn't so bad. Mother is going to Paris, but this perspective doesn't befog the landscape. The world is still there. It's even brighter than usual.

After lunch Mother, still sitting at the table, pulls me into her lap. "Come for a cuddle, my pet," she says. "You know, I'm leaving on Friday, are you going to miss me?"

"Yes," I say. But I'm not so sure. She's never asked before. Has she noticed how different I feel, this time?

"My precious lamb," Mother says. "I won't stay very long, only two weeks."

As soon as she's gone, I even feel a kind of relief. Grandmother is in charge, and it's such a change of atmosphere. Grandmother never tries to please anybody, she just does what she thinks is right. She doesn't take me in her lap, cuddle me, or even kiss me much except when she's going away, or I am, or when I give her a bunch of wild flowers. She doesn't need anything from me, doesn't expect me to love her, wait for her, miss her. She just wants me to behave, and as a whole I do, so we get on well.

On Saturday, after school, Coralie and I don't go home, but Loli takes us to the Vié house. Estelle has invited us to sleep over and spend Sunday with her family. She often does, when Mother is away; and I play with Philippe, her nine-year-old son who's in boarding school during the week (the same school both our fathers went to, in the Montagne Noire), while Coralie romps with little Mireille.

"Can we go round to the garden gate?" I ask Loli.

"Why should we do that?"

I shrug. I can't tell her about the ripe odour I want to avoid. So she rings the bell and Adèle, the Viés' housekeeper, opens the door and kisses us in the entrance. I hurry into the hall, the reek from Bertrand's office on the left is so overwhelming. Bertrand is a doctor, but he doesn't need to work for a living. He just keeps these two rooms in the house, a waiting room and an examination room. When he's around, anybody can come and be treated for free. A lot of gypsies do.

I wonder why I'm such a coward: if Bertrand can welcome them, examine them, talk to them, I should at least be able to bear the smell for a few seconds. It makes me woozy, like cheese does, but I have to try. Father explained that not everybody has the same idea of cleanliness, the same rules. He said that gypsies, if they follow their traditional laws, are only allowed to wash in running water. Not easy when you

112

don't live near a stream but in old houses around the church, where you don't *have* running water!

Philippe is calling me from the top of the stairs. "Hey, Tita," he says, "come and see my new cars. They have windows!"

In his bedroom, he's already set up a chute for the car race. He has more than twenty toy cars, and his favorite game is to set them at the top of the chute, let them slide down and see how far each goes. You aren't allowed to push. When I visit, we share the cars and the competition is between us.

I choose the Renault 4CV and he the Simca Aronde. Mine wins over and over, but today this doesn't bother him. He's trying to elucidate what is special and wonderful about these two new specimens. I can't pay attention, but I like to listen to him, the passionate way he pronounces words like *hub, steering, suspension.*

Adèle calls us to dinner. The grown-ups have just finished their aperitif, and Bertrand excuses himself: he's going to L'Etang, their country house in the Minervois. Three women from Béziers are staying with Estelle for a few days. This evening, they'll all play bridge. Estelle has many friends. Local ones like everybody else, and bridge friends from all over. She's also the head of the *Dames de charité,* and she organizes the *kermesses,* the church bazaars.

After dinner and baths, Philippe falls asleep almost immediately, and I look around his room for a book. There are lots of *illustrés*: *Rodéo, Bugs Bunny, Pépito, Hopalong Cassidy*. Finally, on the top shelf, I find *Sans Famille* and start reading.

Rémi is an eight-year-old who lives happily in the country with his mother and their cow. They never need to eat meat because the cow, who is their friend, gives them everything they need. They never see the father, who's a stonecutter in Paris. Then the father gets hurt while working, he needs money for a lawsuit against his boss, and they have to sell their cow. "No more milk, no butter! In the morning a piece of bread, at night some potatoes with salt."

On the evening of Shrove Tuesday, Rémi's mother has a surprise for him: she's borrowed butter and milk from her neighbors to prepare the traditional pancakes. Just as she slips the butter into the pan, and Rémi watches it melt and splutter on the fire, a man comes into the room. Rémi doesn't know him, but it's his father. No more pancakes! The man wants the butter for an onion soup.

He doesn't look happy to see Rémi, and he sends him to bed. But the bed is in a corner of the kitchen, and Rémi, who can't sleep, listens to the couple's conversation. He finds out that he's not their son, but a baby the man found in Paris "on a step". The man has lost his lawsuit. He doesn't want to keep Rémi, and plans to take him to the Foundlings' Home the next day. The woman says he's exactly like a son to her, but she's not the one who decides.

Rémi is frightened, shocked that the woman he's always loved is not his mother, but happy that this horrible man is not his father. I fall asleep wondering what it feels like to be hungry, to be excited about pancakes, to have no father.

The next morning we all go to high mass, and in the afternoon to the rugby match. Philippe is even more enthusiastic about rugby than about toy cars. He has a notebook where he keeps tabs on each player, and on umpires too. He draws plans of the field at decisive moments, showing where all the players are, what they're doing, and what else they could have done. I don't always understand the fine points of his explanations, but I admire his impartiality. People around us loudly support one team or the other, yelling at the umpire when he rules against their side. Meanwhile Philippe takes notes, devises alternative strategies, and reflects.

"All this chauvinism is pathetic," he says as we leave after the match. "Why would the fact that you live in Cugnac or in Carcassonne obfuscate your judgment?"

Coralie and I join Father outside the stadium and walk back home, where dinner is unusually relaxed. Coralie, after gambolling around the rugby field with her friends, concentrates on the food. Grandmother asks Father about the match, and tells him about her older sister in Nantua, with whom she has spoken on the phone. When Mother's around, you hardly ever hear Grandmother at mealtimes except about practical matters. Tonight, she also has news about a neighbor's nephew who is becoming well-known with his songs in Occitan. When she notices I've stopped eating, she doesn't fuss but negotiates: if I finish the mashed potatoes, I can leave the rest of the fish.

I borrowed *Sans Famille* from Philippe, who said, "Yes, it's a good book, with a monkey and a dog." I read it in bed to Coralie, starting again from the beginning. Coralie is already asleep when I get to Chapter 3 where, instead of being sent to the Foundlings' Home, Rémi is sold to a travelling musician and animal trainer.

Over Monday lunch, Grandmother and I compromise again: if I eat half a stuffed tomato, I won't have to touch the roast. Later, as I'm holding a spoonful of *petit-suisse* in front of my reluctant mouth, I offer a more comprehensive deal: every evening, for a whole week, I'll voluntarily swallow one of these gluey white cylinders; in exchange I'll be allowed to go to early mass on Wednesday. She agrees.

I already go to early mass on Fridays, that's my *jour de garde* as arranged with mademoiselle Pélican. We all have a *jour de garde* — a morning when we undertake to stand watch in the church — starting at our private communion. Mother was against it, she tried to have me exempted because it would dangerous for me to be out "on an empty stomach".

But Pélican wouldn't go along with this, bless her heart, plus our old cousin Edmondine, who attends mass every morning, told my parents that on Fridays, when we come out of church, I eat the croissant she buys me *with good appetite*. So Father said, "Maybe it's better for Tita to have breakfast later, maybe that's what she needs, in fact: to work up an appetite." Mother didn't like that, but there was nothing much she could do. Thank God, because the early mass on Friday is the high point of my week.

Being awake when everybody else is in bed. Walking in the empty streets all alone. The dark, the fresh smells, the wind, the church bells calling out to me. Sitting and kneeling in the nearly empty church, in the second pew on the left. Walking with Edmondine to the pâtisserie Cassagnol. And it's true: I have no trouble at all eating my croissant. I even enjoy it.

So this week I've managed to haggle my way into another morning of bliss. It was uphill work, finishing my *petit-suisse* at the end of every dinner. But worth it. With bits of strawberries, it tasted less offensive, less intimately mammalian. I felt strong and determined, almost heroic. For early mass and its delights, I was ready to face the horrors of the food world, the mush and the stench.

Wednesday. When I open my eyes, the sun has already reached the middle of the carpet. It's too late for mass. I run downstairs in my nightgown. Grandmother is making coffee in the kitchen while Loli puts away plates and dishes.

117

"Didn't you remember?" I cry. "Didn't you remember I was going to mass this morning?"

Grandmother doesn't even look at me. She turns off the stove. "Once a week is enough," she says. "Your mother didn't want you to go twice."

"How do you know?"

"I asked her yesterday, on the phone."

I can't believe this. She'd made a deal with me, hadn't she? "Why didn't you tell me?"

She shrugs. "I figured you'd know soon enough. You were so looking forward to it."

"Why did you have to go and ask Mother?"

"She's your mother. And she'd have found out."

This is unfair, but all I can do is calm down. Grandmother is a practical woman. That's what she has in common with her daughter: words are just tools to help get things done. And she doesn't wield much power. She's like me: she needs to please the mistress of the house. Even when Mother is away, our lives are ruled by her wishes.

Petite Fille Modèle

Mother came back last night. This morning (Thursday) Coralie, in the garden, is mixing gravel and water in a pail. She goes to the laundry room with a shovel, brings back ashes from the fireplace, all the time talking to herself. She tips the ashes into the pail and stirs her soup with a stick. Then she goes over to the laurel tree, pulls some leaves from its branches, and tears them into tiny pieces, which she sprinkles into her concoction.

She looks absolutely focused, and totally happy, in a way I remember from when I was younger. *Happy*: the word makes me think of a book I started reading yesterday. When Grandmother called me for dinner, I hid it in the storeroom behind the scullery, in a drawer under some old seed catalogues. I wasn't sure it was "for children" but now, as I open it again, I think it might be: it has lots of drawings and plans, of a road, a hat, houses, churches, streets, theater stages. Not like the drawings in children's books, though — much simpler, like a friend trying to show you what he's talking about.

This book is like nothing I've ever seen. It's called *La Vie de Henry Brulard*, and it has many sentences I love amidst others I don't understand at all. There are quite a few foreign words in it, but that's not a problem because some are easy Latin and the others (*my life, drawback, dazzling*) I looked up in Father's English-French Dictionary. But the first two chapters are a bit confusing. Henry makes a list of the six women he has loved, who "summarize" his life, and compares their characters. He says that with them he was always like a child. Like a child? On the way, he tells us too about his friends, his brother-in-law, living in Rome, wars, money... What I love is that he speaks to *me*, directly: "I should tell stories, and I write *reflections*! O my reader, you'll need a lot of patience." I need a little patience, yes, but he's worth it.

At the end of Chapter 2 he writes, "After so many general thoughts, I'm going to be born." Chapter 3 starts with his first memory: a cousin of his, a twenty-five-year-old woman wearing a lot of make-up, wants him to kiss her; he doesn't want to, she scolds him, he *bites* her. He's so right! I remember the tribulation of having to kiss all our relatives good night in Paris. But I couldn't bite people, and I shudder when I try to imagine their skin between my teeth.

That's when I hear Mother's voice. "Tita, Coralie, I'm going to town right now, will you come with me?" This, in spite of the syntax and the intonation, is not a question at all. Mother is standing in the tasting room door at the other end of the garden. I close my book slowly, reluctantly. From her I don't need to hide it — she wouldn't notice. Still, I put it safely back into the drawer. Smoothing my dress, I walk across the garden. Coralie is still kneeling over her pail, crushing mint leaves and adding them to her broth. "Hurry up, Coralie, we have to go *now*!" Mother calls.

Coralie doesn't even look up. "I'd rather play," she says.

I stop next to her. "Maybe I'll stay here too, then," I say.

Mother comes forward, adjusts her glasses above Coralie. "I can't take *you* anyway, you're too dirty," she says. "Tita, let's go."

"I'd like to stay here and read," I say. "If you don't mind."

Mother, who had started back towards the house, stops and spins around. She's breathing in the jerky way that means she's so indignant she can't speak. I've just done something unheard of. Something Coralie does all the time. But I'm not Coralie. I'm the one who always wants to be with Mother. Not this morning, though. This morning, I want to be with Henry Brulard.

"I'm coming," I say. Mother takes my hand, and relaxes. We walk through the house, fast, then out and across the avenue de la Gare. As we get into the car, Mother smiles at me. "We can stop at the newsagent's and get you *La Semaine de Suzette*," she says.

Mother always tends to be different when she comes back from Paris, as if she resented being with us and wished she were still at Aunt Caroline's. This time, it's worse. On Friday, when we come home from school at noon, she calls Loli in a stern, fretful voice, and tells Coralie and me to go to the playroom. Coralie runs back into the garden, and Mother doesn't even notice. I don't go to the playroom either, but stop next to the half-open kitchen door and sit on the red-tiled steps that lead to the upstairs storeroom. I want to know what's going on.

"Dolores," Mother says, "what were you doing in front of the *école laïque* ten minutes ago?"

"Doing?" Loli says slowly, as if trying to remember. "Oh, I was just waiting for the children to come out of school."

"The children? What children?"

"The ones my friends look after."

"And why would you wait for *those* children? Why would you spend time chatting with your friends in front of the *école laïque* instead of coming straight home with Tita and Coralie?"

"It was just a minute or two," Loli says. "It depends on which school lets out first. Usually it's the *école laïque* and then my friends wait for me. So that we can walk back together."

"Well, from now on we'll do things differently. Tita is old enough to walk to school on her own. You'll only have Coralie, so you can take the bicycle, it will be faster. And make sure I don't see you wasting time with your friends."

This doesn't sound like Mother, who's usually nice to Loli and proud of being a good *patronne*, loved and looked up to by every person who's ever worked for her. And it's so unfair to Loli, who's at her disposal all day every day except Saturday evening (when she goes to the dance at the Grand

122

Soleil) and Sunday (when Father drives her to her village in the morning, and her parents' landlord drives her back after dinner). Loli chose to work in town, but it must be lonely for her in this house, away from her family. What's wrong with her spending a little time with her friends? Mother doesn't want her to toil nonstop like a slave!

I wonder if she was envious when she saw Loli and the other maids, laughing, arm in arm. Maybe when she was young she had the kind of friends Loli has now, girls who worked like her in beauty salons. She often reminisces about going to the opera with her girlfriends in Lyon — they could only afford the *promenoir* so they must have been standing very near each other, thrilled and happy, the way the maids looked in front of the school.

In Paris, she loves to go out with my cousins and pretend they're all a bunch of friends. She does have friends here too, but they are ladies who sit in armchairs and drink tea. They discuss fashions, films, books, who looks good and who doesn't, what is done and what is not. Mother negotiates it well enough, but it doesn't come to her naturally.

When Mother is gone, I join Loli in the kitchen. She's making the vinaigrette, and there are tears on her cheeks. I kiss her. "You'll have to be careful at noon," I say, "but in the morning Mother is still in her robe, so you can walk back with your friends."

"You little spy!" Loli laughs. "You devil! You're telling me to disobey your mother!"

123

"Not at all. What she said was, 'You can take the bicycle,' but you can also walk with your friends on the way back!"

"Okay, but what about the 'Don't waste time with your friends' part?"

"What Mother said was, 'Make sure *I don't see you* wasting time'. In the morning, she won't see you."

Loli is shaking her head. "I don't think that's what your mother meant."

"You might be right," I say. "But what's important is what she actually *said*."

"I don't know," Loli says. "What's important for me is to keep my situation. It makes me sad not to see my friends as usual, and I don't understand why I shouldn't, but your mother is my *patronne*, and I'll do what she says."

I know there are much worse *patronnes* than Mother. I've heard stories of maids who are given only leftovers to eat, are made to scrub all day and darn at night until they fall asleep. This happens when there's only one maid, and the *patronne* is lazy, stingy, or just cruel.

It's different with us, because Ginette cleans, Grandmother cooks, and Mother goes to the market on her bicycle, does most of the laundry, makes our clothes, and takes care of our bodies. Mother likes cleaning too, especially spring cleaning, taking down the curtains, pulling out the furniture, throwing buckets of water onto the tiles, emptying the cupboards, scouring the wood floors upstairs,

124

waxing them. As a result, our house smells better than most. Mother and Loli get on well most of the time, they work together cheerfully and they relax when they're done. But Loli needs to see her friends, and not only at the dance on Saturday nights. We'll have to find ways. We always do. For instance, when Loli wants to meet her boyfriend in the back street, Coralie and I keep a lookout.

I'm glad that I'll be allowed to walk to school on my own, but I'll miss listening to the maids on the way home. And Coralie will miss walking. She'll have to stay put on the back of the bicycle instead of running around with the other maids' children. She always wants to play with the neighbor boys, but she's not allowed to, because we're supposed to play with girls. Which doesn't make sense, because in Coralie's class half the children are boys, and in the schoolyard she plays with them. Is it because the neighbor boys go to the state school? But the neighbor girls we play with go to the école laïque too, so I don't know.

In most of the books I read, the children don't go to school. At least, the girls. The boys sometimes go to boarding school. In the comtesse de Ségur's novels, boys are sent to boarding school (or threatened with the prospect) when they're naughty, jealous or mean, when they disobey or lie. The girls stay at home, but they "work": they learn penmanship, sewing, sums, history, religion, drawing, piano. They have tutors who come to their house a few hours a week, or a governess who lives with the family, or both.

I don't think I'd like to have all my lessons at home. "How can you like your school?" Eléonore asked me yesterday. "You have to stay until six p.m. instead of five, you recite all those prayers, you get heaps of homework, plus all those lines to write when you're punished!"

Yes, Sainte-Blandine is tough. But grown-ups seem to see that as a good point. I often hear people say about me, "She's so advanced! They do push their students at Sainte-Blandine, you know, they're good at that." I don't feel "pushed" at all. Just the opposite: thwarted. But I don't know what to think, because I've never been to any other school.

There's something I like about school anyway: I don't have to be so *good* there. My *work* is usually good, because I enjoy studying, but *I* am not. My reputation at school is practically the opposite of what it is at home. At home, I'm Mother's dream daughter: clean, quiet and polite. At school I'm restless, I ask too many questions, I mislay my books, and I get punished a lot. It wasn't always like that, and I don't know precisely how it started, or when. But this year I've become something like the class rebel, and it's such a relief from being a *petite fille modèle*.

Eyelash

Just before dinner, as Coralie and I are washing our hands, the phone rings. Through the half-open door, I see Father come out of the tasting room into the hall and go to the phone, which sits on top of a high black cabinet filled with bottles of eau de vie and liqueur. "Yes, yes," he says. "I see." "Yes, I understand." "Of course, I'll be there." His voice isn't warm and relaxed as usual but stiff, almost solemn. Something is happening.

Mother comes downstairs and he says something to her I can't hear. Instead of moving into the dining room, they stand there and go on whispering. Coralie throws some water at me and says, "Come *on*! Can't you smell the soup? Artichoke! And Loli won't bring it till we all sit down!" She pushes me into the dining room, where Grandmother is putting away her knitting. I hear Mother exclaim, "Again!" Father has his hand on her upper arm as they come into the room.

Over dessert (tiny tart-smelling strawberries), Father says, "Tomorrow morning, Justine will arrive on the 7:49 train."

"Yay! Do we get a vacation too?" Coralie asks.

"It is *not* a vacation," Father says. He's doing his best to sound normal, but his voice is weary. "She can't go on at

Sainte-Gudule, so we'll have to find another school for her. Meanwhile, she'll stay here."

"What's wrong with Sainte-Gudule?" Coralie asks.

"She'll tell you when she gets here. If she wants to."

"She's always going to new schools," Coralie moans. "Why can't we go to a new school? We've been at Sainte-Blandine for ever!"

Father laughs. Not a very happy laugh, but he's not making fun of Coralie either. I think he finds it appealing that she always wants something. "Enjoy Sainte-Blandine while you can," he says.

"Enjoy it?" Coralie cries. She's right, "enjoy" is not quite the right word. But compared with what lies ahead of us, with boarding school and being locked up all week...

Mother breathes in noisily. "What I don't understand," she says, "is why something always goes wrong between Justine and those nuns. Justine is such a clever girl, and so affectionate. I never have any trouble with her."

In the evening, when Coralie is asleep, I retrieve *Henry Brulard*, which I've hidden under the cloth of my altar to the Virgin. I read, "My mother, Mme Henriette Gagnon, was a charming woman, and I was in love with my mother. I hasten to add that I lost her when I was seven."

In *love* with his mother?

"I wanted to cover my mother with kisses," he goes on, "and I didn't want her to wear clothes. She loved me passionately and kissed me often, I kissed her back with such fire that she had to leave. I hated my father when he came in and interrupted our kisses. The place I always wanted to kiss was her breast."

His mother died when he was the age I am now. I wonder what would have happened if she had lived. Maybe he would have fallen out of love, the way I have. Maybe not. "She didn't participate in this love," he says. Then what about "She loved me passionately"? But I like the way he contradicts himself after two paragraphs. It's not because he's lying, but because he's trying to capture many kinds of truth.

"I was the criminal, I loved her charms furiously." The way he describes her, though, isn't very furious: "She was plump and fresh, very pretty and only, I believe, not quite tall enough." And why does he call himself a "criminal"? I wonder as I turn off the light. I'm too tired to put the book back under the Virgin, so I keep it close to me under the sheets. It feels more precious to me than any other book. The cover is of an unusual blue, soft and mixed with grey, white, and a bit of green. The letters are black, except for the title and Le Divan, which must be the publisher. Inside, there's a map of Grenoble in 1776. In spite of all the drawings, maps and floor plans, I'm pretty sure this book is not "for children".

In the morning, Father and I cross the street and the station forecourt to welcome Justine, who gets off the train with a suitcase and a large blue bag. She kisses Father over and over, then me. "You can't imagine how happy I am to see you both! How's my dear Odette?"

"Asleep," Father says. "And very well."

As we walk toward the house, Father carrying the luggage, Justine says softly, "I'm sorry. I tried my best, but..."

"I know," Father says. And sighs. And goes into his study.

In the kitchen Justine kisses Loli on both cheeks. Loli shakes her by the shoulders. "How's the bad girl? What did you do this time?"

"Nothing!" Justine moans. "Practically nothing. They just caught a letter I was writing to a boy. As if it were any business of theirs."

"Boys!" Loli laughs. "Here's your tea. Do you want a boiled egg?"

"No, thanks. Just some bread. Loli, honestly, you don't know what nuns are like. Obsessed!"

"There. Try this honey, it's from my grandmother. Pure rosemary. You need to eat, you're so pale. And thin. Are you in love?"

Justine shrugs. "No! Yes! Not really. What about you?"

I'd like to hear more, but it's time for school. Loli has forgotten about my porridge. I discreetly take my bowl into the scullery, holding my breath (the cheese larder) and throw the contents into the garbage. Back in the kitchen, I drink up my orange juice before we leave.

Justine yawns. "I think I'm going to take a nap," she says. "But I'll say hello to Odette first. Is she awake?"

"Yes, she's waiting for you," Loli says.

Justine has been at Sainte-Gudule for five months, I reflect on the way to school. For her, a record. When she first got there, she told me it was a school for stupid girls who have failed everywhere else. "So at least I won't have to work," she said. "I'm far ahead of the rest. They aren't just lazy, like me. They're incredibly slow-witted. Seriously, they don't have a clue."

Then I heard Father tell Monsieur Bonnafous, his accountant, that Justine's new school was extraordinarily expensive. Why would Father want to pay a lot of money for a bad school? Because he didn't have a choice. Justine had already been expelled from five schools in three years.

At noon, I look for Justine and find her upstairs sitting at Mother's dressing table, applying some kind of cream under her eyes. "Look at these rings," she says. "What do you think? Is it a good idea to cover them up? Or do they make me look older, more interesting?"

"You look perfect with or without," I say. And she does. Always. Her ponytail, tied with a black polka-dot scarf, has style. So do her tight jeans, her large white shirt, the thin silver chain around her neck, and her red lace-up espadrilles.

As soon as you see her, you know she comes from Paris. Nobody here looks so completely in control, down to the minutest detail, and so relaxed, so confident about their appearance.

"I hope Father doesn't find another school for me," she says. "It's hardly worth while. Only a few weeks left before summer vacation."

I'm happy she's here, but I wonder why she didn't stay with her mother. I don't ask, because we never talk about her mother. Never. I don't even know her mother's name. I thought I did: when Father mentions her (which is seldom) he uses a word I long assumed was her first name. I'd never heard it before, and I had no idea how to spell it, so I vaguely imagined the woman was foreign, or came from another planet. I finally managed, only a few months ago, to analyse this designation into *Mon-ex*, "My ex".

Father doesn't seem to talk to *Mon-ex* but she writes to him, mostly to ask for money. When he writes to her, he has to wait for ever before she sends him what he needs — some piece of information, or a paper with her signature. I'd like to know more about *Mon-ex*. Won't Justine miss her if she stays here for several months?

"Won't you miss Paris?" I ask.

Justine rolls her eyes. "How can anybody miss Paris? You have *no* idea what Paris is really like, or you wouldn't ask. You only know Aunt Caroline's house in Vincennes, where you're pampered all day by the cook and the maids.

Aunt Caroline's chauffeur drives you to the Eiffel Tower, the Tuileries, the puppet shows in the Luxembourg. You can't imagine what it's like to *live* in Paris, for most people. For us! It's all so drab. The rain, the crowds, the pressure. The *métro*!"

"What's wrong with the *métro*?" I ask.

She shakes her head, fast, and shivers dramatically. "I can't begin to tell you what's wrong with the *métro*! As soon as you get down there, everything and everybody looks terminally sepulchral. All you want to do is kill yourself."

I've been in the *métro* a few times, and what I've noticed is people in all kinds of outfits, some of them speaking outlandish languages. But she and our brothers greatly prefer Cugnac. They like everything here. They always get depressed when it's time to go back to Paris. Justine especially will check her calendar and say, "Only three days of happiness left."

At the end of each vacation, on her last day in Cugnac, she needs to say goodbye to all her cherished locations, and she takes me on a tour. She usually sheds a few tears under the fig trees in La Fourcade, then we bicycle to the church, the place du marché, the pine forest on the hill, and the terrace above the canal. There she'll say, "And now I'll go back to my lugubrious life." Maybe there's something awry with Paris that I can't imagine. Or with her mother?

"I'll take you to the real Paris sometime," Justine goes on, spreading something green on her eyelids. "You'll see.

You don't know your luck. Here, put your hands together and hold this eyelash between two fingers. Don't show me! I'll have to guess which fingers, and if I'm right I won't go to school until October."

I turn my back to her and place the eyelash between my middle fingers. When I show her my hands, she looks at them for quite a while, frowning, and chooses the ring fingers.

"Shit! I lost!"

"You're here," I say. "Let's have fun while we can."

She stands up, and kisses me. "You're so much more sensible than I am."

"Lunch!" Loli calls from the hall downstairs.

As we go through the library and the music room to the landing, Justine says, "This afternoon I have to go and see mademoiselle Verdier. Father wants me to take English lessons with her, and he wondered whether you might like to do that too. Would you?"

I jump so high, I slip and would tumble downstairs if Justine didn't catch me. "Of course! I'd love to speak English!"

Justine shakes her head. "What's with you, always wanting to learn things when you don't have to? Let's hope you're not disappointed. Mademoiselle Verdier doesn't seem to be much fun, but never mind. I'll wait for you in front of the school, and we'll go together. Then," she whispers in my ear as we come into the hall, "we'll be just in time for a few turns on the avenue. I need to catch up."

"Catch up?" I whisper back. "You mean with boys?"

"Exactly."

Mexico

We have a visitor, a man I've never seen before, or heard of. His name is Marcel, and he lives in Mexico. Mexico! Last Christmas vacation when we were staying in Paris, aunt Caroline took Justine and me to the Châtelet Theater, for the operetta *Le Chanteur de Mexico*. The star was Luis Mariano. At the end of Act I the main character, a singer, goes to Mexico — he's from the Basque Country and has already had some success in Paris. I can't remember what Mexico looked like, though. Only the song, "Mexico, Mexi-ee-co-o" — we have it on a record aunt Caroline bought us after the show.

Luis Mariano does this great trick with his voice: "Mexi" in his usual warm timbre and then "ee" a major sixth higher in a tiny, bright, sharp tone that seems to come from another instrument. He goes on with *"Les femmes sont charmantes, ee"*, and again the "ee" (this time a fifth higher), comes from another *world*, although it sounds easy and natural, a cry of pure delight.

At the Châtelet, he started this song with *"Ha, ha, ha-ee"*, very high, in a voice like a girl whooping, with his hands spread out, palms down, as if to say, "Quiet, quiet." Then, slowly, he lifted his arms, swinging them just a little at the same time as his hips. There he was, his arms wide and high,

136

ou dance a tender bolero;
..."

I never tire of listening to

y. "*Une aventure mexicaine*
is quelle semaine, et quel
to Mexico?"

earrings. "I'd love to go to
But passion should last for

or ever," I say.
of flat dark-blue earrings with
rself in the mirror above the
right," she says. "That's the way
rescendo, crescendo, then... all
at's because I haven't found the

at?" I ask.
thing! Mr Right! The love of my

here's a man destined for you?"

mine is so comical sometimes.
God, or what? You said the other day
n God."
rybody believes in true love, don't

and his tiny hands fluttering like leaves in a strong wind. Justine was entranced: "He's so sexy!"

Father's friend Marcel lives in Mexico at the moment, but he's French. He went to a school called Sciences Po with Father, and all through these years they've been corresponding, it turns out. I wonder how many more secret friends Father has. Right now, they're drinking coffee in Father's study, just the two of them (I'm not counting myself, sitting quietly on a low stool) and they sound like they've been neighbors all their lives.

"So, if you'd like to teach at the university, it's possible," Marcel says. "I discussed it with the head of the Business Department. You could start in September. The problem is, you'd be paid in pesos. In Mexico City, it would be about enough to live on with your wife and younger daughters. But how would you pay for all those boarding schools in France?"

Mexico City? Are they actually talking about moving to Mexico?

"In the present circumstances," Father says, "anything to do with wine is practically worthless. If I sold the cellars, the trucks, La Fourcade, and what's left of the vineyards, I could hardly manage to raise enough for a few years of school for my older children. Flying the children back and forth for vacations wouldn't be cheap. And there's the alimony, which will never stop. So I'd have to sell the house too. And even the house wouldn't probably..."

Sell our house! Is that possible? Vineya
Cabarrou, the cellars, the trucks, La Fourcade
our *house*? Of course, people do move. Why is it
to imagine our family outside this house, or t
without us? Maybe because we've been here for evei
family. His father, his grandfather, his great-grandf
heard our great-great-great-grandmother built this
a long time ago. She was a widow, and she came hei
her children. Who told me that? I don't remembei
every time we come home after a vacation the cool,
smell of the entrance hall, like a deep cave, like a well, i.
exhilarating surprise.

"You also need to think about the younger girls," Marc
says. "They'll go to university too, and by then you'll probabl
be retired. And… yes, if you no longer have your house here
where will you…"

"Yes," Father says. "I should have looked for a solution
much earlier. There's no way I can make any money here. In
Mexico, I could. But only for a few years." He slowly rubs his
forehead with his fists. "I need to think."

To think? Seriously? About Mexico? Father is taking
Marcel to meet our neighbor Roger Pujol, so I move to
the dining room, find the "Mexico" record and put it on
the turntable. I'm all alone because this is the time when
Grandmother goes to the kitchen to "see about the soup".
She's very interested in soups, and in the evening all she has
is soup, salad, cheese, and fruit. She says at her age you don't

first night, you go for a walk, then y
the next night you already go wild
"What a song!" Justine says. "
it. It's intoxicating!"
"Yes, the words are great," I s
dure à peine une semaine, m
crescendo! Would you like to go
Justine looks up from hei
Mexico. And passion, sure.
ever."
"A crescendo can't go on f
Justine has put on a pair
white stars. She looks at he
mantelpiece. "You might be
it seems to go with me. O
gone, I'm done. I guess th
right man yet."
"The right man for wh
"For what? For every
life!"
"You actually think t
"Don't you?"
This big sister of
"Destined?" I ask. "By
you don't even believe
"I know! But eve
they?"

and his tiny hands fluttering like leaves in a strong wind. Justine was entranced: "He's so sexy!"

Father's friend Marcel lives in Mexico at the moment, but he's French. He went to a school called Sciences Po with Father, and all through these years they've been corresponding, it turns out. I wonder how many more secret friends Father has. Right now, they're drinking coffee in Father's study, just the two of them (I'm not counting myself, sitting quietly on a low stool) and they sound like they've been neighbors all their lives.

"So, if you'd like to teach at the university, it's possible," Marcel says. "I discussed it with the head of the Business Department. You could start in September. The problem is, you'd be paid in pesos. In Mexico City, it would be about enough to live on with your wife and younger daughters. But how would you pay for all those boarding schools in France?"

Mexico City? Are they actually talking about moving to Mexico?

"In the present circumstances," Father says, "anything to do with wine is practically worthless. If I sold the cellars, the trucks, La Fourcade, and what's left of the vineyards, I could hardly manage to raise enough for a few years of school for my older children. Flying the children back and forth for vacations wouldn't be cheap. And there's the alimony, which will never stop. So I'd have to sell the house too. And even the house wouldn't probably..."

Sell our house! Is that possible? Vineyards, yes, Le Cabarrou, the cellars, the trucks, La Fourcade even... But our *house*? Of course, people do move. Why is it so difficult to imagine our family outside this house, or this house without us? Maybe because we've been here for ever. Father's family. His father, his grandfather, his great-grandfather... I heard our great-great-great-grandmother built this house, a long time ago. She was a widow, and she came here with her children. Who told me that? I don't remember, but every time we come home after a vacation the cool, dark smell of the entrance hall, like a deep cave, like a well, is an exhilarating surprise.

"You also need to think about the younger girls," Marcel says. "They'll go to university too, and by then you'll probably be retired. And... yes, if you no longer have your house here, where will you..."

"Yes," Father says. "I should have looked for a solution much earlier. There's no way I can make any money here. In Mexico, I could. But only for a few years." He slowly rubs his forehead with his fists. "I need to think."

To think? Seriously? About Mexico? Father is taking Marcel to meet our neighbor Roger Pujol, so I move to the dining room, find the "Mexico" record and put it on the turntable. I'm all alone because this is the time when Grandmother goes to the kitchen to "see about the soup". She's very interested in soups, and in the evening all she has is soup, salad, cheese, and fruit. She says at her age you don't need more. Cheese aside, I wouldn't mind this kind of meal. Soup isn't so bad. Well, the ones with pasta in them are dire, not to mention the ones with meat, or Parmesan. But Grandmother makes hers with vegetables and nothing else. When they're cooked she purees them. The color is different every time, and the smells are interesting.

Again I listen to the song, in case I've missed something about Mexico, but no: the women are "*charmantes-ee*" and one forgets everything under the sun of Mexico. That's about it. Except for an interesting verse about Mexican *aventures*, love affairs.

But Mother and Justine are back from shopping in Carcassonne. They've also been to the hairdresser's: Mother's hair is blonder than when she left, and Justine has acquired bangs, which make her look like a film star. I give them a few compliments. Mother gathers up all the shopping bags and leaves. I hear her call Loli, who I think is kissing her boyfriend outside the back door. I hope Coralie had time to warn her. Justine has been laying out, on the dining table, a bunch of earrings she brought back from Carcassonne. She plays with them, moving them around as I do with my farm animals.

I put the needle back on the beginning of "Mexico", to pay more attention to the *aventure* verse: "A Mexican affair lasts hardly a week, but what a week! What a crescendo! The first night, you go for a walk, then you dance a tender bolero; the next night you already go wild..."

"What a song!" Justine says. "I never tire of listening to it. It's intoxicating!"

"Yes, the words are great," I say. "*Une aventure mexicaine dure à peine une semaine, mais quelle semaine, et quel crescendo!* Would you like to go to Mexico?"

Justine looks up from her earrings. "I'd love to go to Mexico. And passion, sure. But passion should last for ever."

"A crescendo can't go on for ever," I say.

Justine has put on a pair of flat dark-blue earrings with white stars. She looks at herself in the mirror above the mantelpiece. "You might be right," she says. "That's the way it seems to go with me. Crescendo, crescendo, then... all gone, I'm done. I guess that's because I haven't found the right man yet."

"The right man for what?" I ask.

"For what? For everything! Mr Right! The love of my life!"

"You actually think there's a man destined for you?"

"Don't you?"

This big sister of mine is so comical sometimes. "Destined?" I ask. "By God, or what? You said the other day you don't even believe in God."

"I know! But everybody believes in true love, don't they?"

"Let them," I say.

"You don't? How can you live, then? What's the point?"

Mother is back. She falls into one of the armchairs by the mantelpiece and sighs, *Ouf!* as if the shopping expedition had exhausted her. She stretches her arms and her legs, kicks off her sandals. "Don't you girls ever tire of this wimpy Luis Mariano?"

"Please don't insult my future husband!" I say.

Mother looks up at me seriously. "You don't stand a chance," she declares. "He's not the kind of man who's interested in women. He's forty years old, and he's never even been engaged."

"Then," I say, "I'll be an old maid. You'll have to rely on Coralie if you want grandchildren." Of course I'm kidding. I'm completely set on getting married as soon as I meet a reasonably agreeable man (one who doesn't eat cheese, kidneys or liver), and having children immediately.

"I know girls need celebrities to admire," Mother says. "I myself used to be crazy about Maurice Chevalier. But Luis Mariano! He has an *accent!*"

"Everybody has an accent," I say. "Especially Parisians, and Lyonnais! Luis Mariano's accent is Spanish, and very much like ours. Like Father's. Don't you like Father's accent?"

Mother is stumped for a moment. She purses her lips, while the big toe of one foot taps against her discarded sandal. "Luis Mariano is short!" she finally says.

"Not so short," Justine remarks, trying on a pair of dangling silver earrings. "He's five-seven. Taller than me."

Mother sneers. "For a *man*, that's short!"

"Well," Justine says, "why should that be a problem?"

"A problem?" Mother says. "Of course it's a problem. What woman would be seen with a short man? She'd have to be desperate."

Justine is still in front of the mirror, lost in thought. "Or the man," she says after a while, "would have to be... fascinating?"

For once she is practically disagreeing with Mother (who's just bought her quite a collection of earrings). Could she be attracted to a short boy? Yes! I saw her exchange several glances last night, on the avenue, with Hervé Barral, who is definitely shorter than her even though he's seventeen. Cute guy, and a good rugby player.

"You'll see," Mother says. "As you grow taller, your life won't be easy. Most men will be shorter than you. Yes, believe me, there will be very few men for you to choose from."

This makes me wonder. Did Mother choose Father because he was the only man who was tall enough for her? His height, his appearance, are traits she always mentions with wholehearted approval. Mother is five foot nine. On the one hand, she's very proud of it. She despises short people. Justine is already pretty tall, and Mother expects her to become as tall as herself, which is, I think, one of the reasons she's so fond of her. Coralie too is tall for her age, and our brothers are giants. I'm the only one in the family who's about average, and Mother hopes this will change if I eat more meat and petits-suisses.

On the other hand, being tall has always created problems for her. When she left school, she was apprenticed to a dressmaker. For a whole year, she got terrible back pain, bending over the machine, crouching to pin up hems on customers. That's how she decided to become a beautician, which suited her much better anyway. But her main problem was with men. She often says that she had to move to Lyon because, when she went to dances in her village and nearby, the men were all too short for her.

"I don't think it matters much whether a boy is taller or shorter than I am," Justine says. "That's a minor detail. His personality is what I care about."

"You can't be serious. How could a topsy-turvy couple look good? And short men have unpleasant personalities too."

"I haven't noticed that," Justine says.

Mother is breathing hard and fast, her shoulders bunched up to her ears. The record has run its course. I go and stand in front of her. "*Mexico, Mexi-ee-co-o, les femmes sont charmantes-ee!*" I sing, moving my hips and hands in

Luis Mariano style. "Wouldn't you like to live in Mexico?" I ask her.

She shakes her head. "Don't be ridiculous," she says. But her shoulders have relaxed, and she's almost ready for a smile.

Dots and Stripes

We all came to Narbonne this morning, then Father and Marcel drove on to the lagoon to sail with Bertrand. I wanted to go with them — I love the lazy smells of the lagoon, the turbulent winds — but they didn't ask me. Instead, as Mother has been planning some new outfits, we visit Monsieur Picq in the rue Droite.

He is from Lyon, like Mother, and as he takes out the rolls of fabric and unfolds them with his dainty fingers, he addresses her in the subdued voice of a co-conspirator. Many shades of flowered cotton sateen (for Mother's dress) pile up on the counter, then corduroys for Justine's jacket. The three of them discuss textures and colors for ever and ever. I'd normally stay on the bench outside and watch the busy street, but this time I'm on the lookout. What Father said about blue made me want to try something.

The ladies are done. Now for our dresses. Mother decides on a blue chequered fabric for Coralie plus the same in pink (maybe a concession to Father's wish). I call Coralie, in case she wants to express an opinion, but she's too busy pursuing Monsieur Picq's orange cat into the back of the store. Monsieur Picq has taken out only four rolls, so the other two must be for me: bright red, and white with red dots. "Can I look at something else?" I ask. I've never done this before.

"Certainly," Monsieur Picq says, and turns to take down another roll. Mother immediately looks very tired of standing in this store. She starts her blustery breathing, as if she'd been running up stairs.

"I like these stripes," I say. They are light green and light brown, unlike anything I've ever worn.

"Very good choice," Monsieur Picq says, stroking the fabric with one hand as he lightly pulls up my chin with the other. "This green is exactly the color of your eyes." I hadn't thought of that. My eyes. Greenish, like Father's, and Justine's. Monsieur Picq smiles at Mother. "Your daughter has excellent taste."

Mother, ignoring him (and me), looks down at the fabric for quite a while. She adjusts her glasses. "How much is it?" she finally asks.

"Three hundred and thirty francs a meter."

It's ten francs more than the first ones. And we only need 1.8 meters.

"I'll take the first ones," Mother says. "The red and the dotted."

"Could I have only one dress?" I ask. "With the stripes?"

"Nonsense," Mother says. "You need two dresses."

"Maybe we could get something cheaper for the other one then? Do you have any fabric at three hundred and ten francs or less?" I ask Monsieur Picq.

"Certainly," he nods, and turns back toward his shelves. "Here. Light muslin, two hundred and ninety francs. In white, blue, or yellow."

"I'd love a yellow dress!" I say. "This fabric is so soft! And all in all, the total would be 36 francs less than with the others."

Monsieur Picq widens his eyes. "Exactly. Good calculation!" But when he looks up from the fabric to share his appreciation with Mother, his smile freezes.

"I'll take the red and the dotted," Mother says.

Monsieur Picq bows. "Certainly. Anything else?"

"No, that'll be all." Mother has never spoken so coldly to her compatriot.

"Why?" I ask. Asking why has never got me anywhere with Mother. I go on all the same. "Why can't I have the stripes and the yellow? It would even save some money."

"Don't be tiresome," Mother says.

Justine, outside the store, is studying the window display. She slid away as soon as the situation became tense. She can't take my side, not with Mother, not openly. She needs Mother on *her* side. And it doesn't matter, because it wouldn't have helped. Nobody can change Mother's mind, not even her darling stepdaughter.

Now we're going to have lunch at Les Glycines, a restaurant with a terrace above the canal and a view of the promenade. The wisteria above us is in full bloom, its heady scent seeps through my skin. The wind from the sea is humid, invigorating.

"It will rain tomorrow," Mother says. She studies the menu and decides on cassoulet. "They make it very well here," she says, "with big lean pieces of goose. Justine, will you have the cutlets with cauliflower? That way, you can give me some of your cauliflower. I'm sure they'll bring plenty." Justine nods meekly. As usual, Coralie and I will share a bouillabaisse. I like to share with Coralie: if I don't eat much, it doesn't show. But I seldom have trouble eating in restaurants.

Mother's cassoulet appears in its earthenware pot, with its golden crust of beans, tomatoes, pieces of mutton, sausage, goose confit. Into our plates, over slices of grilled bread spread with *rouille*, the waitress ladles the bouillon, fragrant with garlic, basil, fennel and saffron. Between us, on a platter, boiled potatoes, bits of fish. And sea urchins, one of the few foods Coralie ignores and I like.

Mother has ordered a bottle of côtes-du-rhône, a wine from near Lyon that we never drink at home. She and Justine clink their glasses, "To the sun!" Is it because they have lived further north? They are both obsessed with the sun. They try to get as tanned as they can, which in my opinion does nothing for their looks. We locals hide from the hot sun. We like the sea wind and its fickle showers.

Mother is eating cauliflower directly from Justine's plate. If someone did that to me, I wouldn't touch what was left on my plate. It wouldn't be my plate any longer, it would be theirs. But Justine encourages Mother: "There's a lot, and I don't like cauliflower particularly."

Mother also seems to enjoy her cassoulet. The waitress brought a plate, but she hasn't used it. She eats directly from the pot: "It keeps hot that way." But the pot is deep. All of a sudden Mother stops eating and drops her fork on the table, as if she couldn't imagine why she ever agreed to hold such a nasty object in her hand. She looks down at the cassoulet. "I am so satisfied," she sighs, wrinkling her nose. "I couldn't eat one more bite." As if anybody wanted to make her. "Justine, will you have this? It's really good."

Justine has just finished her lamb, and there's still some cauliflower on her plate. "Here," Mother says, "have a taste," and she dishes out the rest of her pot into Justine's plate.

"I'm no longer very..." Justine says.

Even if she were starving, getting the remnants of someone else's dish, from the pot they've eaten it in, couldn't be too inviting. Justine cautiously brings a forkful of beans to her mouth. I know for a fact that she doesn't like beans. At all. She's not like me, she can manage most foods, at least when she's hungry, but beans are always a hardship.

"Isn't it lovely?" Mother asks. "The goose, especially. Here!" And with her fork, she points at a large piece of meat.

Justine chews, and tries to smile. Laboriously, she eats up everything Mother has put on her plate, only leaving a few pieces of fat she carefully cuts from the meat. Mother pours the rest of the wine into their glasses, and sighs, "This wine is really great. These côtes-du-rhône, they're the best. I don't like the wines from around here so much, do you? They're more... ordinary. Flat, I'd call them flat."

Justine has been silent for a while. She seems to have a hard time keeping her eyes open. There are traces of sweat along her forehead. She's probably eaten much more than she wanted to. And there's the wine. Two glasses. Not quite full, but Father wouldn't let her drink that much.

Mother orders coffee, lights a cigarette and, through her sunglasses, gazes far into the horizon. "And this whole region is so flat," she says. "Nothing stands out. Maybe that's why people here are so unenterprising. With the Alps in front of you, of course you have to aim for the stars."

Flat is good, I decide. I think I'll dedicate myself to celebrating what is flat. Like Charles Péguy in the poem Pélican made us learn about his "plate Beauce" and his "Beauce plate". Meanwhile, I need to stand up for the truth.

"It is flat because you're looking west," I say. "On your left, behind that house, are the Pyrenees. And if you turned around, you'd see all the hills between here and the sea."

Mother snorts. "Hills! With nothing on them but dried-up scrub. And the Pyrenees hardly compare with the Alps."

I think of what Henry Brulard says about himself and his father: "Never had chance brought together two persons more essentially antipathetic to each other." The difference is that Henry never felt any affection, any attraction for his father. Simpler, I guess.

The waitress brings Mother a cup of coffee. "I only need one sugar," she says. "Justine, will you have the other one?"

Justine tries to sit up. Her cheeks are red. "Thank you, no," she says. "I don't... feel too well."

"I'll have it!" Coralie cries.

Mother hands it to her. "Maybe you ate too much," she says to Justine. Her voice is solemn. "You should be careful. You look very good now, but around your age a lot of girls eat just a little too much and before they've even noticed what's happening, they're fat. Once you're fat, it's almost impossible to get your figure back again. I've seen so many cases. Friends who could have been quite good-looking and just because they didn't pay enough attention... Yes, when you're fat, there isn't much you can do about it. It's very sad."

Aperitifs

When Mother came to kiss us good night yesterday before going to a dinner party at the Viés', she found me coughing, so this morning she took my temperature and decided that I had to stay put and wait for the doctor. She said I could get up if I felt like it but shouldn't go out of the house, not even into the garden. And she made me wear socks even though it's warm.

I'm still coughing, my throat hurts, and there's something going on deep in my left ear, but I don't feel too bad. The beautiful side of being ill is that I'm practically released from eating meals. For breakfast, I had just a cup of rosemary tea with honey, not in the kitchen but in our parents' room. Then a long cuddle in Mother's lap. Since Mother came back from Paris, I've noticed that while I still enjoy her kisses and caresses, I no longer need them. I feel the same about our Holy Mother Church. As if I were outgrowing all my mothers.

Now I'm sitting in Father's office typing addresses on envelopes for Simone, Father's secretary. So much more fun than school. Simone is talking on the phone. "Maybe he didn't really need a new fishing rod, but come on, we'll get the fish, won't we? Think of all the husbands who spend their money on aperitifs." She listens for a while, then bursts out laughing. "Okay, *apéritif* then. The Conti at seven-thirty. No, just the two of us, Alain will be playing pétanque. Yes, you're right, pétanque is a good deal, the metal balls are quite durable. But it doesn't get you any fish!"

The office has bay windows that open onto the garden, above Mother's hydrangeas, now adorned with quite a few big blue and pink flowers that don't look quite real, they're so trim. Two double desks sit in the middle of the room, facing each other, and two smaller tables near the windows. Simone does more of the typing and Berthe more of the calculations, but they share the rest of the work as it comes.

Berthe is the chiropodist's daughter, she can look shy or haughty to people who don't know her well but, when it's just the three of us in the office, she relaxes and her conversation becomes extremely interesting. She's unhappy about her skin (pimples), her hair (not enough) her weight (too much), and her mother. She keeps discussing possible solutions. Simone is pretty, skinny, and quick. People call her "a live wire". She talks to everybody, so she knows all the gossip in town. She got married last year, to Alain, a car mechanic who looks like Gérard Philipe. I was her only bridesmaid.

"You're having *apéritif* with your mother?" Berthe asks Simone. "That's nice."

"Yes, she seems to be a little lonely. She should go out more. She complains about my father spending too much money on fishing tackle, but what she really resents is his going away to the lagoon without her. She'd like to do things with him. But he needs some quiet after driving his truck all week."

"Couldn't she go with him to the lagoon?" Berthe asks.

"She's tried it, but she finds it so boring. Actually, I think she should get a job. In a store or something. She's like me, she needs to be active."

"It's no longer so easy to find a job around here," Berthe says. "The wine crisis is dragging everything down and..." She glances at me, and stops. I think she's worrying not only about the wine crisis in general, but about Father's business, and about her own job.

Berthe busies herself with the account book. Simone comes and watches over my address typing. "Incredible! You don't look at the keyboard at all now!"

"For the numbers, I do. Maybe I could manage not to, but I don't want to make a mistake and ruin an envelope. I need to practice."

Simone goes back to her own typing. "This girl!" she says to Berthe. "If the little pigs don't eat her up..." I have no idea where those little pigs would come from, but I think I know what Simone means: if I escape the little pigs, I'll make my mark, somehow. I just need to watch out for the little pigs.

A knock on the door: Ginette. "Tita, the doctor is here for you."

154

A blond, brawny young man in a light-green polo shirt is talking to Mother as I enter the sitting room, "Yes, I'm Dr Pauli, Dr Barral's substitute during his vacation." Can this be the doctor? He shakes hands with me. "Good morning, Tita." He looks as different as possible from our Dr Barral, who is tall, very thin, bald with a grey moustache, and always wears a dark three-piece suit.

Mother helps me undress as she explains my condition to the doctor with quite a bit of head-shaking and eye-rolling. I sit on a chair in front of Dr Pauli, and he examines me with his various cold tools. He listens to me coughing naturally as well as on purpose, looks into my ears with his light through a funnel-shaped instrument, then puts everything back into his bag and takes out his prescription pad. "The left ear is slightly infected," he says. "And there's tracheitis. But she should be better in a few days."

"It never stops," Mother says. "How many times has she been ill this school year? Ten, at least! No other child catches so many infections. Is it because she doesn't eat enough?"

Dr Pauli is still writing sedately. He finishes with a large, dashing signature, then looks up. "The important part, if you want to avoid or to fight infection, is fruit. Fresh fruit, vitamins. Does Tita eat enough fruit?"

"Well, persuading her to eat her main dish is so much work," Mother says. "And her white cheese! She doesn't eat any other cheese, you know. So when it's time for fruit..." She sighs. "We're all exhausted."

"What fruit do you like?" Dr Pauli asks me. *Me!*

"Figs, pomegranates, apricots, peaches," I say. "Actually, there's no fruit I don't like."

"Excellent! Then you should eat fruit as an hors d'oeuvre," the doctor says. "As many different kinds as possible. Start each meal with it. Breakfast too."

Mother's mouth falls open and her face, for a few seconds, is like wood. "But," she breathes, choppily, twice, "won't that spoil her appetite?"

"Even if it did," the doctor says, "vitamins are essential, so fruit comes first. And don't worry about her appetite. Fruit might even work as an *apéritif.* You'll see."

Apéritif? Apéritif is the time when you get together before lunch or dinner to drink orgeat or *menthe à l'eau* (or Cinzano, if you're a grown-up), with olives, anchovies, bits of carrots and cucumbers. What has it got to do with fruit? But now I remember a prayer we sometimes say before mass, *Aperi, Domine, os meum,* "Lord, open my mouth". *Apéritif,* then, could also be something that *opens* the appetite. I'll have to look it up.

Mother's frown is getting deeper as she stares at Dr Pauli's white boat shoes. When she finally notices that I put on my dress backwards, she turns it around mechanically. After a while, she sees my red cardigan on the armchair, picks it up, takes me in her lap and starts pulling one of the sleeves over my arm.

Dr Pauli looks at me. "Are you cold?"

156

"No," I say. "I'm really hot."

"Then you don't need a jacket."

Mother stops with the sleeve up to my elbow, my hand inside. "But she catches cold so easily!"

"Don't worry," Dr Pauli says as he picks up his big black bag. "If she's cold, she'll know to put it on."

Mother shakes hands with Dr Pauli and walks him to the front door. I can hear her, as soon as the door bangs shut, talking to herself. "As if children knew anything!"

I'm going back to the office, but Father calls out from the tasting room, "What did the doctor say?"

"Ear infection, tracheitis, the usual."

A short grinning man is taking out sample bottles from a case and setting them on the pink-and-white marble counter. "This is Tita, my number four," Father says. "And Tita, this is monsieur Espardelier from Peyriac-Minervois."

Instead of lunch, I'm allowed to have a nap. As soon as I'm alone in my room, I retrieve *Henry Brulard* from under the Virgin. After his mother dies, Henry likes to be with his uncle Romain, his mother's brother, a young lawyer who sometimes takes him to the theater, to the opera. "He laughed with me and allowed me to watch him as he took off his beautiful clothes and put on his robe, every evening at nine before supper. These were delicious moments for me. Then I walked downstairs in front of him, holding a silver candlestick." Romain has many beautiful outfits he couldn't have paid for, and this creates problems with his father. "When I saw my father coming into the Xes' salon," Romain tells Henry, "I had to run away and change into an ordinary outfit. Meanwhile, madame Y was waiting to see me in the splendid suit she'd bought for me!"

Henry explains that, at the time, there was nothing wrong with taking money from ladies, provided you spent it *hic et nunc* — didn't hoard it. But when questioned by his father, Romain says that he won the money gambling. So it looks like, for his father, gambling was better than ladies. Henry thinks that Romain shared his winnings: "He took money from his rich mistresses and gave it to the poor ones." He must have had lots of mistresses. Which I know is a word for a woman lover, but why isn't a man lover called a master?

I also wonder why Romain, a grown-up man, is still afraid of his father. Maybe because his father gives him money, and an apartment in the family house. When I grow up, I won't let anybody give me money, or tell me what to do. I love this house, leaving it will hurt. But I want to be free and on my own.

Henry's family members are: his grandfather, his great-aunt, his uncle Romain, his aunt Séraphie ("a female devil"), his father Chérubin ("an extremely disagreeable man") and his two younger sisters. "These are the characters in the sad drama of my youth, of which I remember mostly pain and deep moral vexations." This, just after he told us about all the fun he had with his uncle Romain. But I understand. If you're alive, you're bound to enjoy yourself at times, even if mostly drenched in spite and gloom.

Again Henry thinks of us before he starts in on the details of his calamities: "The reader here could skip a few pages, and I beg him to do so, for I'm writing haphazardly and this might well be extremely dull." I skip pages and paragraphs all the time, especially about politics, which I can't follow at all, but I want to know about Henry's troubles. Everything he says feels both illuminating and enchanting, as if I had, for the first time, a friend who is my kind.

But he also makes me grateful for all the friends who are *not* my kind — for school, for neighbors, for my bicycle, for the vineyards and the pine forests. Henry has to study at home with a stern priest he detests. He sleeps in an alcove in the priest's sunless room, next to the noise and stench of a cage holding the priest's thirty canaries. He's never allowed to play with other children because his father feels superior and doesn't want him to mix with *des enfants du commun.*

After a while, I feel drowsy. I sleep, then Grandmother comes in with a cup of linden tea. Later, Father brings me a large flat package with a gold ribbon. When I open it, I see a paper doll set. "And here are your scissors," Father says.

The doll's name is Pepita, and she smells of cinnamon. "You got this in Spain!" I say.

"Yes, I found it last month in Gerona and kept it for an occasion like this, when you shouldn't read too much or it will hurt your head."

I love this chubby little figure with her old-fashioned outfits.

"Have fun," Father says, "and try to rest too, that's how you'll get better."

I cut out Pepita and her frilly one-piece bathing suit. I leave the other clothes for later, and I sleep some more. When I wake, the clock says it's four-thirty, and I feel almost well, so I go and see what's going on downstairs.

In the kitchen, Justine is deep in a *roman-photo* in *Nous Deux*, "the magazine that brings you luck". She couldn't do this anywhere else in the house, because only maids are supposed to read *Nous Deux*. But Berthe told me she likes it, too. "If you don't have a boyfriend, you can always dream," she said. Meanwhile, Loli is arranging petits fours on two plates. "Hey," she says, "you look better already, would you like your *goûter*?"

"No, thanks. Just some water."

Loli takes the tea into the sitting room, and I carry the cakes for her. Mother is there with Estelle Vié and Denise Pujol. I'm glad to see Estelle. Whenever she's around, the conversation takes a brighter turn. Denise is more predictable. Their contrasting voices greet me: "Here's the sick girl, how do you feel?"

"Pretty good, thank you," I say, and go to sit on my low stool. As soon as they've poured the tea they've also forgotten about me, and I can listen.

"Have you seen this Dr Pauli?" Mother says. "Rather handsome, but I don't trust him. He wanted Tita to eat fruit *before* her main dish! Imagine! Why not candy?"

"Bertrand likes him," Estelle says. "Finds him brilliant. He's young, of course. From Perpignan. Fruit first might not be a bad idea, you know. Why not try it?"

Mother is staring at her cup, her mouth set. Estelle, in matters of the body, is respected as an expert.

"Still," Denise says. "Fruit first, that's very unusual." "Unusual", for Denise, is the equivalent of "horrendous" for someone else.

I slide away, back to the kitchen, where Loli is peeling aubergines. There's a basket of morello cherries on the sideboard. "May I have a few?" I ask her.

"Sure," Loli says. "As many as you like. I can get more from the orchard. Help yourself."

English

Justine is gone. Father didn't find a school for her, but something much better: she's in England. In Sussex, in the country, near a town called Eastbourne. Father has friends there, who invited her to stay with them until September so she can improve her English. She was ecstatic when she left: she loves riding, and these people have horses. She'll speak French with their two children, who are about her age and take French at school. I so wanted to go with her, but Father said maybe I'd go later, when I can really speak English.

I'm learning. I have a lesson with mademoiselle Verdier every Tuesday after school. Then I bicycle back home, and all I want to do is find Father and practise what I've just learned. He likes to speak English with me, but we have to skid back into French as soon as Mother comes near. She gets intensely irritated if she hears anybody speak a language she doesn't understand (i.e. anything but French). That's probably why I hardly ever speak Occitan or Spanish with Father. It's okay, because we both share these languages with many other people. For English, though, Father is my only partner: mademoiselle Verdier teaches English, but she doesn't speak it.

She lives at the other end of town, in a small house with only four rooms. Two upstairs, which she rents out; downstairs her bedroom, and a dim kitchen which opens onto an overgrown back garden. That's where our lessons take place. Even though it's warm outside, the wood stove is always going, with several pans whispering on it, one of which remains on the corner closest to us and contains permanent gruel. Mademoiselle Verdier is withered and bent, her thin face nothing but wrinkles. When you meet her in town, she always wears a convoluted hat, and a whole fox around her neck. Even now, in June.

At her kitchen table I read from an ancient book she gave me. Every double page starts with a picture: a boat, a battle, a cliff, a town between two rivers or at the top of a hill. Father says they are called woodcuts because they are printed from carved blocks of wood. After the picture comes a story about Romans, Angles, Picts, Saxons, Jutes, with names like Cadwalla, Oswiu, Willibrord, Ecgfrith, Biscop, or Offa. They're all men, so I don't pay much attention to their exploits, but I delight in every word. I don't know how to pronounce them but it's obvious they shouldn't sound like French or Spanish, so I just try for a different sound.

Once in a while, mademoiselle Verdier corrects me. She sits in an armchair on my right, near the stove. After I finish reading each sentence I'm supposed to translate it. If I can't, she helps me. Sometimes she glances at my book, but mostly she seems to understand what I read. Maybe she knows it all by heart, this book seems to have been used so many times.

For Justine, the book was a different one, slightly more recent, but the lessons followed the exact same pattern.

Justine thought it was weird. "This woman teaches English as if it were Latin!" she said. In her various schools, the English teachers usually tried to start a conversation of sorts, usually with little success. "Do you think mademoiselle Verdier can speak English at all?" my sister wondered. Maybe she can't. She went to England when she was a *jeune fille*, she told me. So many years ago. Before World War One. And here I guess she doesn't know anybody who could speak English with her. Except Father, but they don't see much of each other these days.

They've known each other for ever, though. Father told me that mademoiselle Verdier, when they were growing up, used to live on the ground floor of the Maison Bousquet around the corner from us. She was a few years older than him, and friends with his sister Caroline. Once when he was about twelve he ran into her house on some errand and when he opened the door of their kitchen, there she was standing naked in a basin of water, with a sponge in her hand. He muttered something and ran away, but he says it was the first time he'd ever seen a woman without any clothes on, and he never forgot it. "For me, she will always be this beautiful vision, like a marble statue in the middle of the kitchen."

Mademoiselle Verdier was an only child, and she doesn't have any family here, Father said. "Her parents left her the house she lives in now, which used to be her mother's parents'. But that's all she has. Nothing else, no money at all.

It must not be easy for her to make a living. And she needs to maintain the house, or she couldn't get tenants."

Today, in mademoiselle Verdier's kitchen, when we're done reading and translating our double page, we talk. In French. She offers gruel and I say no thanks, after which she hands me a white napkin embroidered with tulips and a plate of plump, juicy apricots from her garden. I eat a few while she sips her tea. She's very interested in marriages, especially the kind that end up not happening, or that shouldn't have happened.

"Is your father still trying to find someone for Cécile Barniol?" she asks. The Barniols are distant cousins of ours, who live around the corner from mademoiselle Verdier.

"Well," I say, "he invited her to dinner last month with a sailing friend of his from Perpignan, a nephew of the Viés'. I don't think they liked each other at all. The man was telling Father about sailing along the coast of Andalusia last fall, and Cécile immediately announced that she couldn't stay on a boat, she was always seasick. Then Father mentioned the fact that Cécile likes to paint, and the Viés' nephew went on about Matisse — he'd just seen an exhibition. But Cécile said she couldn't even look at a Matisse painting, they were all so ugly."

Mademoiselle Verdier is amused. "What Cécile does is hardly art: she just copies reproductions from books! Your father is so generous. He will do anything for her. I don't

165

think he'll ever get anywhere, though. She's too stuck up. And she's getting old, nearly forty, isn't she? She had her chance when the new *notaire* came to town, remember?"

I love that mademoiselle Verdier speaks to me as if I were her age. As if I could be familiar with what happened ten years ago. But she's going on about cousin Cécile. "She was not even thirty at the time, she still looked good enough. Although she always wore too much make-up. He would have married her, but... I think her mother is to blame. She's always set her sights much too high. And Cécile is entirely under her thumb."

I say goodbye, and hurry home on my bicycle. I want to speak English. Father is in his study, reading a Série Noire novel titled *Touchez pas au grisbi*. "What is *grisbi*?" I ask in English.

Father explains and, miraculously, I understand: *Grisbi* is a slang word for "money". We go on like that for a while, and I learn (without any explanation in French, without any translation) the words "title", "street", "stove", "boat", "novel". I already knew "what", "book", "read", "I", "like", "go", "back", and a few more. Father and I are swimming together in this whirling stream, where short, crisp words twist and jump all around us. Then Father says something that I don't get. Or I'm not sure. "Do you mean that I shouldn't read detective novels?" I ask in French.

"Right," Father says.

"Because they are 'not for children'?"

"No, not only because you're too young. You *are* too young, I'm sure you wouldn't be interested in these novels now. But I'd like you to keep away from them even when you're older."

This doesn't seem to make sense. Father reads them all the time, so why shouldn't I? "Is it because they are for men?" I ask.

"No." Father seems to think. "No, it's just because I'd like you to choose a more... substantial kind of literature. Something larger, more complex, more... real?"

I wonder if he means something like *Henry Brulard*. The book is pretty worn out, he must have read it many times. I'd better not mention it, but I have an idea. I go to the shelves, where I've seen several other books by Stendhal, the author who wrote *Henry Brulard*. I take one out. "Do you mean books like this one?" I ask.

Father strokes the front page, which has a small drawing of a jumping horse. "*Armance*," he says. "Stendhal's first novel. I remember buying it in Paris at the librairie Honoré Champion, near the Palais du Luxembourg, a long time ago. Yes, it's a beautiful and very strange book."

"Can I read it?" I ask.

Father shakes his head. "You'll have to wait. It wouldn't make sense to you now. It's about a dramatic, morbid kind of love, and you'd have to know first about healthier kinds. You'd also need to know some history. Look at the subtitle:

'*Or some scenes from a salon in Paris in 1827*'. Eighteen-twenty-seven probably means nothing to you right now."

"What does it mean to you?"

"The Restoration."

"The Restoration?"

"That's the time when the monarchy was restored in France. The Bourbons were back, after the Revolution, after Napoleon. Stendhal is a republican, and he sees the Restoration as a time of ennui and decay."

Father is right about the Restoration but thanks to Henry Brulard I know something about the Revolution. Henry witnesses, from the window of his grandfather's room, what he calls "the first blood spilled by the French Revolution": a hatter, supported by two other men, blood spurting from a bayonet wound in his lower back, walks up the six flights of a house across the street. All this is clearly visible through the large windows of the staircase and Henry can't stop looking. When the worker gets to his room, he dies. Henry's parents are for law and order and against the revolution, but Henry sees "the anger and the strength of the people".

I open *Armance*. There are many pages of preface and *Avant-propos bibliographique et critique*, ending with a photo of Stendhal's manuscript — his handwriting looks even worse than mine. I read the first page of the novel itself, which starts with a few English words. Then the story: Octave is twenty, just out of *Ecole Polytechnique*, and he'd like to enter the artillery. But he is an only child and his parents want to keep him in Paris, so he gives up his plan. "Do I have to wait until I am twenty to read this book?" I ask.

"Maybe sixteen?" Father says.

Sixteen! "And I shouldn't read detective novels at all? Ever?"

He sighs, his elbows on the table, his cheeks between his fists. "Some of them are very good of their kind. I'm not saying you should avoid them altogether. But they... I... don't really... enjoy them so much, as a matter of fact."

I love it when he says "as a matter of fact". It took me months to analyse this expression, which felt like a single word. As with *Mon-ex*. "Why do your read them, then?" I ask.

"That's..." he laughs, "what I'd like to know. I guess it's.... to take my mind off... things. The way I do crossword puzzles, or play bridge."

He looks around, stands up, takes my hand. "Let's go into the garden," he goes on in English, "and before it gets dark let's try to call some flowers by their English names."

Hosts

This evening Coralie is already asleep when Mother, smelling of carnation in a pink and green floral-print bustier dress, comes to kiss us good night. Our parents are going to a dinner party at the Viés'. As soon as I hear them walk down the hall and close the front door, I go back to the last pages of *Henry Brulard*, about the "five or six months of celestial, complete happiness" he spent in Milan. I love "five or six" because it means that he doesn't know exactly, and he admits it. Mother would never say "five or six". She always knows exactly, because she doesn't care about the truth.

Milan, for Henry, becomes the most beautiful place on earth. "I don't at all feel the charm of my fatherland," he says. "I have for the place where I was born a repugnance, a physical disgust, like sea-sickness. Milan, from 1800 to 1821, was where I constantly yearned to live." Milan! A place I'd never heard of until now. I try to think if there is a place in the world where I could yearn to live. Maybe Paris, in spite of the bad reputation Justine and our brothers give it.

"Reader, forgive me!" Henry writes. "If you are older than thirty or if, younger, you are on the side of prose, close this book!" He's always telling us to close his book, or asking his future editor, if he ever gets one, to cut his digressions. It's a bit much but I like him so I decide that I'm not on the side of prose either.

Henry starts telling us about the woman he loved in Milan: "She did love me, somehow. She had other lovers but I told myself that, if my rank had been on a level with theirs, she would have preferred me! I had other lovers too."

This is what I'll do. I don't know if I'll go to Milan, it might be some other place, but I won't stay in my fatherland either. I'll be happy sometimes, celestially, and I'll have quite a few lovers, like him. He doesn't say much more about these times: "How can I paint the extravagant happiness everything gave me?" The last sentence of the book is, *On gâte des sentiments si tendres à les raconter en détail*, One spoils such tender feelings by recounting them in detail.

I hear Grandmother and Loli go up to their rooms. The house is totally quiet now. The clock on the mantelpiece says ten to eleven, so our parents should still be safely away. I decide to take *Henry Brulard* to Father's study, and look up *prose* in the Petit Robert.

I don't quite understand the definition, but the word came into the French language in 1265, from the Latin *prosa oratio*, "speech that goes in a straight line". And I can see that Henry does exactly the opposite: as soon as he starts telling us about something, he remembers something else.

I also look up *porridge*: it was first an English word, which only settled into the French language in 1901, when Father was already four years old. I wonder what Father had for breakfast before 1901. If I ask him, he'll say he doesn't remember. He remembers practically nothing that happened

171

before he was seven and was sent to boarding school. But could he have had porridge anyway? By another name?

The Robert says that porridge was originally an English word, a "corruption" of the French word *potage*. It doesn't say when *potage* became *porridge*: for this, I need to look into the Shorter Oxford English Dictionary — two heavy dark-blue volumes, each much larger and thicker than the Robert. All in English, but I understand that *porridge* was born in 1532 and came from "altered f. POTTAGE". "Altered", so much more polite than "corruption". So, *potage* became *pottage* at some point (in English), and then *porridge*. This English dictionary is engrossing. But I need to be in bed before our parents come back.

I abhor porridge, I think as I turn off the light. Since Dr Pauli asked me what fruit I like, I've been looking at food in a different way. I've always eaten fruit of my own accord, especially from trees, but I didn't think of fruit as *food*. Food was something people wanted to thrust into me, so I automatically shrank from it. Now I see that what I dislike is meals. Meals at home. Because that's where you're supposed to eat up whatever they put in your plate Or Else. That's where you have to sit and endure all kinds of repulsive smells while others make conversation and ingest their food without worrying about it. That's where your duty is to pick up bits of seared flesh, haul them to your lips one by one, shove them inside your mouth and keep them there until, in desperation, you make up your mind to swallow.

But there are foods I actually like. Fruit, bread, fresh almonds, tiny raw artichokes, hazelnuts... Even at meals once in a while there are good moments. Grandmother's soups I always found okay, but now I try to guess what vegetables she put in them. Potatoes, carrots, celery are staples, but I especially like fennel, cucumber. And there are some other dishes I enjoy: sautéed string beans, chard, aubergine-and-tomato gratin.

The problem is, the more I let myself enjoy some foods, the more I abominate others. I used to be able to let Loli stick porridge into my mouth. For a while now I've been doing it myself and it means that I have to be *there*, to *taste* the actual putty. Gruesome. Why should I eat something that makes me sick?

In the morning when I see Loli taking the box of oats from the shelf, I say, "Please, may I have a different breakfast? Something I like?"

She turns towards me, the box still in her hand, and grins. "*Is* there anything you like? Anything serious?"

"Yes!" I say. "I could have fruit first, because the doctor said I should, and then... bread? With your grandmother's honey?"

Loli seems to think. She puts the box back on the shelf. "Will you have a banana? A banana, that's nourishing", she says, as if to herself.

"Okay!"

So she brings me a banana from the storeroom, cuts a slice of *gros pain*, spreads beautiful liquid honey on it. This is so good! The best meal I've ever had. And I just needed to ask?

I arrive at Sainte-Blandine in a strangely energetic mood. As soon as we're done with mass, Pélican demands our complete attention, opens her desk, and takes out a round box. There are a hundred hosts in there, she says, unconsecrated. When we have "earned" them all she'll give the box to the priest, who will consecrate them. *Earn* them? We look at each other with wide eyes. What can she mean?

"Exceptional sacrifices". We're supposed to come up with these ourselves, but Pélican gives us some examples: not saying a word to anybody in school (except when the teacher asks us to) for a whole day, not eating any candy for a week, giving away our toys to the church bazaar. If we succeed in these extraordinary feats of goodness, we "earn" a host. Or several.

Break, and brainstorming in the yard. "I could try to save my weekly allowance," Noëlle says, "and give it to the poor. Put it into that box at the back of the church. I couldn't buy any cardboard for my puppets, or any paints. But for a week, I guess I could try."

"If there's something you need, I can give you my candy money," I say. We don't get an allowance, but Father gives us

174

a few francs every day after lunch. I like liquorice, but I can easily do without it.

"Thanks!" Noëlle says. "And that could be *your* sacrifice. Going without candy."

I can't say it aloud, but I don't think so. Our sacrifice needs to be something difficult.

Anne-Claude is frowning. "This doesn't work," she says. "If Noëlle gets money from you, where will be her sacrifice?"

"It will only be a few francs," I say. "For an emergency."

"Okay," Anne-Claude says. And I could try not to smack my brothers. For a whole week! That will be really really... I'll have to keep away from them. Stay in my bedroom. I won't even be able to play in the yard."

"You can come and play at my house," I say.

"It's too easy not to smack them if they aren't around!" Noëlle says.

"That's where you're mistaken," Anne-Claude says. "I guess at first I hit them because they annoyed me. They never stop crowding me, and the only possible reaction is to smack them when they come too near. But now, when I think of a whole week without them, I realize I've got used to the whole... Tita, what about you? Do you hit Coralie?"

I have to laugh. "Sometimes, I'd like to," I say. "But she's very strong. And she enjoys fighting, which I don't."

My friends are amazed. "She's not even six!" Anne-Claude exclaims. "You can't be afraid of her."

175

"But I am. And it's not only that she's stronger. I don't like to be too close to her. She often smells of butter, of cheese…" This gives me an idea. "I know what my sacrifice will be," I say. "What I hate most is the smell in the passage between the pâtisserie Cassagnol and the rue de l'Horloge, where several gypsy families live, with lots of small children. I always take a wide detour to avoid that street. What I'll do is, I'll take a bunch of my toys to that street. I'll actually go inside a house if they ask me."

"That will be two sacrifices then," Noëlle says. "The smell, and giving away your toys."

"The toys won't count," I say. "I only care about my dolls, and I won't give them away, because they're my children."

But Noëlle is right. I'll tell Pélican about giving away my toys, although it doesn't mean anything. I won't mention the stench. Pélican probably has no idea what a torture it can be. Her house reeks of stale sausage and moldy fabrics.

Back upstairs in the classroom, we announce our vows. My toy sacrifice doesn't make much of an impression, but when Anne-Claude explains about her brothers, I can see Pélican's face contracting in horror. When we're all done, she says, "Some of you have deeply reprehensible, shocking behaviour to get rid of, and should be grateful for this opportunity. Remember, if you practice violence, it is not enough to give it up for a week. Except if you plan to go to hell."

My-ex

On the shelves in Father's study, I found another book about a child. Its cover is white, with only the title, *Jean Santeuil*, in red letters. The rest is black: "Marcel Proust" and "Gallimard". Around the writing there's a triple frame — two thin red lines and a black one. As usual, I skip the preface. Before the introduction there's a small paragraph, all alone on the page: "Can I call this book a novel? It is less and much more, the very essence of my life. This book was not made, it was gathered."

The introduction itself I can hardly follow: two men are spending their vacation on a farm in Brittany, and are all excited when they realize that a writer they admire is also there. They write him a note and manage to meet him but nothing much happens. Nobody has a name: there's "a duchess" and "the princess of ***"; the other characters (and even some places) are just initials.

But as soon as Chapter 1 starts, I'm enthralled. Jean is a seven-year old boy, and he doesn't address the reader (like Henry), but someone tells us about him. His mother has decided that this evening, for the first time, she won't go and kiss him good night in his bed. His parents' guest, a doctor, politely hopes that he's not the reason why madame Santeuil won't go to her son's room. "No!" madame Santeuil answers, "we want him to give up these little-girl habits, we want to bring him up *virilement.*" I'd never thought about this. Do parents treat boys differently from girls? Maybe. Philippe doesn't get a good-night kiss. I thought it was just because Estelle is not a kisser, but I'll have to look into this.

Jean is not happy about his mother's decision. He comes back into the garden, three times, to say good night. Then from his room he calls his mother, who hurries upstairs because she's afraid he'll catch cold standing at the window. Meanwhile, she's told the doctor that she wants her son to become a judge or a lawyer. "But I thought he had a gift for music and poetry," the doctor says.

"Even if he were Mozart or Beethoven," she replies, "I'd much rather he found a respected, remunerative position in the Foreign Service or the *haute administration.*"

"What about medicine?" the doctor asks.

"Oh, no!" the mother says, even though she seems to admire the doctor's achievement.

I hope Jean does what he likes, not what his mother wants. My parents don't seem to have any plans for us; maybe I should start thinking about the future myself. It's probably going to take place somewhere else. I don't hate Cugnac (where I was *not* born) the way Henry Brulard hates Grenoble, but Father seems to assume that there's no room here for me.

Today, after our lesson, mademoiselle Verdier remembers her former student. "So, how is Justine doing in England?" she asks.

"Very well. She says she learns new words all the time, and everybody is inexplicably nice to her." What she wrote in a special secret letter to me (half of it in English) is that she has *three* suitors, and that over there it's completely normal to go out with boys. Different boys on different days. Even the parents don't mind.

"A clever girl," mademoiselle Verdier says, handing me a plate of peaches. "And very well behaved. Let's hope she doesn't take after her mother."

Her mother! Am I finally going to learn something about Mystery Woman My-ex? I wait. Mademoiselle Verdier is deep in thought. "People should never get married in such a hurry," she finally says. "There she was, a guest of the Pujols, the older couple, I mean, Roger's parents, who'd met her at some spa in the Pyrenees. Nobody knew anything about her, except she was a good tennis player. It all happened in September of... 1934." Mademoiselle Verdier, once again, becomes abstracted for a while. "Of course, your father would be interested," she goes on. "He was the best tennis player in the *département*. So, they play together every morning for three weeks, then they come home one day and announce that they're getting married!"

She sits up, reaches for the kettle, and pours some hot water into her half-empty cup. "Pure recklessness!"

she exclaims. "Utter folly! There they were, in their tennis clothes, all sweaty and full of smiles, announcing, 'We're engaged'. As if it were completely normal to marry someone you'd never heard of three weeks earlier."

"Did you play tennis too?" I ask.

"I?" she shakes her head, fast, pushing her shoulders up and shivering, as if my question were utterly absurd, or even offensive. "Certainly not."

Then how did she know exactly how this came about? She sounds like she was there when Father and My-ex announced their engagement. Well, she lived practically next door at the time. Did this happen in the garden, and was she spying from the other side of the wall? Or did she see them pass her window in their tennis clothes and then someone told her what they'd been up to? But who? Aunt Caroline must have been married by then, and living in Paris.

"And your father was *not* so *young*!" mademoiselle Verdier goes on. "He should have known better. Your grandmother was not happy, I could see that, but for once there was nothing she could do. She said they should wait, and they didn't pay any attention. Most likely your father was sorry he had obeyed her when she made him come back from Japan to take over the business after your grandfather died in 1932. Such an unfortunate idea. He had a brilliant career in front of him, and she put an end to it just because she didn't want to live alone in that big house. Not that she was really alone. She had a housekeeper, a cook and a maid at the time, plus Ginette of course, but Ginette never lived in. She didn't mind using your grandparents' bed, though. Ginette was so giddy, as a girl. I was surprised to see her settle down with Joseph Sens. Once, it was in August, your grandparents came back from their house in the Montagne Noire a day earlier than expected, and found her *in their bed* with the gardener, a married man. Why on earth did they need to use your grandparents' bed, when the house was full of guest rooms? Both of them should have been dismissed, but your grandfather just laughed it off. He was a magnificent man, but he never took anything too seriously. Your father too errs on the side of leniency with his employees. He has such a good heart."

Again mademoiselle Verdier loses herself in contemplation of my father's goodness and of its downside. I often hear people say that Father is "too good." Why should that be a problem? Obviously, My-ex was not too good, in mademoiselle Verdier's opinion. But what was wrong with her?

"I'm not saying that your father's wife was the only guilty party," mademoiselle Verdier goes on. "Your grandmother was not an easy woman to get along with. She was in her house, with her servants, her only son. She was not ready to share. Do your remember your grandmother?"

"Yes, I visited her in her room when I was little. She showed me her treasures: gloves, postcards, prayer books."

"Good, you do have some idea of... She was a *grande dame*. From Paris, one of the best families. Jewish, originally, but Catholic for generations. She played the harp beautifully, and her embroidery was outstanding. She was always kind to me, and taught me a few stitches I'll never forget — except now my poor hands are not much use. It might have worked out if your father's wife had been more docile. Maybe. But that Odette had a mind of her own. And her manners were not... She couldn't fit in."

Odette! Was that really the woman's name? Or is mademoiselle Verdier getting her confused with my mother?

"By the time Justine was born," mademoiselle Verdier goes on, "the house was already divided in two: your grandmother had the street side of the first floor, and your father's ex-wife took the garden side. The second floor, of course, was for the children and the servants."

"What about my father?" I ask.

"Well, he had his study and offices on the ground floor, where they are now. His mother and his wife stopped coming down for meals, the maids had to carry everything up. When he had guests in the dining room, he asked one of the women, never both at the same time. It worked for a while, but eventually he had to make a choice. That's how it ended up in divorce. But it took years. You father seemed to like that woman in spite of it all. But the house was his mother's."

182

I wonder where Father slept. "Couldn't he and his wife go and live in another house?" I ask.

Mademoiselle Verdier sighs. "No, I don't think it was a possibility."

This is so much to take in, I'm glad it's time to get on my bike. I choose the long way around the stadium, where the acacia trees are covered with flowers. Their intoxicating scent competes with brisk wood and sober cement when I pass a building site: about twenty houses, white and clean above the mud. Two floors, and a bit of bare land in front of each. Windows on all sides but no glass in them yet. Slightly different from each other in size and shape, but every one of them pretty. That's where Monique and Nicole are going to move in September. I wonder which house will be theirs.

As I pedal back along the river, I try to imagine Ginette as a giddy girl. Not too hard, actually. Easier than picturing mademoiselle Verdier naked in her kitchen. But it's hard to imagine her in bed with the gardener, Achille, a small shrivelled man I've never seen without his beret!

Father is not in the office. "I think he went to the cellars," Simone says. I get on my bike again, and there he is in the yard, talking to Célestin, one of the cellarmen. Célestin goes inside, and Father comes toward me.

"How was your lesson? I'm going to La Fourcade now," he says in English. So I leave my bike in the cellar yard and take his hand. Today, I need to speak French first.

"Mademoiselle Verdier says that, before you became a wine dealer, you had a great career. What kind of career was that?"

Father shakes his head. "I worked for a few years as a commercial attaché, in three different places. All over the world, you could say. Doesn't it sound thrilling? I liked the idea of living abroad, but... it turned out, none of these places felt like abroad. The work was insipid, for me at least. There were long periods of having very little to do, and my plan was to use them in order to read and to write. I did read, and I did write. But somehow I got more and more discouraged. With my job, with what I wrote, and with myself for staying on."

Mademoiselle Verdier mentioned Japan, and I'd like to know the names of the other countries he worked in, but I don't think he wants to talk about this any more. I remember his mentioning Morocco once, but maybe he just sailed there. So mademoiselle Verdier was wrong about the brilliant career?

"Were you happy when you came back here to sell wine?" I ask as we walk along the narrow path between the sawmill and the pond.

Father slows down and, gazing at the stagnant water, rests his hand on the nape of my neck. "I was relieved, in a

184

way. I was doing what my mother wished. I no longer had to decide."

"Didn't you decide? To come back? To do what your mother wanted?"

Father stops completely, and pulls my plaits, gently, one after the other. "You're quite right. I did decide. I made a bad decision. I was disappointed with where I was, and there was an obvious place to go back to, where I was needed."

We're entering La Fourcade, where Achille is pulling up weeds under the cherry trees. He looks up, waves, and I try to see him as a lover. Maybe he didn't have that bumpy red nose when Ginette fancied him? "Good evening," Father says. Achille grunts and nods. Then he looks at me, and the right side of his mouth moves up. In a smile. Just for me. He stretches up, picks a few *guignes*, crisp wild cherries, from a high branch, and lays them in my cupped hands. "To eat, or as earrings," he says. Father takes out a list from his pocket, and they go into the shed discussing fertilizers.

What about Odette? Shall I ask Father if that was actually his first wife's name? No, I won't. Because now I'm pretty sure mademoiselle Verdier *didn't* make a mistake. That's why the first wife's name is never uttered in our house.

Confession

At the end of the week, Pélican wants news about our sacrifices. Seven of us have managed to do (or not do) as we promised. Doing appears to be easier than abstaining, especially doing one thing once. For me, it was painful, but achieved in a few minutes. I got my toys together, attached them to my bike's rear rack, and went to the smelly street, rue du Mimosa. There were at least twenty children playing outside. A woman took the boxes from me and said, "Thank you". She didn't invite me in, so what could I do? I tried not to hurry back home, but I pedalled fast enough. I was done. Noëlle put her allowance in the poor box. Whereas poor Anne-Claude couldn't completely keep away from her brothers. They came into her room on Sunday morning and tried to drag her out of her bed. What choice did she have then? She tried to play dead, but one of them tickled her while the other pulled her hair, so how could she help hitting them?

According to the level of our vows and the quality of our success, Pélican decides how many hosts our sacrifices have won us. The net outcome is, we've only earned less than half the box of a hundred hosts this week, so we have to make new vows to earn the rest. A few of the kids in Group One jabber about abstaining from rude words and doubling the usual amount of rosary decades they recite every day. Anne-

186

Claude, annoyed with her failure, comes up with "abstaining from impure thoughts," which completely stumps Pélican. I say that every morning I'll kneel in front of my altar to the Virgin for ten minutes, which is no sacrifice at all. We didn't want to cheat the first time, because what's the point of cheating if what you're going to come by is nothing anyway? But by now all we want is to get Pélican off our backs.

In the afternoon Pélican starts reading us a story about saint Marguerite-Marie Alacoque, my least favorite saint, who practically invented the Sacred Heart — without her, we wouldn't have to stand and kneel, twice a day, in front of a bland-faced Jesus, almost life-size on his low pedestal, opening his arms wide to let us admire, blazoned over his tunic, his bleeding heart, adorned with cross and thorns.

In the middle of a description of teen-age Marguerite-Marie carving the name "Jesus" into her chest, a kid from downstairs comes to call Pélican, who looks flustered and leaves the room without even saying which one of us is in charge. We can hear her shoes clattering to the bottom of the wooden stairs, and I go to the window (getting up from our seats without permission: strictly forbidden). She's walking across the yard to her house, hurrying as much as she can, which isn't much. "Let's take a look at the hosts!" I say. The babbling was getting louder as Pélican got farther from us; now the room becomes very still. I'm standing near Pélican's desk. Noëlle and Anne-Claude join me.

187

"You wouldn't dare!" Elisabeth cries from the other end of the room.

"What if we go to hell?" Maryvonne mutters.

I open the desk. There on the left is the metal box of hosts, which looks exactly like a box of biscuits. I take it out for all to see. The girls are watching me in complete silence. I start working on the tape that keeps the box shut. Anne-Claude takes the box from me and deftly pulls all the tape off. Now we can open the box. But that again is hard. Anne-Claude tries, but the lid is stuck. Noëlle finally succeeds. I remember Pélican, and move to the window: she's not in the yard. We have to watch the yard. When we hear her footsteps on the stairs, it might be too late.

There Noëlle stands, the open box of hosts in her hands. "Who wants one?" I say.

"Don't you think she's going to..." Elisabeth shivers, looking sideways at the box.

"Come on! I'm taking one anyway," I say. Anne-Claude eats one too, then Noëlle, and one by one all the girls. They're hurrying now, while I watch the yard. "Anybody for seconds?" Noëlle asks in a shaky voice. Silence. Maryvonne is coughing, as if a host got stuck in her throat.

"This isn't a mortal sin anyway," I say. "These hosts aren't consecrated. So it just comes down to disobeying the teacher. Or not even that, since she never *said* we shouldn't touch the hosts."

"We're not supposed to open her desk," Elisabeth says. "Let alone take things from it."

"Has she ever actually said so?" I ask. But I haven't been looking out. "Stop!" I say. "Here she comes!" Pélican is already in the middle of the courtyard.

Noëlle quickly puts the box back into the desk and we're all in our seats when Pélican enters the room, her wig awry, her glasses in her hand. "Where are your notebooks?" she says. But we were ordered to put our notebooks away to listen to the Alacoque story. "Take out your notebooks this minute," she croaks, "and Group One, do exercises number 4, 5 and 6, page 28 of your grammar book; Group Two, in your math book problem 6 page 57, you'll come to the blackboard in fifteen minutes; Group Three...", etc. The woman has completely forgotten about saint Marguerite-Marie.

When we sit down to dinner Loli, as usual, brings the soup tureen. Meanwhile, I notice a bowl of bigarreau cherries on the dresser. Their pale, sleek skins make me want to break the sturdy flesh, taste the juice. "May I start with these cherries?" I ask.

Mother frowns. I go on, though. "Remember, the doctor said..."

She doesn't seem to hear. Maybe I should have reminded her earlier? Every morning, since the first banana, I've had fruit for breakfast. Pear, raspberry, apricot, melon, whatever

189

Achille brought or Loli picked. Then two large slices of *gros pain* with honey. Loli keeps saying that doctor Pauli is clever, that he's practically turned me into a normal eater. But we've both kept quiet about this. Just to be on the safe side.

Mother is serving the soup.

"Doctor?" Father asks.

"Not Doctor Barral," Mother says, her eyes on the ladle. "That young man who came last time, his substitute. Tita, eat your soup before it gets cold."

"What did the doctor say?" Father asks.

Mother is eating her soup. Ignoring him. Can I say something? Or is it rude to answer a question if you're not the one who was asked? But *Mother* is being rude.

"That I should eat fruit to start every meal," I say. "For vitamins. And as an *apéritif*."

Father stands up, gets a small plate from the sideboard, and drops a handful of bigarreaux into it. "Here," he says. *Bon appétit!*

In the evening, Mother doesn't come to our room to kiss us good night. Coralie doesn't notice. She's reading *Buck John*, whose covers always feature a man wearing a cowboy hat, with a little yellow scarf around his neck and a gun in his hand. When she's finished, she strokes the cover and sighs. Her eyes are bright. "When I grow up," she says, "I'll dress like him. With a red shirt, a yellow scarf, a cowboy hat. And a star!"

"Do you know what the star means?" I ask.

"Yes! It's a sheriff's star. I'll be a sheriff!"

I'm going to tell her that there are no sheriffs in France, but I stop myself. Maybe she'll live in a country where she can be a sheriff.

I tell her a story I make up where Sophie and her cousin Paul go to America like at the end of *Les Malheurs*. There's a murder, and the sheriff needs the children's help to find the murderer. I'm in pretty deep water, as I have no idea what a sheriff is supposed to do, or what Americans are like. But Coralie falls asleep after five minutes, and I go back to *Jean Santeuil*.

Jean doesn't go to school, not because his parents are snobs like Henry Brulard's, but because he's considered too fragile. He's not shut up at home, though. "In Paris, with his legs bare to let them get tan, he stayed all day on the Champs-Elysées, sitting on a bench. Little boys invited him to play, little girls approached him, his maid threatened him, but he kept desperately silent, hiding his face against the back of the bench." This goes on until he falls in love with Marie Kossichef, "a Russian girl with long black hair, clear mocking eyes, pink cheeks, and the sparkle of health, life, joy, of which Jean was deprived." But his parents think that Jean's *surexcitation* about the girl is dangerous for his health, and they decide that he shouldn't see Marie any more, shouldn't go to the Champs-Elysées. Instead, he will have a lesson with a private teacher. Jean starts yelling, "Not go to the Champs-Elysées! Not to the Champs-Elysées! Yes, I'll go, I don't care about the teacher, if I run into him I'll kill him, that hideous monkey, I'll kill him, do you hear me?"

This is not the only time Jean becomes very angry at his "cruel" parents. He often shouts and curses in such a way that they think he might be crazy. When his father tells him that he is going to Henri-IV (a school), Jean says "I won't set foot there!" and "This is the last Latin translation I'll ever write!" But in the end he has to do what his parents want, so I wonder if all the drama is worth it. Maybe it is, though. Maybe it's better to show that you don't agree.

The next morning, when we come into the classroom, Pélican doesn't tell us to sit down, so we all remain standing as she gives us a long lecture. A terrible misdeed has been committed, and the only way for the culprits not to remain in a state of sin and risk going to hell is to confess immediately. I reflect that she shouldn't have used the word "confess", because it reminds me (and probably all of us) that we have another way of dealing with our sin: we can just tell the priest at our next confession, which is tomorrow. So even if we've committed a mortal sin (which I don't think is the case), we'll only risk hell if we die within the next twenty-four hours. And the priest couldn't tell Pélican: seal of confession.

We all keep silent, and Pélican finally tells us to sit down. But at break time she says, "I'm sorry to announce that there will be no breaks for this class until the culprit of the terrible deed I alluded to earlier has come forward. Meanwhile, all breaks will be spent in the Sacred Heart room kneeling with your rosaries".

Okay, she wins. What's the good of having everybody kneeling in front of the Sacred Heart? I'd rather do that on my own. I put up my hand.

"I did it," I say. "I'm sorry."

"You stay here," Pélican says. "Everybody go down to the yard." When the rest are gone, she makes me stand in front of her desk. I look down, of course.

"You of all girls," she says, "who should know better. Aren't you ashamed of yourself?"

"Yes, M'selle," I say. I watch her out of the corner of my eye as she sits for quite a while glowering at me. I try to imagine what she could do to me. Beatings are out. She could give me a thousand lines, but I wouldn't care. I get lines more or less every day, and I manage to do them in school mostly, between exercises. I'd hate to get so many lines that I couldn't play with my friends in the evening but, if she tried that, Father would object. So I wonder. Maybe she too is wondering. What if I got myself expelled? I'd stay at home, like Jean Santeuil and Henry Brulard. Read all day. Learn Latin with Father, and English with mademoiselle Verdier. I'd be rid of Pélican, all her works and her pomps. But I'd miss my friends!

"We are going down to the schoolyard," Pélican finally declares, "and when we get there you'll do exactly as I say."

What's going on? I was ready for the Sacred Heart, the rosary, endless detention. She must have thought up something worse.

When we get to the middle of the yard, she says, "Now you are going to get down on your knees in front of me and ask my forgiveness." The games around us have slowed, and all the girls surreptitiously look in our direction. Anne-Claude rolls her eyes and makes as if to clap. I look at the ground: yes, I can kneel. If that'll make the woman happy. But I don't feel like it right now. So I don't move. "I'm warning you," Pélican says, "you'd better comply or…" I glance at her for half a second. She's trapped. She has no "or". She's staring at me with stern eyes behind her round gold-rimmed glasses, but she's cornered herself and she knows it.

She steps towards me and tries to push my shoulders down to make me kneel, but I resist. She pushes harder. I don't kneel but keel over and fall. My left knee hits a stone and starts bleeding. Not a lot. Madame Riu, the downstairs teacher, comes up to us, takes my hand and says, "Come with me, I'll clean that, put a plaster on it." As we go to her classroom I notice that, under her dark-blue gathered blouse, her body doesn't have its usual clear shape. She bends over my knee to disinfect it, but not easily. Something's going on around her waist. Yes! I remember when this happened to Cami. Madame Riu must be pregnant. Good for her!

I don't get any lines, don't have to kneel in front of the Sacred Heart. The next day, I add to my scanty list of sins, "At school, I took unconsecrated hosts that didn't belong to me," which is the most specific sentence I've ever pronounced in confession. I go on to describe the opening and eating and inciting. The priest responds as usual, "My dear Euphémie, my little friend, you will say three Our Fathers and three Hail Marys". He absolves me in Latin, both of us making the Sign of the Cross.

Black

Everybody looks at me askance because I don't eat cheese, hate the smell of cheese, can't be near cheese. I don't know why people are so much more exercised by cheese than by the other foods I shrink from — liver, kidneys, snails, beef tongue, andouillette. Maybe it's nationalistic.

Even Father. He knows there's no hope with Camembert, but this morning as we're getting ready for a picnic, he says, "It would be so nice if you could eat a little cheese. Not the fusty kind. A bit of Emmental. Could you try? If you do, I'll give you a reward. Whatever you like. Book, toy, board game... "

Father asks nicely. Not like Maxime and his friends, who used to pursue me with chunks of fetid cheese in their hands, squealing, "Choose between eating this wedge of Brie and being scalped (whipped, strangled, drowned, burned at the stake)!" That's how I learned to run fast. Mother never tries to make me eat smelly cheese, but she sighs and shakes her head a lot. Father once told me in confidence that, as a child, he didn't like cheese either. Now he's inciting me to explore, and I feel ready to defy grisly threats to get... what? I know what. Something strange, as strange as the idea of eating Emmental.

"I'd like a black baby," I say. "Small. I saw one in the toyshop in Narbonne." Not too expensive, I think.

"Black?" Father asks.

"Yes, I already have quite a few pink dolls."

"It's a deal!" he says.

We have lunch along the canal, and nobody pays much attention to what I eat: two celery sticks and half a small melon. I'm saving my appetite for the Emmental. Father cuts me a thin slice, I stick it between two hunks of baguette, and I divide this into tiny bites. I chew them, one at a time. Swallow. Emmental is too salty but dry, tart, not soggy like cream cheese. Not too bad, actually. I don't let on, though. I keep very quiet. Only Father notices and, when I'm done, gives me a small nod and a smile.

We stop in Narbonne on the way back and visit the toy store in the rue Droite. Mother tries to make me take a blond doll, she says it'll be so much more fun, she'll help me make dresses and suits for her. What do I want with a black doll — a boy too? He won't wear any interesting clothes. But I'm adamant. Father says, "I promised".

My black baby's name is Aurèle, after Marcus Aurelius, a Roman emperor who didn't like complainers. He wrote: "Is your cucumber bitter? Throw it away. Are there brambles in your path? Turn aside. That is enough. Do not add, 'Why were such things brought into the world?'". I found it in a notebook where Etienne copies quotations.

Mother gives me a leftover ball of blue yarn to knit an outfit for Aurèle, but I don't feel like knitting, and he looks good with just his diaper, like an Infant Jesus in the crib. "You can't take him out half naked!" Mother says.

"Why not? It's blazing today."

I'll need to make him some clothes for next winter, though. I go to the dining room and look up "Africa" in the first volume of the big red Larousse encyclopedia. There I find a cross-reference to a "costumes" article, which has a full-color page on the way people dress in various parts of the world. It shows men and women of all heights, widths, skin colors, hair colors, with their clothes, ornaments and headgear. I decide that Aurèle's outfit will be a long robe, which I'll embroider around the neck with backstitch.

I look at all the men on this page and try to think which ones I'll choose when I grow up and have children. My original plan was to have four children, but now I realize that I should have more, there are so many shapes and styles of men to have them with. I'd like them to be as different as possible from each other. For the time being, I single out a few: Tuareg, Nuer, Trobriander, Khoikhoi, Samoan, Kalahari, Iroquois, Dogon... I copy the names of their countries into my notebook, and look them up in the atlas.

"What are you doing?" Grandmother asks. She's knitting in her armchair near the window. "Geography?"

Grandmother often asks me about my schoolwork, she wants to know everything. That's because she didn't go to school much. She grew up on a farm in the Jura. The school was two hours away on mountain paths that were impassable during the winter months because of the snow. Then in the spring there was a lot to do on the farm.

"Well," I say, "not exactly." And explain my project.

Grandmother shakes her head. "You should have all your children with the same man," she says. "With your husband."

"Father had his with two different women," I object.

"Two, not eight! And it's better to stay with one, if you can."

"Why?" I ask.

Grandmother sighs. "Why why why!"

"I'd like to experiment. See what kind of baby comes out of the mix, every time. And it would be fun for them, to be so different from each other."

"It isn't done," Grandmother mumbles, "and that's that."

Yes, I guess it isn't done much, and not *bonne façon* (one of Grandmother's special expressions), but why should I care? Father said I'm not going to live here anyway. Maybe I'll live in New Guinea, or in the Sahara. I could also move to a new country each time I change husbands.

And maybe I don't even need to change husbands. I could stay with the same man and just have children with various others. It's probably not *bonne façon* either, but I know it *is* done. I heard Berthe and Simone discuss the fact that Philippe Vié is not Bertrand's son. Of course he is, officially, but Estelle had a lover at the time, a blond man who was the director of the distillery, and Philippe looks like him. Philippe's older brother seems to be Bertrand's but about Mireille they weren't sure. And Simone says that she herself was conceived with a grape picker from Andalusia during the grape harvest. Her father (the legal one) was not happy at first, but he himself was fooling around at the time so there wasn't much he could say. And Simone was always his favorite. "Maybe because I'm different," she said, "with my curly hair and darker skin. And more outspoken! You don't necessarily want your children to be like you."

Intense attraction is essential if you are going to get close enough to a man to have children with him. But Justine is right: it doesn't last. I've been very attracted to several men or boys already, and it passed. At the moment there are three: Luis Mariano (whom I've seen only once and from a high box far away from the stage, but his voice is enough), Bertrand Vié, and Jordi Puch. My predilection for Bertrand is pretty obvious. Last year, I was such a baby I didn't think anything of declaring my love to him every chance I got; he laughed, kissed me, reminded me that he was too old for me and directed me to his son Philippe. I'm more sensible now. Luis Mariano is even further out of my reach, but he completely inspires me as I bicycle into the hills among the lavender and pines, alone, singing *La Belle de Cadix* at the top of my lungs. Sometimes I am the Belle de Cadix, with her languorous eyes, sometimes her disappointed lover.

Nobody knows about my penchant for Jordi Puch. It's not even a secret, it's something that cannot be told, because it's unimaginable. How can I, almost eight years old and in Group Two upstairs with all the older girls, be attracted to a younger, tinier boy who's still in the infant class? Grandmother's "It isn't done" doesn't begin to say how impossible this feeling is. But it's real. I love Jordi. He smells of trees and pine cones. His little body exudes fresh energy, the "sparkle of health" Jean Santeuil sees in Marie Kossichef. I want to touch his chestnut curls, feel their springy texture.

His father is a carpenter. Whenever I can, on my bike, I swerve into the back alley, near the bowling ground, where he has his workshop. The Puch family lives above the shop, but I don't particularly look for Jordi. What I like is that the whole width of the quiet street is covered with wood shavings. Under my tires, in the heady smell of resin, I crush the cracking wood.

Reports

July 12, last day of school, which also happens to be saint Olivier's day, i.e., our priest's name day. In the afternoon we'll celebrate with a *goûter* in the downstairs classroom, which is more than large enough for all of Sainte-Blandine's denizens.

Before we go down to the party, Pélican reminds us that, during the summer vacation, we shouldn't forget to say our prayers (at least a whole rosary every day), go to mass on Sundays (mortal sin if we don't) and take communion at least once a week, preferably twice. She also encourages us to read only the right kind of books and — her voice tight and dark — warns us about magazines. The devil is always out to entrap and confuse our souls, so we need to remember: *Coeurs Vaillants* (for boys) and *Âmes Vaillantes* (for girls) are highly recommended, but *Vaillant* is something we should avoid at all costs, as it's an organ of pagan Communist propaganda.

I'd never heard of *Vaillant*, and now I'd like to take a look at it. *Âmes Vaillantes* I've seen around, and it didn't look attractive at all — more like an organ of Girl Guide propaganda. But Pélican has already gone on to her next subject: today's celebration. We need to walk down the stairs in an orderly file and, one by one, on our way to our seats, congratulate monsieur le curé, who will be sitting in the middle of the room in front of the cold stove. We should then wait until everybody is served before starting to eat and never, never look at our neighbors' plates to check if their portion is bigger or smaller than ours.

"This is extremely important!" Pélican insists. "You should be grateful for what you are given, and never compare it with what the others get, for *that* is the beginning of Envy, one of the Seven Deadly Sins!"

Envy. I've never thought of that sin before, and I don't think I've ever envied anybody — especially not for getting a bigger piece of cake! What a funny word. Where can it come from? Latin, I guess. *Video*, "I see"? Yes, *invideo*, exactly what Pélican was describing: I look into (my neighbor's plate).

By the way, for "neighbor", i.e., the other students, Pélican used the word *compagne*, literally "someone with whom you share bread". It's the official word at Sainte-Blandine (and nowhere else, in my experience — but maybe it's normal for Catholic schools, I need to ask Justine). At the *école laïque*, and in the wider world, one says *camarade* (literally, "someone with whom you share a room"). But *camarade* is avoided at Sainte-Blandine as a godless Communist word.

Downstairs, I curtsey to the priest, who holds my hands for a few seconds. He's wearing a white cassock with gold and brown embroidery: flowers, leaves and letters. He looks benign, and tired. Everybody likes him, but I don't think he has much influence on the school. Or on anything else.

Each large, plump, crown-shaped brioche has already been cut into a dozen clearly unequal pieces. They're all capped with candied fruit, and lie on lacy paper mats, the trademark of pâtisserie Cassagnol. Anne-Claude's parents donated the Cartagène, a sweet wine they make, in which you can smell the grapes just as if they were being crushed in front of you. Cami and another mother are pouring full glasses of the golden liquid for the priest, the teachers and themselves. For us, two fingers, which they top up with water.

"What's this green thing on the brioche?" I ask Cami. "It looks like leek."

"It's angelica stem. You only eat it candied. And look at this." She shows me a pale yellow cube. "Citron. You don't eat it raw either. But candied, it's delicious."

Yes, this one smells a bit like lemon but deeper, mellower. When I put a bit of it in my mouth, though, I taste nothing but sugar. And the texture is so thick.

So I give it to Coralie with my pineapple, angelica and orange peel. Coralie loves candied fruit. She always gets some for Christmas, from her godfather. I don't even understand the *idea* of candied fruit. Why take something fresh and aromatic to turn it into these sorry, sticky relics? But the brioche itself is nice, not too sweet, with a tang of orange blossom.

When the *goûter* is over, the priest leaves after a short, grateful speech, and each teacher gathers her students at one end of the room to give them their reports, in unsealed envelopes. Pélican explains that the results of our end-of-term exams are inside, but we shouldn't look at them before we give them to our parents. Of course we'd like to know, she says, and it would be easy to take a peek, but we should resist temptation and exercise our willpower. This is what she tells us every term. For me, usually, it's easy: I mostly get top marks except for geography and conduct, and anyway my parents have never punished or even scolded their children for a bad report. When we give him a report, Father comments in a nice way. Even if she's around, Mother doesn't even look. She's proud of mine, I know, but doesn't need to go into details.

So my willpower has never been tested yet. This time, though, for us in Group Two, it's different: except for Francette (who's already twelve and a half so will have to join Group Three), our reports should tell us whether we're staying in Group Two one more year or going on to boarding school. It makes a big difference. What difference exactly, I'd like to know. And I can't, because I've never been to boarding school. I'm not at all sure I'll like Sainte-Trinité or Assomption. But I'd rather not stay put. Even if boarding school is horrible, at least it will be an adventure. I'll learn something.

We don't go back upstairs, we don't say our prayers in the Sacred Heart room, but we play in the yard until it's time to go home. When the bell rings for the last time of the school year, as each group lines up in front of the gallery, Anne-Claude whispers in my ear, "I looked at my report in the loo. I couldn't wait. I didn't do particularly well in the exams, but it says, 'Admitted to *sixième*.' What a relief! I was so afraid she'd keep me for another year."

"So you're going to boarding school in October?"

"Yes! To Assomption."

"Are you happy?" I ask.

"Sure. Noëlle too is 'admitted to sixième'. And Sabine. What about you? You *must* be! Have you looked?"

I haven't. My willpower is entrenched.

Coralie too has got her report from madame Riu. At home we find Father in his study and give him our envelopes. We wait while he opens Coralie's first, takes a look, says, "Very good, so you'll be in mademoiselle Pélican's class in October, congratulations!"

"I want to stay with madame Riu!" Coralie cries. "She's fine! I don't want to go upstairs!"

"Why?" Father asks.

"Be-cause!" Coralie wails.

"You can't stay with madame Riu anyway," I say. "She's leaving. She's having her baby in October, and next week she and her husband are moving to Montpellier." Madame Riu herself told me this yesterday. I didn't even ask, but I couldn't help looking at her waist so she laughed and explained.

"I like it downstairs!" Coralie squeals.

"But there will be a different teacher downstairs."

"Never mind! I'll be with the different teacher! I just want to stay downstairs! Please!"

Father takes her in his lap. "Don't you want to read books? Write, count?"

"I like comics!" Coralie says. "And the other books Tita can read to me! I want to stay downstairs with Jean-Luc and Jordi and Alain! There are only *girls* upstairs. I won't walk up those stairs. I won't let them carry me! I'll get my bow and arrows! Just wait!" And she runs out of the study.

Father shakes his head. "Well," he says, "she has two and a half months to get used to the idea. Let's look at your report." He opens the envelope. "Excellent!"

I'm standing in front of him, waiting, so he raises an eyebrow, and hands me the report. "Here, everything is fine."

I read. Yes, my marks are even better than usual. But I'm not "admitted to *sixième*". Is this a mistake? Did Pélican forget to write it in? But Pélican doesn't make this kind of mistake.

Why should I be kept back then? Why? Is it because I'll be eight in October, and all the girls who are going to boarding school are ten or eleven? But what am I going to do? Stay at Sainte-Blandine for two more years? In the same group?

"What's wrong, sweetheart?" Father asks. "Even your conduct is rather good, this time."

Weird, after the hosts incident. Maybe she'd already filled out the reports when it happened. But can I say something? I'll try. "Three girls in my group are admitted to *sixième*, and I'm not. It doesn't seem fair, because my marks couldn't be better except in geography and embroidery."

Father takes up my report and studies it. "I see. Do you feel ready for boarding school then? As a matter of fact, I was pretty young too when I got into *sixième*, so maybe... I'll have to talk to your teacher."

3

Brothers

Justine is still in Sussex, but our brothers have come as usual for the summer vacation. Maxime spends most of his time with his local buddies fishing, sitting outside cafés, smoking, playing cards. He's always kept his gang here, from the time he was in the infant class at Sainte-Blandine. He says he's never made such good friends in Paris.

So he's happy, even though he won't go to university because he's just failed his *bac* again, for the third time. He has a friend here who has also failed after repeating his class twice, and they keep joking about it: three years in *terminale*, they think they should get a prize for holding out so long. His friend is going into the Merchant Marine, and Maxime will take an exam for a photography school in Paris. Father asked for the syllabus, and he makes Maxime study some of it every day, but Maxime only wants to hang out with his crowd.

This morning he's trying to do a math exercise in Father's study (Father is in the tasting room). In the office next door, I'm concentrating in front of a typewriter. I have an idea for a new play, and I'm copying bits of dialogue from various notebooks and loose pages. Alas, when I look at it now, a lot of what I wrote, which seemed to work at the time, doesn't make me laugh any more. I have more work to do. What I'm happy about is Coralie's character.

Coralie wants to be a devil, more precisely *une diablesse*. Her name, I decide, will be *Diavola*. She says she's always dreamed of wearing horns. I think the idea came from Grandmother who, when Coralie talks back to her, says, "Look at your horns", sticking up her index fingers on each side of her *own* forehead. I wonder if Grandmother invented this or if it's something they do in the mountains where she grew up. I find it odd, because with this gesture *Grandmother* looks like she has horns, not Coralie. Anyway, I like Diavola. I wonder if I'll have an angel too. In a white tutu.

At the other end of the room, I overhear Simone whispering to Berthe. "Isn't it a shame, the way this Pélican woman won't let her go into *sixième*? Supposedly because she's still too young and fragile to adjust to boarding school!"

"Yes," Berthe says. "The excuse is so lame!"

Yesterday, Father looked sorry when he told me he hadn't managed to persuade Pélican. "I know it's hard to stay put when you could go forward," he said, "but it will be nice to have you with us one more year. Just one year. Mademoiselle Pélican promised me that after a year she'll have no problem with your going on to *sixième*."

I'm trying to reconcile myself to my fate. But if I'm not going to boarding school, I need to find ways of keeping *out* of Sainte-Blandine as much as possible during the next school year. Already this year I missed at least five weeks with throat and ear infections. I could completely stop eating fruit, so I'd catch more infections. And if this doesn't work, accidents are another possibility.

With my bike, for instance. I could imitate the boys who crash a lot as they try to outdo each other racing downhill on the rocky track from the top of the Mourel Pardos: no hands, or back wheel only, or feet on seat. I'd have to practice — I don't want to hurt myself badly, just enough to keep me at home.

Simone sounds so angry at Pélican, she's not whispering any more. "It's so unfair! Tita is more than able, the termagant herself gave her the best marks. Why can't she just let her go?"

"Yes," Berthe says. "Unfortunately, Pélican is the one who decides. Most likely she doesn't have enough students, so she makes up pretexts to hold on to them."

Is this at all possible? That Pélican just needs one more student in her class? Actually, it could be. In my group, three girls are leaving, and four in Group Three. This leaves five of us, and only four girls are coming up in October. Next *rentrée*, there will be nine of us upstairs instead of twelve.

Maxime comes into the office to ask Berthe for help. He's been trying and trying, but he has no idea what the math questions mean. Berthe explains and helps him find the answers. He writes everything down, then kisses her hand. "Thanks *infiniment*, Berthe. Father will be so happy with this. Goodbye now."

"Are you done?" Simone asks. "I thought you had some chemistry too."

"Oh, I'll do it later!"

"Do you think this is the way you'll pass your exam?" Simone scolds. "Working ten minutes a day?"

"Dearest Simone, please don't harass me. I won't pass this exam anyway. Exams are not for me."

"Then what will you do?"

"I'll come and work with you, of course. Aren't you looking forward to it? I feel I was born to be a wine dealer. I'll go on with photography on the side."

Simone's face becomes unusually serious. "Did you discuss this with your father?"

"Not yet," Maxime says. "And now I'm sorry to leave you, but Dominique will be waiting for me at the Conti." And he's gone, waving to us in his carefree way.

Simone is frowning as she puts away some files. "This kid has no idea," she says to Berthe. "Absolutely *no* idea. He's twenty-one, he's supposed to be an adult, and he knows *nothing*. He's just spent three years in *terminale* in this expensive school, doing nothing, and he's ready to go on doing nothing. He really thinks money grows on trees. He's a nice boy, and he isn't stupid, so what went wrong? Why doesn't his father..."

"Divorce," Berthe says. "Parents feel guilty. They want to do their best, and... Monsieur Henri is such a good man. Not strict enough, I guess. And maybe the boy's mother doesn't realise... "

"With my children," Simone says, "I'm going to be *more* than strict. They'd better do well in school, and they'd better behave. I'm not even sure I want to have children. Maybe one. And I hope it's a girl." I can hear her drumming her fingers on her desk. "I wouldn't mind having a daughter like you, Tita. You understand you're not going to work here when you grow up, don't you? You understand there's no future in this business?"

"Yes," I say. "Father makes it pretty clear."

"Why doesn't he tell your brother, then?"

"He's told him too. Many times. But Maxime likes it here. He believes that everything can stay the way it is."

"I'm glad he likes it here," Simone says. "But he'll have to make a living, that's what he'd better wise up to."

I wonder why she takes Maxime's situation so much to heart. Maybe she's thinking about Father too. Father worries about what's going to happen to all of us. Especially Maxime, at the moment. But at least there was a *reason* for Maxime to stay in *terminale* for three years: he didn't work. *I'll* be repeating a year for no reason at all.

Thinking about this makes me type more slowly. Simone comes up behind me. I'm aware of her hands on my shoulders, and her scent — mimosa. "It's okay," she says. "Don't listen to me. This is none of my business. It just baffles me that

Maxime, who's almost my age, knows so much less than *you* do."

"That's because he doesn't live here," I say. "For Justine too, this place is paradise. They can't see what's going on." But Mother, who does live here, can't see it either. Or won't.

Simone kisses my cheek. "Never mind. You just type your play, do what you need to do."

Actually, I'm not too concerned about Maxime. Why should I be? He's happy. And I think he'll manage somehow, because everybody likes him. But I wonder what's going on with Etienne. He's not acting like himself this summer. One of the reasons might be that we no longer have a tennis court.

Before the Cabarrou was sold, he used to play tennis every day, but now he and his friend Laurent Vié have to bicycle to Castelet, which is nearly an hour away. The court needs to be reserved and paid for, so they only go twice a week. Is this why Etienne spends so much time in the kitchen? He brought quite a few cookery books, and he also improvises.

At first, I thought he'd fallen for Loli. Which might have been a problem, because Loli already has a fiancé, a secret one: his name is Kamel, she met him at the dance; they've been seeing each other for quite a while. He's nineteen, he comes from Algeria, and he works for the railway. After watching Etienne for a while, though, I decided that he's not in love with her. He just likes her, and he loves to cook.

215

He's good at it too. Mother was taken aback at first, but now she compliments him. He's been asking Grandmother about recipes from the Bresse.

This afternoon, Etienne is rolling out and folding his dough on the kitchen table, rolling out and folding, in total concentration, with flour not only on his hands but on his nose, cheeks and shirt. I'm oiling a tin for him. Father, on his way from the hall, stops and watches us for a few minutes with knitted brows, and goes out through the garden, to the cellars I guess. When I'm done oiling, I wash my hands and get on my bike. I find Father in the cellar yard, checking deliveries with Alban, one of the drivers, so I take another turn around the yard. When I come back Alban is getting into the truck, and we wave as I lean my bike against the wall. Father is standing there, waiting for me to tell him what I want, but I don't know how to start.

"About Etienne," I say after a while. "He doesn't only cook. He also tidies up, cleans the pots. Everything. He doesn't make more work for Loli. And he doesn't waste anything, he's careful."

Father nods. "Good to know. And I'm glad he likes to cook. It's just... I don't think it's a good idea for him to drop out of school."

"Drop out of school? Why would he drop out of school?"

"I hope he doesn't. It's... something I'm discussing with his mother."

Adrien, Alban's brother, comes out of the cellar, so I say hello to him and get back on my bike. What does this mean? Etienne loves school. All of it. He can happily draw maps, heat up powders and solutions in test tubes, dissect frogs — he doesn't mind the smell. He just wants to learn *everything*. He always gets *félicitations*, and first prize in every subject, including sports. So what's going on? I'd like to ask him, but I don't dare. I would, if it were just about him, but his mother seems to be involved, so I don't feel I can.

But I can listen. On Sunday, Father and Bertrand take us all to the lagoon to sail. Only Coralie and Mireille stay in Cugnac with the mothers. For the first time, Philippe and I are allowed to get on a little dinghy together, just the two of us. We do pretty well for a while, but we have trouble getting back to the harbour. We make it, though. While I'm drying my hair and changing back into my dress, the Vié boys and my brothers decide to have a final race. Our fathers settle down to Cinzano Bianco and *tapas* outside the clubhouse. I go and sit nearby, under the pine trees.

Bertrand is shaking his head. "But that doesn't make any sense!"

"What she says is, if Maxime can't get his *bac*, Etienne shouldn't. There should be no difference between them. It would make for bad feeling. This is entirely in her head. Maxime never liked school, he's glad to be rid of it, whereas Etienne loves studying and is exceptionally good at it. How

217

can there be no difference! And she's persuaded Etienne that it's the right thing to do. That he should sacrifice himself for his brother! He likes cooking, so he'll go to hotel school."

"But does Etienne *want* to go to hotel school?"

"It's his mother's idea, and he's going along with it. What can I say? I asked him if he couldn't get his *bac* first and go to hotel school later. I could see that the mere question upset him. He can't go against his mother."

"Did you discuss it with her?"

"Of course. When I tried to argue for the *bac*, she said I was stingy! That I didn't want to pay for hotel school, which is very expensive, and wanted Etienne to go on to university because it costs practically nothing."

"Can't you just tell Etienne that she's wrong? Because she *is* wrong. Anybody can see that."

"Anybody but her son. And what's the use of his seeing that she's wrong if she makes him drop out anyway? As she will. So I'll just have created more of a mess." Father rubs his forehead with the back of his hand, back and forth.

"Bertrand," he says, "it's my fault. I shouldn't have agreed to her getting custody. The children were young, I didn't think of the future. I didn't realize she'd get to make all the decisions. When she said I could have them for every school vacation, I just... Why do I never think ahead?"

In the kitchen the next day Etienne is making ratatouille, and I'm his assistant again. I can't help him when he works with meat or fish (the smells), but I like ratatouille, and I think this one is going to be outstanding. First I peel the aubergines, slice them lengthwise, very thin, set all the slices side by side on four dishtowels, and sprinkle just a little coarse salt on them to draw the liquid out. In about an hour, I'll dry them with the towels. Meanwhile I'm peeling the garlic cloves. Etienne has been blanching the tomatoes. He's in the garden now, getting bay leaves and thyme. "So you want to be a cook?" I ask him when he comes back.

"Yes," he says. "I'm taking the hotel school exam in October."

"But you were contemplating math, history, philology, archaeology... you never mentioned cookery."

"That was..." Etienne considers. "That was before circumstances made it necessary that I..." He hesitates again. "I can't stay at Saint-Ignace, I can't take my *bac*, so I have to choose a métier *now*," he finally says. "And I like to cook, so..."

Why can't you stay at Saint-Ignace, I want to ask. Why can't you take your *bac*? But I know why.

"Is this what you want? Really?" I finally ask.

"It's what the situation demands."

Lourdes

Every morning before breakfast Mother listens to a fitness program in the bathroom, and she does all the exercises on a mat covered with a blue towel. Meanwhile, we're all around, brushing our teeth, shaving, getting dressed. There's ample room for all of us — the bathroom is nearly as large as our bedroom. It's also very sunny, with a view of the avenue, wide and windswept, the Café de la Gare, and the railway station's forecourt. Often, you can even see the Pyrenees in the background. This morning the radio is still on as Mother brushes her hair and rubs cream onto her face. The next program is about vacation camps for children, where you get to climb rocks, sail and row, with instructors, and without any parents around.

At the end of the morning, I catch Father alone in the tasting room and ask him if I could go to one of those camps. "Youth camps?" he says. "I heard about them during the Occupation. Pétain set them up. But they were for boys. Paramilitary, I think."

Forget it. He doesn't have a clue. I ask Mother just in case, and as usual she doesn't seem to hear. But in the afternoon as she's having tea with her friends I mention the idea again, and Cami Espeluque brightens.

"You know, I'm going to look into this," she says. "Vacation has hardly started and the girls are already complaining about being bored. I don't feel like going away this year, we'll just spend some time with my mother in the country. Fine for the twins, but Anne-Claude is always so restless there." Cami seems to remember that an acquaintance of hers from Narbonne once mentioned a camp somewhere in the Pyrenees; maybe her daughters could go, with Coralie and me. Mother says why not.

Cami soon comes up with the news: we can all go in August, for two weeks. Coralie is enthusiastic, so are Anne-Claude and her sister Sylvie. The camp takes place far away in the Pyrenees, near Lourdes, a town famous for apparitions and miracles, where millions of the crippled and sick go to drink the water or bathe in it. And get healed (or not).

On the first Monday in August, before sunrise, Cami drives the four of us, with our bags, to a place near Narbonne and leaves us in the yard of what looks like a convent, with scores of other girls who all seem to know each other. When she kisses me, I have a hard time keeping back the tears. Cami is so cute with her black curls, her big red mouth, her scent of hyacinth and peach. I want to get back in the car with her.

But here I am, and here are my friends. I look around. Coralie is climbing a statue — an angel with large worn-out wings. Anne-Claude is looking for something in her bag. Sylvie sucks her thumb, huddled against her sister. All the other girls are busy talking to each other, laughing, jumping around and making faces. No, there's one near the chapel door who doesn't seem to belong. I go over to her. She's tall, muscular, with a wide placid mouth. "Hello," I say. "I'm Tita, I come from Cugnac."

I don't know who starts it, but we shake hands like grown-ups. Her hand is big and strong. "Françoise," she says. "My mother's family is from Narbonne, but we live in Berlin. Where's Cugnac?"

Françoise doesn't know anybody here, but she knows that this place is a *patronage* or *patro*, a club her mother and aunt used to attend every Thursday when they were kids. They didn't have camps for girls back then, and her mother was envious because the boys' club went camping in the summer.

"When my mother talked about a camp," Françoise says, "I thought we'd sleep in tents. Then the nuns told us we wouldn't, and I wasn't sure I wanted to go any more. But my mother just inherited a house in Sigean, full of all kinds of stuff. My parents are busy sorting it all out, so they said I'd be better off in the mountains. We'll see!"

A nun in the middle of the yard is telling us to get in line, two by two — the bus is outside. "That's Mother Honorine, the camp leader," Françoise says. She also points out Sister Brigitte and Sister Gisèle, Mother Honorine's assistants. She met them last week when she came to register with her mother. Nothing but nuns? How are we going to sail, let alone climb rocks? Will they take off their tunics, their coifs and veils and wimples?

Sister Brigitte is busy making Coralie climb down from the angel's wing she's been riding. Coralie takes my hand to get in the bus. "Can we go home?" she asks in a small helpless voice I've never heard before. I settle her next to me, give her the latest issue of *Mickey* before shoving our bags under our seats. "I'd rather you told me a story of little girls who hide in garrets," she says. So I do, until she falls asleep in my lap.

After many hours in the bus, we stop in front of a long white house on the flank of a mountain, with a view of Lourdes far away in the valley. The nuns make us fill glass jugs with water from the sinks and carry them to the Formica tables in the refectory.

"Choose a seat and drink some water as an apéritif," Sister Brigitte says. "Lunch will be ready soon." But there's something very wrong with this water: the smell is revolting. I don't even try to bring the glass to my lips, but others do, and they all start hollering. "What's this? Horrible! Poison!"

"Shush! There's nothing to worry about," Mother Honorine barks. "We had it checked. The pipes are new, that's all. It will get better by and by." Everybody's still grumbling, but some girls let themselves be persuaded, Coralie among them.

The whole place has a dismal odour of plastic, burned coffee and dishwater. I run outside through the back door. Mountains all around. I decide I don't like mountains, not when they're this close. Their shapes: the silly folds, the pompous peaks.

An electric bell: lunch, inside. A girl they call Delphine, who looks around twelve, brings a large transparent gratin dish from the kitchen, and shovels the contents onto our plates: hard potatoes in lukewarm milk, stinky bits of veal. I'd die rather than touch any of this. Coralie, Anne-Claude and Sylvie hesitate. Françoise cuts a slice of meat, brings it to her mouth, chews for two seconds, then puts down her fork and runs to the bathroom. The other girls at our table are half-heartedly moving the food around, nibbling bread.

Françoise is back. "If the cook hasn't arrived," she says, "why didn't they just give us sandwiches?"

Sandwiches, like for a picnic? Is this something they do in Berlin?

Delphine shakes her head. "There won't be a cook. Last year and the year before, my mother came along to organize the cooking. This year she couldn't, because my grandfather broke his hip. So in the kitchen it's just Sister Bri and a local volunteer who looks terrified of her. I asked if I could help, but I was only allowed to carry the dishes."

"Why didn't they bring Sister Anne?" another girl asks.

"Sister Anne needs to stay at the convent to cook for the nuns," Delphine says. "And for the visitors. There are quite a few Spanish girls at the school who came for the summer to learn French."

Convent, *patro*, school, camp — all these words are floating dizzily around in my head, touching, separating, blending. I keep my hands in front of my nose so as not to smell the gratin. The other girls sigh and wait until Sister Gisèle, who has a soft, quavering voice and looks more tractable than the other two, comes to tell us that for once she'll make an exception because it's our first meal and we must be tired from the bus ride. As a rule, we won't get dessert until our plates are clean.

"Try to eat as much as you can," she says. "When you're done, you can go and empty your plates into the big plastic pan on the kitchen table. But remember, this... shouldn't happen again. You have to eat, because you're going to get a lot of exercise."

Dessert, in another of their long transparent dishes, smells of burnt milk. The *patro* girls call it a tart: over a hard black bottom, lumps of flour and... something watery. Coralie and Sylvie, after some shilly-shallying, scrape off as much as they can from the charred crust and actually eat a few spoonfuls of the filling. I'm not in the least hungry, but horribly thirsty, and I can't imagine what to drink. Not that water. Then Mother Honorine growls that we must all take our bags into the dormitories, put them away in the boxes by our beds, and take a nap.

A nap! I don't think I've had a nap in the last five years. Naps are for babies. Coralie and our friends are muttering, but the other girls seem to be taking this in stride. I catch sight of Sister Gisèle. "Do we *have* to take a nap?" I ask. "If we're not sleepy, can we just play quietly?" I'm trying to be diplomatic.

"You do have to take a nap," she says. "And you'll feel the need for it when we've started our activities. There will be days when we do whole-day outings, and you'll miss it. You'll see."

I doubt it. But at least this woman has a soft voice. From my bag, I take out a heavy book with a tacky cover: a woman with golden hair, half-closed eyes and glutinous lipstick on her chunky mouth; below her, a city skyline, high buildings, before a setting sun.

Yesterday I was wondering what book I'd take to camp. Mother said we were only allowed one book. We could only have in our bags what was on a list they sent her. Mother called to make sure. Her problem was that the list said only one woolen sweater, and she worried about what would happen if it got wet, or dirty. The camp leader was adamant: our bags would be checked before we got on the bus, and anything that was not on the list would be given back to the parents.

One book for two weeks! I'm definitely into grown-up books now, but I didn't feel I could steal one from Father's shelves. I was walking around the house, trying to think. In one of our attics I found, at the bottom of a heap, a thick collection of *La Petite Illustration*, but the cover looked fragile, with a corner already torn off, so I thought I'd better leave that for later. Then I wandered into Justine's room. On her desk was a book that seemed to be waiting for me. As soon as I opened it I knew I'd want to read on, even though the main character was seventeen, not seven.

Her name, Marjorie Morgenstern, is also the title of the novel. No! I can see now that the title is *Marjorie Morningstar*, the name she chooses for herself as an actress. Marjorie reminds me of Justine, but she lives in a place called New York. Last night before going to bed I looked at the globe in Father's study and found New York, a city on the other side of the Atlantic Ocean.

Last night! I was in my own bed, with only Coralie in the room, in our comfortable-smelling house, doing mostly what I liked. What madness made me want to come here? Why did I believe the words of a stranger on the radio, who was probably talking about something completely different anyway? And the net result is that not only I but my sister and my friends are exiled for two weeks in this realm of reeking water, noxious food, and preposterous naps.

The whole dorm has been whispering and tittering for quite a while. Coralie wiggles out of her bed. "Mother Ho is a witch!" she enunciates in my ear.

"Mother Ho?" I ask.

"That's what the *patro* girls call her."

"Quick, get back to your bed," I say. Mother Ho, from the other end of the dormitory, is booming, "Shush, all of you! I don't want to hear a peep!" Soon she's standing in front of my bed, a malevolent look on her tiny slat of a face. "You must sleep, not read!"

I look her straight in the eye. "Yes, Mother," I say, and set the book on my night table. *Marjorie Morningstar* is certainly not a children's book; I hope the cover won't give this away. But Mother Ho doesn't even glance in its direction. She's scrutinizing me as if I were an incongruous insect. But she's not going to spend the whole afternoon checking on us. As soon as she starts back to the door, I take up my book. I don't even wait.

The Bronx. What a strange word. It rumbles inside the mouth before hissing out. Marjorie no longer lives in the Bronx but in Manhattan, and she's very happy about this. El Dorado is the name of her building, her flat is on the seventeenth floor. Seventeenth floor! And it sounds real, I mean possible, not like a fairy tale. She's been to a dance at a place called Columbia, with young men who "live in the dormitories".

In our dormitory, the whispers are back. Coralie in the next bed is masturbating. I learned this word from Etienne last week; he said everybody does it, so I must be an exception. He also said that it's good for your health. Sylvie, her eyes on Coralie, sucks her thumb and fondles her fluffy tiger. Anne-Claude's eyes are closed. Françoise is at the other

228

end of the dorm. There are no curtains on the windows, so the room is inundated with light. I go on reading for a while. Suddenly, a lull: Mother Ho is again stalking the narrow passage between the two rows of beds. I go on with my book, and she doesn't stop.

Grotto

After our nap, time for bread and chocolate in the dining room, and tinny water flavoured with grenadine. The syrup can't overcome the foul taste, but my mouth is parched so I drink a whole glass anyway. I also have a slice of bread. The bread at least is okay, huge loaves like you find in villages.

After this, Mother Ho and her sidekick Sister Bri take us out in front of the house. They have whistles hanging from their necks. As they start wielding them, the girls jump into rows. Then, each time a nun blows her instrument, the first girl in a row turns around towards the others, shouts something and makes weird gestures, imitating maybe some animal. The rest of the row yells something back. With the next round of whistles, each row of girls, in turn, recites something in unison, with words like "faith", "obedient", "cheerful", "heart" and "Jesus".

The four of us Cugnacaises are standing against the wall with Françoise, and nobody's paying any attention to us, they're all so busy with their thrilling rites. When they've exhausted themselves shouting and moving around the place in rows and circles, they scramble down into the forest, apparently on some kind of mission. There we are, alone on the terrace, and the two nuns finally catch sight of us. "What are you doing here?" Mother Ho says. "Which is your patrol?"

"No patrol," Anne-Claude says. "We're from Cugnac."

"I'm not from Cugnac," Françoise says, "but..."

"Oh, I see. Well, just follow the rest."

Françoise dashes down the slope, leaving us to dawdle. At the bottom, she turns around. "Are you coming?" she calls. "Shall I wait for you?"

Anne-Claude and I glance towards the house: the nuns have gone in. "No, thanks!" Anne-Claude shouts back to Françoise. "Go ahead!"

We stroll down to the forest and sit on tree trunks. "Do you think these girls are Guides?" Anne-Claude asks me. "Last year I read a novel about Guides. I think it took place in England, though."

"What are Guides supposed to do?" I ask.

"I'm trying to remember. Sleep in tents? Wear uniforms? Have a totem, exchange their name for an animal's? Get badges? Play hare and hounds?"

"At least the *patro* girls don't have uniforms," I say.

"Why do they shout at each other so?" Sylvie whimpers. "They don't even sound like they're angry, but they hurt my ears."

I feel especially bad about bringing Sylvie to this place. In Cugnac, I hardly paid any attention to her. She's nearly my age, but for me she was just Anne-Claude's sister, a quiet kid in Group One. Since we came here I've been worrying about her, because she's not grown-up and sensible like Anne-

231

Claude, or energetic like Coralie. She's sweet and dreamy, unprepared for hardships.

"We'll have to blend in somehow," Anne-Claude says. "We might even need to become like them. Or pretend."

"I want to be an Indian!" Coralie cries. "In this forest! Why didn't Mother let me pack my Red Indian outfit? I'm an Indian anyway. Sylvie, you're a cowboy. Look at that branch over there! That can be your horse. Let's play!"

Anne-Claude and I say we'll be the cowboy's mother and the Indian's wife; we'll keep house here while Coralie fights Sylvie and her horse. I don't feel like moving.

Anne-Claude could remind me that this was all my idea, but she just lies down on the moss and hides her face with her arms. Her long black hair is spread out around her head, and bedecked with pine needles. "Tomorrow we're supposed to go to Lourdes," she says after a while. "There's holy water there. Maybe we can drink some! Or could it be the same as the water here? Is it the holiness that tastes so rank?"

"Then we can buy Vichy," I say. "I have some money."

"At least we'll get away from here," Anne-Claude says.

The *patro* girls are back, stumbling and puffing. It sounds like the first patrol won: they tracked down whatever booty they were supposed to find.

Anne-Claude stands up. "I guess we'd better head back to the house," she says. "Sylvie, Coralie, come on! Time for prizes and prayers!"

232

We wash our hands while the bell rings again. When we come into the refectory, we see Françoise sitting with a bunch of older girls at a table where two seats are still free. "Shall we?" Anne-Claude asks me. "No," I say. "You go, and I'll sit here with Coralie and Sylvie."

Dinner starts with soup, certainly made with the stuff we threw away at lunch, mixed with water and boiled. The potatoes have mostly melted but there are still gristly bits of veal floating in it. At our table, only two girls seriously try to eat some. The others taste it and moan. I'm trying not to breathe. Coralie looks at her soup with a wide-open mouth and furious eyes. Sister Bri comes by and says we all have to eat up what's in our plates. Sylvie says she can't, and Sister Bri gives her the usual blah-blah about hungry children in China. As if our making ourselves sick with this pig-swill could be of use to anybody, let alone Chinese kids.

The nun is gone. One of the *patro* girls takes out a plastic bag from her skirt pocket, and deftly pours her soup into it. She passes it on to the next girl, and so on. Sylvie and Coralie are grinning. I'm last: "What shall I do with it?" I whisper. The bag is half full by now. "Keep it on your thighs, with your skirt over it," Delphine says. "If your skirt isn't long enough, pass it on to Lauriane." But my skirt is long enough, and I might need the bag later.

Delphine takes the empty dish to the kitchen and brings back a pasta gratin covered with stale-smelling cheese. Everybody else looks happy with it. Lauriane, after the first forkful, says, "It's not as good as my grandmother's, but definitely better than what we get at the canteen, don't you think?" "Yes, more cheese than at Assomption," another girl says. The rest agree.

"Are you at the Assomption school?" I ask.

"Yes," they all nod. "Except for the five of you, everybody here is from Assomption. The *patro* goes with the school. On Thursdays some little girls stay at home, but most of us go to the *patro*. All the boarders anyway."

So that's it? But Assomption is where Anne-Claude's supposed to go in October! And I don't think she's aware of the connection.

"Are any of you boarders?" I ask.

"Most of us. In the nursery and elementary sections, if your parents live in town you can go home in the evening, but starting in *sixième* you have to be a boarder."

After dinner we sit on the grass outside and sing. We don't know the songs, but they're easy, and surprisingly refreshing. *Au bord de la rivière, m'allant promener*, "As I walked along the river". Maybe tomorrow we'll find a river, water we can drink, water in which to swim and forget.

In the dorm, there are no lamps apart from the night light above the door. I'm not sleepy at all and, as soon as Sister Bri leaves us, I go and sit in a bathroom stall with *Marjorie Morningstar*.

234

Marjorie is studying to become a biology teacher, but what she wants to be is an actress. Meanwhile, she goes riding in the park with boys. She seems to be enormously interested in clothes, and in making boys fall in love with her, especially boys who go to Columbia or live on the Upper West Side. Her fiancé is in the Bronx, though. There seems to be a huge difference between these neighborhoods, and I think it has to do with money, but not only.

The neighborhoods are stacked on top of each other. "Above the West Side, the older and wealthier Jewish families of the Upper East Side. Still above, the well-to-do Christian families of Park Avenue and Fifth Avenue." Is New York built on a hill? I'd need a map. And does this mean that people of different religions live in different parts of town?

Is "Jewish" the opposite of "Christian"? I know there are several religions, but I don't know anybody who isn't a Catholic or an atheist or an agnostic. I'm trying to remember my catechism: there are heretics who disagree about some tenets of Catholicism, schismatics who don't want to obey the Pope, apostates who have left the church... for another religion? And infidels! I think infidels are people who have never heard of Jesus. But the Jews have heard — they're in the Gospels.

Marjorie's mother is called Rose and when she was young she spoke Yiddish. Yiddish? In Brooklyn. I stand up, close my book, lay it on the toilet seat, stretch my arms, pronounce the exotic words a few times: Yiddish, Brooklyn, Bronx.

But I *am* sleepy now.

The next day, there's milk for breakfast, in large metal jugs, and the girls say it tastes fine. But I don't drink milk. Milk smells like the inside of someone else's body. Which it is. Still, breakfast is by far the best meal here: good bread (though it's rather hard now), okay plum jam. I try to swallow some water, but I give up, the aftertaste is so dire.

The good news is, we won't have to take a nap today. Just after breakfast, the nuns give each of us a paper bag ("your lunch") and we trudge down to Lourdes with our backpacks. The *patro* girls, in their patrols, sing loudly, and we bring up the rear, shaking our heads and giggling. We wouldn't giggle if we knew what's in store for us.

As soon as we enter the streets of Lourdes, I want to run back into the woods. Lourdes must be the ugliest place in the whole world. Every house in it is a café, a restaurant, or most likely a souvenir store. The streets are packed with people, mostly moving in herds, like us. Wheelchairs, crutches, distorted bodies and faces, but also many ordinary-looking people who don't seem particularly in need of miracles.

We are taken to the Grotto. Now we all have to hold hands in case some of us get separated from the group, the crush is so bad. We hardly get a glimpse of the Virgin in a little hole above the entrance to the Grotto before Mother

Ho leads us around and behind the rock. She looks excited. "You're going to walk the Stations of the Cross," she says. "On your knees."

It sounds like the privilege of our lives. Some older patro girls mutter that they've done it before, but we all get on our knees and start. Coralie is lucky, she's wearing trousers. But I have a flimsy cotton skirt that doesn't want to stick under my knees. Nobody looks uplifted. Anne-Claude, behind me, whispers, "Why don't the nuns do it themselves if they think it's such a treat?"

I'm thirsty. God, the sun is burning now. And I need to pee, but there are people all around us, and no public lavatory in sight. After the Way of the Cross, the nuns say we're going to a park for a picnic. The park turns out to be a bare piece of ground with one bench (for the nuns). We sit in the trodden grass, and open our paper bags: there's a sandwich in there, soaked with runny omelet. I shut the bag fast, and hide it behind me. Most girls eat a few mouthfuls and throw the rest into the garbage can. The nuns made us put water in our flasks, which I use to wash an apple I retrieve from the bottom of the paper bag, all sticky with omelet juice. After I dry it with my skirt, it's fine.

A crowd of Spaniards marches into the park, and I slip away. There's a grocery shop further up the road. I buy two bottles of Vichy water, and I ask the woman about a public lavatory. She say's there's one near the parking lot, then decides to let me use hers at the back of the shop. The water there is okay, so I drink a lot of it, and fill up my flask — I'll keep the Vichy in my backpack, for later. I'm all set now, practically happy.

When I get back to the park, Mother Ho is explaining that we're going to take a look at the souvenir stores. We're not supposed to buy anything until later, but she's sure we'll be interested in checking out the wares.

So we visit three of these emporia, with the nuns, each time, waiting for us outside. Rocks with a Virgin in the background, figurines of saint Bernadette, shells, crucifixes, shawls, brooches. When I see dolls dressed in Pyrenean costumes, I think of Eléonore's collection. I wonder if I'll get her one. I so object to the whole idea. Collections. Showcases. Junk. At least I don't have the kind of parents who would want grottoes and Bernadettes. Or any kind of souvenir. Grandmother might like something, though. But what? Everything here is so ugly. So I have two problems on my hands: Eléonore, and Grandmother. And nearly two weeks to decide. God, two weeks of this!

Waterfall

We plod back up to the camp in the heat. When we get to the forest everybody wants to rest, and the nuns agree — it must be worse for them with their long dresses, wimples, and veils. I find a bush to hide behind, take out one of my bottles of Vichy and discreetly offer it to Coralie and our friends. Anne-Claude declares that I'm a genius. "Hush," I whisper. Sylvie and Coralie kiss me, then start building something with pine cones. Anne-Claude and I are sitting against tree trunks.

"I heard that the patro is part of the Assomption school," I say. "So some of these girls are going to be in your class, I guess."

Anne-Claude looks up, startled. "Who told you that?"

I tell her about the conversation at dinner. "Delphine is going into *cinquième*, but Lauriane is your age, I think."

Anne-Claude gives a long sigh, then lies down, her head on her backpack, her yellow cardigan hiding her face. "These girls might be okay, don't you think?" I say. "In school they're not going to do the Guide stuff. Only on Thursdays."

Anne-Claude stays silent for a long time, and I hold her hand. But here is Mother Ho's whistle, followed by her screech: time to go. We stand up.

Back at camp, we're all sweaty and exhausted. I ask Sister Gisèle if I can have a shower and she says no, we're not allowed upstairs during the day.

"Why not?" I ask. She looks embarrassed.

"It's a rule. We can't have girls running all over the house. You'll wash at the basin this evening. Showers are on Saturday mornings."

Does she mean we won't shower tonight? Last night, we *did* go to bed directly after brushing our teeth. I didn't pay attention then, because everything was so strange.

"Why can't we shower every day?" I ask.

Sister Gi hesitates. "Hot water is expensive," she says.

"I can use cold water, I don't mind at all."

"You should learn to abide by the rules," the nun says. "You argue too much. Be careful, you could get into trouble with Mother Honorine."

"What kind of trouble?" I ask. I know I shouldn't, but I'm curious. How could Mother Ho make this Gehenna worse? Is she going to lock us up in a cell, beat us?

Sister Gi looks at me pensively. "You're not used to this, are you?" she finally says.

After the *goûter*, the *patro* girls get ready to line up in their patrols, run up and down, dance to the whistle. This time we sit behind the house, out of sight. There's a smell of disinfectant and turnips coming from the kitchen, but we're too discouraged to go into the woods. "This place is like *Les*

Malheurs de Sophie," Coralie says. "Mother Ho would be madame Fichini. She really likes to make girls suffer."

"And the worst thing is," Anne-Claude says, "these girls look like they're used to it. It makes you wonder. Can people get used to just anything? After a while, do you automatically line up and jump to the whistle? Are we going to like this water eventually? I mean, not *like* it, but... drink it without disgust?"

"I'm already eating some of their food," Coralie says. "I can't do without food. But it makes me sad. It's the first time I've ever eaten meals without enjoying them at all."

"Same here," Sylvie says.

Françoise, who seemed to have joined the *patro* pursuits, is now plodding towards us. "How are you?" I ask as she sits down against the wall.

She shrugs. "Fine, thank you. Actually, you were quite right to stay here. I tried. And it was okay for a while, but now they're meeting in small groups and they say I can't sit with any of them because I'm not a member."

"A member?" Anne-Claude asks.

"It isn't their fault. They have all these rules. They made a promise — it's a solemn ceremony, where you recite the law, you get a totem, whatever. They said I could become a member, but it's a whole... It takes a lot of time, months, years maybe. So here I am."

"Are you going to join?" I ask.

"No. If I could do it here, today, I would, but according to them it's completely out of the question."

"At Assomption, in October, we'll have to," Anne-Claude says.

"I'm not going to Assomption," Françoise says. "I live in Berlin. I go to the French lycée."

"Berlin!" Anne-Claude says. "The capital of Germany?"

"Used to be. Now it's more complicated, with the division... East Berlin is the capital of *East* Germany, but I live in West Berlin, in the French sector."

"Are you a boarder?" I ask.

"No, there are no boarders in our lycée. It's around the corner from our house. What I love is that we have a German-style timetable: we start earlier than here, at 7:30, but at 1 we're free. We have the whole afternoon to do what we like!"

"Amazing!" Anne-Claude says. "What do you do in the afternoon?"

"Long-distance running, swimming, chamber music — I play the cello. In winter, ice-skating..."

"You're so lucky!" Anne-Claude says. "Your school sounds like the exact opposite of... ours."

"I want to go to the lycée! I want to live in Berlin!" Coralie cries.

Françoise laughs. "You don't have to live in Berlin, there are lycées in France too. My father went to the Lycée Arago in Perpignan. He was there at the same time as Charles

242

Trenet, can you believe it? Not in the same class. Charles Trenet was older."

"Father's favorite singer!" Sylvie says.

Coralie leaps up and starts singing, *Boum! Quand notre coeur fait Boum!* She jiggles and jumps from foot to foot. *Tout avec lui dit Boum! Et c'est l'amour qui...*

The bell. As we walk towards the refectory, Anne-Claude presses my arm and sighs. "Looks like I'll have to go through the whole rigmarole then, promise-patrol-totem... Tita, pray for me."

Before bed, while we're all brushing our teeth in front of the basins, I take off my skirt, my blouse, and start soaping my shoulders. I'm not even naked, I've kept my underpants on, but the girls around me mutter, "You'd better not, careful, she's coming," and two seconds later Sister Bri is behind me. "What are your clothes doing on the floor?" she asks.

I go on lathering my arms and torso. "I didn't know where else to put them," I say.

"You shouldn't take them off until you go to bed and change into your nightgown."

"Am I supposed to wash with my clothes on?"

"You will wash in the morning," the nun says. "With your nightgown on." I turn to look at her. Again I'm staring at a nun, and I know I shouldn't, but I want to make sure she's joking. She isn't. "Tomorrow you'll wash your face and

243

neck, your hands, your feet; and you'll have a shower on Saturday."

"I can't stay all dirty until Saturday," I say. The nun gives me a tense little smile.

"Well, you'll have to, like everybody else. You shouldn't worry so much about your body. Just make sure your soul is clean."

I'm not sure my soul is so clean, but I can't stand the smell of my body. So I wait until everything's quiet in the dorm, and take *Marjorie Morningstar* to the bathroom with me. Also a towel, and soap. But I can't go to the showers — they're at the end of the passage next to the nuns' rooms. In front of a basin, I lather my whole body up, very fast, with my hands. But then, how can I rinse it? If I wet my towel, I won't be able to dry myself.

There are quite a few flannels hanging from pipes under the basins. I borrow one. When I'm done, I wash and rinse it carefully and put it back on the pipe. Perfectly dry, in my nightgown, I can go and sit in a toilet stall with Marjorie. I feel so comfortable now. I take out the scented card with which I mark my page, an ad for Roja Flore brilliantine featuring a bunch of blue, red and yellow flowers, and start reading.

Marjorie too is going to camp! In Camp Tamarack, she teaches dramatics to "twittering little girls". Like us. Except nobody here teaches us *dramatics*, which I suppose means acting. A pity. But I'm not sure Marjorie is a good instructor. She doesn't seem to pay much attention to the little girls. In fact, the novel tells us nothing about her work and practically nothing about Camp Tamarack, except that Marjorie is extremely disappointed when she realises it has a rule that forbids its counsellors from going to a place called South Wind, an "adult camp" on the other side of the lake. South Wind is what Marjorie is really interested in — the real reason she took the job at Camp Tamarack.

I wonder why adults would want to go to camp. Finally Marjorie's girlfriend who works with her at Camp Tamarack takes her to South Wind at night, secretly, on a boat. They have to go, because so much is happening there (as opposed to *nothing* at Camp Tamarack with the little girls).

There they are fascinated by a "celebrity" called Noel Airman, "a thin man in a black turtleneck sweater". I don't know what a turtleneck is exactly (I'll ask Justine), but I decide that I'll wear a black turtleneck sweater. I like the idea, and I've never had anything black. Noel Airman writes songs and holds forth about his audience, "college kids" he describes as the new leisure class, "a transient class but a solid one," living "off the sweat of parents" as callously as the French aristocracy used to exploit its peasants.

I'd never thought of this. Leisure classes. Even though most of them can't be called aristocrats, there *are* people around me who don't have to work, who don't really work, like Bertrand, or Anne-Claude's father. *Propriétaires*, who could be said to live off the sweat of peasants. And most *bourgeoises* don't work, even if their husbands and fathers do.

I'm going to work, as soon as I can. I want to study too, but I'll work at the same time. I know some children actually make money picking grapes. I'll ask Loli, and Simone. They both do the grape harvest every year. Practically everybody does, in Cugnac, except the bourgeois.

I don't want to live off the sweat of anybody. Not that my parents sweat much, now that they no longer play tennis.

The next day, first thing after breakfast, we're detailed to peel potatoes and scrape carrots. All the girls, in circles in the yard, around big pots. Delphine has a great scraping technique, which I try to imitate.

"You're good at this," I say. "How did you learn?"

"My mother showed me," she says. "I like to cook with her on Sundays. And I do quite a bit of peeling, scraping and chopping at Assomption. Because I chatter a lot in class. I can't help it, most of the lessons are so dull. When we're caught doing something bad, as a penance we're made to help."

"Don't you get lines?" I ask.

"Sometimes. But they need help in the kitchen, so their first choice is always kitchen duty. When they have enough of us in the kitchen, then they start giving lines. Which is worse, actually. The sisters in the kitchen are okay, they're

246

glad to have us. Whereas if you get lines you have to stay in the classroom during breaks, with Sister Bri staring down at you."

"Sister Bri?" I ask. "In your *school*?"

"Sure. Sister Bri is our history teacher; she also does study hall and detention."

I knew that some teachers were nuns in these boarding schools, but I imagined a different kind of nun from Sister Bri.

"Mother Ho is chief supervisor at Assomption," Delphine goes on, "and Sister Gi teaches music in the elementary section."

"What about the other teachers? Are they all nuns?"

"Practically. This year we only had one lay teacher, for biology. But the only difference is the habit. Mademoiselle Ferrand has a room in the convent, she never goes anywhere, I don't know why she isn't a nun."

Now I'm worrying not only about Anne-Claude, but about myself too. Assomption is where I'll end up in a year, if Pélican finally decides to let me go.

"What's your favorite subject?" I ask.

Delphine stops scraping. "Subject?"

"Yes, do you like math, for instance? English? Latin?"

"Oh, I see. Well, there's no Latin, no English. Only Spanish. Favorite subject, that's a strange question. Music was okay with Sister Gi, but this year our teacher was totally out of it, she played records and we just talked and read magazines. Well, at least we could relax — in the other classes we're supposed to listen. I could imagine... yes, Spanish, why not? With a different kind of teacher, I might like Spanish. But if I ever got interested in a subject, I'd be seen as a freak, even by the teachers. So better not."

"Do you mean the teachers themselves aren't too keen on their..."

"Right, what's important at Assomption is good conduct, i.e., keeping your head bowed and your mouth shut."

When we're done with the vegetables, Sister Bri and Sister Gi give us smaller pots and pans and take us down the hill at the back of the house to pick red currants in the sun. The *patro* girls look unenthusiastic but unsurprised. Coralie and Sylvie don't pick anything, they just eat. I should eat too, I rather like red currants and I've swallowed nothing in the last three days but bread, jam, and two apples. But I can't. It's too hot. I fill my pan like a robot, a nun takes it from me, empties it into a tub, brings it back. As in a dream, I go on pulling the tiny berries. My fingers are red, the sky is red. Then black.

A torrent. A waterfall. I'm burning. The cascade is an inch from me, but I can't move. I'm stuck in the desert, or is it hell? It can't be hell, because I'm all alone. Alone, with sand all around me stretching to the horizon. I am a stone statue in the middle of the Sahara. Then I am on my bed. The dorm is empty, but there's a noise in my head. Of water, waterfalls. Sister Gi comes by after a while with a glass of water. I moan when I smell it: I don't want to drink this. She tries to make me. There's water all over my face, my neck, the sheets. I won't let this into my mouth. I want my bottle, I still have a bottle in my backpack, but I can't move, and I can't speak.

She leaves, I doze, I dream of a small fast river. I can't drink because I don't have a mouth, but I can drown. When I open my eyes, small furry animals with long tails are crawling on all the beds around me. I kind of know they aren't real, but I'm not dreaming either, I'm not asleep. The other girls come and go. Anne-Claude gives me daisies and non-sparkling, non-metallic water, Coralie a drawing, Sylvie a kiss. Sister Gi brings camomile tea, and I drink some, although the stink is there, just under the gentle surface. Slowly, I start moving my toes, my fingers. Sitting up.

One afternoon, Sister Gi asks me if I want a shower. It's Saturday, she says. The next morning, I'm given a clean dress, and I go downstairs. A priest has come to celebrate mass in the chapel. He does it very fast. No singing, nothing. He must be in a hurry to get to a real church for a real mass. I take communion like the rest, although I haven't been to confession. I've never done this before. I vaguely wonder if I've committed a mortal sin since last time. I don't think so, and I don't care.

At breakfast, everybody is excited: another outing, another picnic. They went to Lourdes again while I was ill, but this time we're hiking in the opposite direction, up the mountain, to a lake. There'll be no Way of the Cross, only pleasure.

Squirrel

Again we're given our lunch in paper bags. Again we start along the paths to the strains of martial songs. But this time we're walking upwards on a steep path. Coralie and Sylvie look wan. Anne-Claude's face is sunburned. "Are you okay?" I ask her. We've been here for six days, but it feels like for ever.

"I don't know," she says. "I'm waiting for a letter from my mother. It's the only thing I'm interested in. And getting out of here. By the way, Françoise *did* get out. She asked Sister Ho if she could call her mother, and Sister Ho said impossible. But on Friday when we were in Lourdes she managed to sneak into a café, she talked to her mother, and yesterday around noon her mother came and took her away."

"Would you like to run away?" I ask. "It would be easy to run into the forest while the rest have their picnic."

She sighs. "I don't know. We'd have to take Sylvie and Coralie. Sylvie is slow. And what if we get lost? Maybe we'd better wait it out. But I can't believe we still have lives in Cugnac. In little more than a week we'll be there. And then everything will be like a normal vacation, which I hadn't realised until now is practically heaven... but in October... I'll be back with Mother Ho and Sister Bri. At first, I thought this camp was just a bout of purgatory, but it might be a foretaste of hell!"

I'd like to contradict her, give her some hope, but I have exactly the same impression. "Would you rather stay with Pélican another year, if you could?" I ask.

She shrugs. "Yes, at least I'd eat and sleep at home. But I don't have a choice. I can't stay at Sainte-Blandine for ever."

"Except if you went into Group Three."

"It would mean that I leave school in three years, don't take my *bac*, don't go to university. My parents would be so disappointed. They're so happy when I do well in school. And there's something I learned from this camp: I like my parents. I mean, of course I do, but I resented my father for driving too fast and playing more with the twins, my mother for wearing bright colors and laughing too much... You know how it is. They're not perfect. But now I can see that, with all their faults, they're kind and funny and... real! Don't you think?"

"Anne-Claude, I love your mother! I always have! But do you think Assomption will be as bad as this?"

"Worse! Here at least we have each other. We have the forest. And the air smells good, even if the water doesn't. At Assomption we'll be inside, or at best in the yard. For seven years! I just... I'd rather not think about it. Until it happens. Sometimes I just wish I could fall seriously ill at the end of September. Not tuberculosis, because you have to go to a sanatorium. Something that would keep me at home, for ever. Well, until I'm old enough to get married or work or..."

Old enough to be done with school. It was clever of you to get sunstroke. I wish I had. But I'm strong."

Yes, she is strong. And now I notice that she looks older somehow than before my little illness. "At least we're going to a lake," I say. "Swimming will be a relief. But we didn't take our swimsuits!"

"You're dreaming," Anne-Claude says. "The *patro* girls didn't even *bring* swimsuits. Those weren't on the list, remember, we had to count them with the underpants. We get to *look* at that lake, that's all we get to do. The nuns keep their clothes on, we keep our clothes on."

We all sit near the lake, take out our paper bags, and that's it. Our sandwiches are filled with the most awful-smelling dirty-looking slices of... stuff. Delphine says it's called liver sausage. The mere words! There's also a banana, but it's black and squashed, and smells almost as bad as the sausage. Coralie eats both hers and mine. I wander away around the lake and find a cascade like the one in my dream. Under the pouring water I drink, drink, drink. Then I fill up both Vichy bottles and put them back in my backpack. The Vichy water is long gone. Anne-Claude filled the bottles in Lourdes on Friday, and this morning we shared the last drops.

Anne-Claude was right. We're too tired to run away. But I can say some prayers. *Jesus, Mary, Joseph, saint Rosalie, deliver me from this place of darkness, or if you can't (I'm afraid they can't) then give me the strength to stay in a good mood and not despair, but learn from this slight (and self-inflicted) predicament, as well as from the hardships to come.*

I have a special devotion to saint Rosalie. A year ago, Aunt Caroline gave me a rosy-cheeked plastic doll, and I was wondering what to name her. I asked Father, who said "Rosalie". I knew it was a joke, he didn't really think Rosalie was a beautiful name, but I liked it. I looked it up in the Grand Larousse and found that saint Rosalie had lived near Palermo in the twelfth century.

I had no idea what Palermo was like, but I enjoyed pronouncing the name, and *Sicily*. The Larousse also said that Rosalie had been a hermit, and the Robert told me that *hermit* comes from a Greek word that means "solitary", which suited me perfectly. So I called the doll Rosalie, and I decided that saint Rosalie would be my patron saint.

After lunch, the nuns doze in the shade of a weeping willow near the lake, and most of the girls start a game. They lie down at the top of a meadow, at right angles with the slope, and let themselves roll, or push each other down. There's a lot of poking, tickling, and giggling, they seem to be having quite a good time, and I'm surprised the nuns let them. But the nuns look dazed. Maybe there was wine in their flasks. Sylvie and Coralie are building a castle near the lake, pulling up grassy soil with their hands and consolidating it with a few sticks, carrying water for the moat. Anne-Claude joins me. "Do you still want to be a nun?" she asks.

"I never wanted to be this kind of nun anyway. Maybe a contemplative nun, who does nothing all day but pray."

"Wouldn't you get bored after a while?"

"I don't think so. But I don't want to be with other nuns. I could be a hermit."

"A hermit! You'll live alone at the top of a mountain?"

"Not a mountain. I'd be near the ocean. I want to swim."

"Do hermits swim?"

"I can't see why not. Do you know what you want to be?"

Anne-Claude picks up a small pine cone, inspects it, smells it. "Not really."

"Do you think you'll live in Cugnac when you grow up?" I ask.

"Yes. Or maybe in Carcassonne. It depends on… the man I marry," Anne-Claude says, blushing.

"You could decide to go somewhere first and find a husband there," I say.

"Go where?"

A girl is throwing up at mid-slope, and Sister Gi shambles towards her. Anne-Claude notices two other girls being sick further down. A whole group near the lake are holding their bellies. Mother Ho heaves herself up. "Enough rolling in the sun, young ladies, come and rest here before we go back to the house."

That evening, I am the (more or less) healthy one, and nearly everybody else is sick, including the nuns. They say it comes from rolling down the meadow, but did the nuns roll down the meadow? Or Sylvie and Coralie? And they're all very sick, you just need to look at their faces. Green. Anne-Claude is almost all right but, as she said, she's strong. The smell in the dorm is terrible. Thank God sister Bri, who looks like a ghost tonight, staggers away as soon as we're in bed. I can go back to my stall and to *Marjorie Morningstar*.

Marjorie's father, when she's twenty, tells her that he'd like her to have as many children as possible, as soon as possible. Marjorie is an only child, I wonder why her father didn't have more children. Maybe he couldn't, or his wife? Anyway Marjorie doesn't agree with him. She's not completely against children, but she doesn't want to have them until she's thirty and ready to "retire from the human race and become a breeding machine." As if she were going to have thirty children! She also says that she doesn't want to be "just one more of the millions of human cows."

Why cows? Wolves and tigers too have children. The difference is that, if they live in the wild, their children are not taken away from them and killed for meat. Neither are human children, usually, so why the cow comparison? Maybe it means that, for Marjorie, marriage is a kind of slavery? She seems to be afraid that if she had children she wouldn't live in Manhattan but in "the suburbs". I've never been to a suburb, so I can't imagine what's so scary about them. And her parents live in Manhattan, for her the exact opposite of a suburb, so why couldn't she? She seems to be incredibly particular about neighborhoods. "Living north of Ninety-Sixth Street", even though it's still Manhattan, she considers "disqualifying".

What Marjorie wants is "to have everything in life worth having". I wonder what she means by that. When her father asks, she says, "the finest foods, the finest wines, the loveliest places, the best music, the best books, the best art." Like her father, I don't know much about all these things except for books, and I can't see how having children would automatically deprive her of them. I also wonder what she means by "the finest, the loveliest, the best". For me *Henry Brulard* is the best book in the whole world; I'm pretty sure Marjorie wouldn't want to read it, though. Anyway she doesn't seem to read books at all, ever.

Her dream: "Amounting to something. Being well known, being myself, being distinguished, being important, using all my abilities." She wants to be famous, like Noel Airman, to be looked up to. If that's what makes her happy, okay, but I can't see the attraction. What about the idea of using all her "abilities"? She feels she has a gift for acting, so she wants to act. Okay, but what she wants most is to be with Noel Airman, and then she doesn't mention any other abilities.

It makes me wonder if I have any abilities. Not for acting. My friends are clearly better at this than me. No, I can't think

257

of anything I am particularly good at. Anything *useful*, anything you can do for a living. Except typing, maybe. But I hope I'll be good at picking grapes. I love the smell of vine leaves, of ripe grapes. But this can't be my vocation — the grape harvest lasts only a few weeks.

Marjorie's father says that "the main thing is happiness." Maybe. But how do you know what will make you happy? Mother Ho likes us to suffer, I guess that makes her happy. Mother and Justine, like Marjorie, need people to adore them, to admire them, to do what they like. They think they'll be happy if men or boys find them irresistible. I'm not sure I want to be happy. What I'd like is to be free. From Pélican, from boarding school, from Father's money. But still more from... how can I explain? From needing things.

I drink some cascade water from the Vichy bottle I keep in my backpack — Anne-Claude has the other one. Then I hide under the sheets with my four scented cards.

The next day, after breakfast, we're told to stay in the refectory and write letters to our parents. I write, "Dear Parents and Grandmother, I hope you are all well. We went to Lourdes and walked the Way of the Cross on our knees. The water here has a weird taste. We are only allowed to shower on Saturdays. We miss you."

I don't say anything about the food because I don't want to sound too pathetic. *I* put myself (and the others) in this situation. Our parents are not responsible. But the shower detail might upset Mother, and the Way of the Cross, Father. They might come and get us, if it's not too much trouble.

Coralie writes, "Hi mum dad com I don want stay hir sisters ar min food disgustin I want my Red Indian soot."

Sister Bri surveys our letters. Most *patro* girls are allowed to put theirs into envelopes, but the four of us are in trouble. The nun tears up our papers and tells us to start again.

"Why?" Anne-Claude asks.

"Your parents want to read interesting news about camp," Sister Bri says.

"I don't know what else to write," Anne-Claude says.

The nun looks at her sternly. "You'll stay here until you've written an adequate letter."

So we spend the rest of the morning at our table. Sylvie tries, she thinks Sister Bri hasn't liked her handwriting, so she prints all the words, but she writes almost exactly the same as before: "Dear Mum and Dad and Jeannot and Hervé. My head hurts. We eat potatoes at every meal not like at home, burned and mushy. We have to walk on our knees. The *patro* girls play stupid games because they are Guides."

Anne-Claude and I decide not to write at all. Coralie is drawing a squirrel. There are dingy smells from the kitchen, noises of dishes being shoved into the oven. When it's time for lunch, Mother Ho comes in. She looks at Sylvie's letter, shakes her head, and goes to throw it in the garbage. When she comes back she turns to us. "Where are yours?"

"Sister Bri tore them up," Anne-Claude says.

"She told you to write better ones. Do this immediately or you'll go without lunch."

How scary!

"I can't think what else to write," Sylvie says. Mother Ho goes out and brings back a letter one of the *patro* girls wrote.

"This will give you some ideas," she says.

Anne-Claude and Sylvie start copying the *patro* girl's sentences. "My Patrol got nine points on the Weasels in yesterday's treasure hunt", "We prayed in front of the grotto where the Virgin appeared to saint Bernadette." I won't do that. I don't care what Mother Ho does to me. When she comes back, the *patro* girls have already set all the tables. "Well then," she says, "just sign your sister's letter." So I write my name under Coralie's squirrel.

Sulk

Why don't I try to call my parents? Françoise did. Maybe I'm too proud. What about Anne-Claude? I think camp is the least of her problems. There's Assomption, which she can't escape, waiting for her in October. Waiting for me in a year. We're doomed. Since there's nothing we can do, we'd better forget about it. I decide to hibernate. Mentally, which you can do even in August.

I go through the motions. Meanwhile, I stay in New York with Marjorie as much as I can. I read in the morning before the bell, I read while we're supposed to nap, and in the evening. At mealtime, prayer time, Lourdes time, not-being-allowed-to-shower time, Marjorie keeps me company in my head even though she can be pretty silly as she grows older. At least she's not *here*.

The summer after Camp Tamarack, she manages to go to South Wind, the adult camp: paradise. She acts in plays, and she's in love with Noel Airman. Marjorie's father accuses Noel of being an atheist and Marjorie says no, he believes in God. As if not believing in God would really be the limit. But how can you disapprove of someone for that? You can't help what you believe, can you? Actually, the parents also seem to object to Noel's left arm, which is crooked — another thing he can't help. The parents are so upset, they're ready to give Marjorie a lot of money so she can travel to the West Coast instead of staying at South Wind with Noel. They're very scared that Marjorie will end up having sex with Noel.

After camp she goes on seeing Noel, and they explore the city, "ride a ferry for a nickel, hugging each other to keep warm in the icy river breeze, watching the jagged line of black skyscrapers slide past in the moonlight." This makes me want to ride the ferry too, watch the skyscrapers, walk on those streets that have numbers instead of names.

The problem is, she no longer likes to kiss him. But she does kiss him all the same. I wonder why. Noel doesn't seem to be her ally any longer. "You're not an actress," he tells her, but "a good little Jewish beauty, with a gift for amateur theatricals." You can "direct all the temple plays in New Rochelle". Right after these insults, Marjorie finally decides to have sex with him, at a time when she doesn't have "the faintest desire to do it". Why do it then? After a year Noel leaves Marjorie and goes to France. Marjorie marries a man named Schwartz, a lawyer. She ends up living in Mamaroneck, near New Rochelle!

The ending feels totally hurried, as if the author had a train to catch. Or as if he didn't quite believe in what he finally does to his heroine. His conclusion is that Marjorie was wrong about herself from the beginning, that Noel was right (at least, about her). It's a bit like the comtesse de Ségur's *Quel amour d'enfant* where Giselle, when she grows up, is punished after being spoiled by her parents. Giselle's fate is dire: lousy husband, financial ruin, social disgrace.

What happens to Marjorie is that she just becomes ordinary: gives up acting, gets married, lives in the dreaded suburbs. I don't know why this should be so awful, but for her (for the Marjorie we get to know through the bulk of the novel) it's the worst possible fate.

I'm glad I took this book with me here: it helped me escape from the nuns, into a part of the world I didn't even know existed, where exotic characters worry a lot about neighborhoods, receive their degrees in costumes, are afraid to eat pork, and are obsessed with what they call success. But Herman Wouk, the author of this book, is not my kind. Like the comtesse de Ségur, and unlike Stendhal or Marcel Proust, he tries to make a point: a spoiled girl like Marjorie, who wants to do what she likes instead of what she's expected to, is misguided, and can only fail.

The camp lasts until Monday, August 19, but our parents called Mother Ho last night to tell her they'll come for us on Saturday morning on their way to Saint-Jean-de-Luz. We're all going to stay there for a week with Aunt Caroline, who has a villa on the ocean.

"We get to leave two days early, hurray!" Coralie cries.

"Yes, you're lucky," Sylvie says. "We'll have to ride all the way back with the *patro* girls." Not that we think ill of the *patro* girls. They could have flouted or even tortured us, and they haven't, at all. They've all been so busy with their Girl Guide stuff, they've mostly ignored us. I remain grateful for

263

the way they tuned us in to the plastic bag trick from the first soup. And Delphine's description of her school gave me a lot to think about. They're all right.

Our parents are supposed to arrive at eight, and breakfast is usually at eight thirty, so on Saturday Coralie and I are told to sit outside in front of the house, at the table where the nuns usually bring the vegetables to be peeled and scraped. There we are served an extraordinary meal. Someone has built a kind of tower with small crescents of butter. Three jars stand open in front of us, with a different kind of marmalade in each. And boiled eggs. And canned peaches. I nibble on a slice of bread, but Coralie looks stunned. She stares at the butter tower for a while, weeping quietly. That's when I hear our parents' car. Here they are, smiling down at us and patting us on the head, more elegant than ever, Mother in a new low-cut dress, red roses on a cream background, Father with his light-green short-sleeved shirt.

Mother Ho comes out and asks them if they want to sit down to breakfast with us. They say no thanks, they've had breakfast, they'll just wait for us. Coralie has tears all over her cheeks and chin. "What is it, my pet?" Father says, taking her in his arms.

"I think she wants to go away," I say. "We're ready."

Sister Gi brings our bags, we say goodbye, and we leave in the 402. Coralie goes on crying. Mother mutters, "What's wrong with her? Isn't she happy to see us?" Then she turns on the radio.

When we drive into Dax Father says, "Let's stop and have something to drink, shall we?" We sit outside a café in front of the church. I say I'd like grapefruit juice, but Coralie can't speak. "Chocolate ice cream?" Father asks, and she nods, sobbing louder. But when the waiter brings her three scoops in a beautiful blue dish, with two wafers on top, she quiets down and eats.

When she's done with the ice cream, the wafers, and a tall glass of water, she jumps into Father's lap and starts sucking her thumb.

"Are you all right now?" Father asks. Coralie looks up at him, then at me. She nods, closes her eyes.

Mother shrugs. "Just another fit of the sulks! And I thought camp would straighten her out."

Father watches Coralie for a while, then looks up at me. "What happened?" he asks.

How can I explain? I'd rather forget about it all. "I'm sorry I started this," I say. "It wasn't a good idea. We didn't like the camp."

Father shakes his head. "Nuns!" he says.

Rooftop

September first. We're walking to church, Mother in her green suit with grey lapels, low-heeled grey shoes, and a green-and-white contorted hat, like a winkle, with a tiny veil in front. Grandmother: black coat, black hat adorned with a feather and a token veil. Coralie and I have the same white pillbox hats above our perfect plaits, the same dark-blue pleated skirts, the same black patent-leather shoes. Only our jackets are different, because she's wearing my faded crimson one from last year. Mine is brick red.

Being dressed up makes me sad, and like a doll in Eléonore's display cabinet. For Coralie, it's worse: she needs to climb and crawl and get dirty. But she finds ways to escape. Mentally. Right now, for instance, she's telling me what she calls "a Back When story". She always starts these with, "Back when I was very little, before I was born…"

This time, she goes on, "I climbed to the top of the steeple, and then I flew from the steeple to the church roof, and with my spear I dug a hole in the roof to watch the people inside the church. They couldn't see me, but they could feel the wind. When they thought of looking up, I was gone. I was flying again, into the hills."

Because she doesn't like school and doesn't talk much to adults, people say that Coralie isn't clever. They couldn't be more wrong. Coralie is a genius at doing what she likes.

She doesn't worry about being nice and approved of. "I flew above the pine trees," she goes on, "and I shook them. Some pine cones fell down and they hit a rabbit. The rabbit looked up, and he saw me. I said, 'Sorry'. I didn't mean to hurt him. The rabbit said, 'Come and share my breakfast'. His breakfast was *pain au chocolat* and *chausson aux pommes.*"

"Stop that," Mother says to Coralie, "you shouldn't lie." Coralie looks the other way and sticks out her tongue.

"She's so little," Grandmother says, "she doesn't know the difference."

"She shouldn't lie," Mother says.

"She's not lying," I say, "she's telling me a story."

"A story?" Mother says. "She claims she did this and that. It doesn't even make sense."

"You can tell a story in the first person," I say, "and it's still a story, not a lie." I could mention *Claudine à l'école*, which I borrowed from Anne-Claude's grandmother, but better not. Claudine is in love with a young teacher at her school, who teaches the smaller girls. In love with a woman! I'm not sure Mother has even heard about women who are in love with each other. Anyway we're already walking into church.

Choirboys with their lace collars, priest going back and forth, holding up the host in the sparkling monstrance. We bow because our mortal eyes are not supposed to espy the Real Presence. I can't take communion, because to do so I'd have had to abstain from eating. Which I'm allowed to do for the early mass on my *jour de garde*, but on Sundays we go to the High Mass, at ten, and Mother doesn't want me to go that long without food. Food is what she cares about. She never takes communion. I wonder if she's even baptized. Actually, why was *I* baptized? Nobody in my family has any interest in religion.

After mass, Mother talks to her friends for a while in front of the church. While the women dissect each other's outfits, I join Coralie, Anne-Claude and Sylvie, who are admiring the window of a small bakery. "My mother is furious about the *patro* nuns," Anne-Claude says. "She wrote to the bishop, she called lots of people to warn them never to send their daughters to that camp. And I might not go to Assomption after all!"

"That's great news! But where will you go?"

"I'm not sure. Mother's calling around."

"What did you tell her?" I ask.

"Not much. But Sylvie prattled on about the water, the food, the Way of the Cross on our knees, so Mother asked why we didn't mention any of this in our letters. I explained. And that's what made her most angry: that they didn't let us write what we wanted."

Coralie and Sylvie, in front of the shop window, are trying to decide which cake they would most like today: *religieuse, millefeuille, saint-honoré*? Noëlle joins us. "I'm so glad I didn't go to Lourdes with you. These Assomption nuns sound even worse than what my neighbors tell me about Trinité."

"Sainte-Trinité?" Anne-Claude asks. "That's where Sabine's going in October! Is it that bad?"

"Well," Noëlle says, "it's supposed to be so chic and all but, according to Geneviève and her sister, quite a few of the teachers are loons, and most girls don't even take the *bac*. The only edge Trinité has over Assomption is that the school doesn't have a chapel, so the girls get to go into town. They line up in twos and walk to the church for mass three times a week. At Assomption, apparently, they never even leave the school, and their yard is pretty small. But it's closer to Cugnac, and less expensive, that's why so many people choose it. I visited both schools with my parents in July but they didn't like either so they asked around and..."

Noëlle's father is calling her, and they get in their car while we set off towards home. To cross the avenue, Mother takes Coralie's hand and Cami takes Sylvie's. I am behind them with Anne-Claude, who comes closer to me and whispers, "Do you know what's going to happen at Sainte-Blandine?" I don't. "I overheard monsieur le curé telling my father, but it's supposed to be kept secret until the *rentrée*, or more parents might back out. When the bishop received Pélican's estimates in June, he said he needed to know precisely how many students the school could count on for this October. He said that he wouldn't recruit a new teacher to replace madame Riu if there weren't nine at least in each class."

"But there *will* be nine in each class. Just. Upstairs too, thanks to me!"

"Maybe not. Elisabeth might not go back, she helped at the record store during the summer and now they've offered her a job. Pélican is trying to persuade her parents to keep her in school for another year but I don't think they will. Pélican was also thinking of putting little Roxane upstairs even though she can't read at all. But then there wouldn't be enough kids downstairs. It was touch and go, so the diocese decided last week that there will be only one class this year. Only Pélican's. If more students enroll next year, then maybe they'll appoint another teacher."

Further along the avenue, we run into Father in his car. "I'll take the girls to the cemetery," he says to Mother, and we climb into the back. I try to imagine Pélican alone with students from two to fourteen years old, six groups in the same room. It will all take place downstairs, certainly — the room upstairs would be too small. Pélican never even *looks* at the little kids. Someone who can't read doesn't exist for her. And even when you're in her class, as soon as you cut your finger or your nose bleeds, she sends you down to madame Riu. How will she manage on her own?

In the cemetery, we have several tombs. The main one is at the end of the first row, you see it as soon as you walk through the gate. It's huge, with a fat column on each side. On its front are the names of my paternal grandfather and grandmother, aunt Marta, and aunt Madeleine. There are two empty spaces still, where you could engrave the names of two more people. Who? I don't think Mother will want to be in there, she hardly ever comes with us to the cemetery. Aunt Caroline?

We tend this tombstone every Sunday. Sometimes we bring fresh flowers, or new plants, but today we just water the ones that are there, yellow freesias, small white chrysanthemums. Coralie is rubbing wet soil between her hands. I recite a *Requiem aeternam* for each of the four dead people, and a special *De profundis* for Marta. What I like about this prayer is that it speaks in the dead person's voice, trying to reach God from the depths of the tomb. *Clamavi ad te*, "I called you," I enunciate — but softly. *Exaudi vocem meam!* "Hear my voice!" But I have no idea what Marta's voice was like. Father must remember. He's standing there, his eyes closed.

We walk on to the back of the cemetery, Coralie skipping in front of us, singing *Nous n'irons plus au bois*. We have three more tombs there, all full. I don't know exactly who the people are in these tombs. Many of the men are called Auguste or Gustave, and most of the women are Clara or Marta. "Which of my names will be on my tombstone?" I ask.

Father looks startled. "You'll have to choose," he says.

271

"Which one would *you* choose?"

"I chose Euphémie when you were baptized. I needed to find a saint's name in a hurry. And now I think it rather suits you."

"So I don't need to be Lakmé at all, after I die?"

"You can decide what's on your tombstone," Father says.

"But not what's on my passport?"

"No. You can't change your legal name. At least, not easily."

"What about you? Do you like Lakmé?" I ask.

He looks embarrassed. "Your mother…" he starts, but doesn't go on. "For Coralie too the priest asked us to find a different baptismal name," he says after a while. "There's no saint Coralie. Your mother chose Christine."

When we get back in the car Father says, "I need to stop by Laget's." Laget is the blacksmith, and we all go into his shed. Father and monsieur Laget start looking at metal rods while Coralie plays with the little dog. Father nods, and shakes monsieur Laget's hand.

At home, Father warns us: "Keep away from the garden!" Through the window, we try to see what's going on. A man is digging a hole. There are metal bars on Mother's gravel.

After lunch, Father takes us into the garden. In the middle of the gravel area, between two flower beds, there's a huge contraption with a slender crossbar at the top from which hang a trapeze, two rings, and a swing. It looks homemade: the texture of the metal is rough, not like in public parks. Coralie jumps up, kisses Father, gets on the trapeze and hangs from her knees as if she's done this all her life. Mother says, "What is this?"

Father smiles. "It's for Coralie," he says, "she's such an acrobat!" He puts his hand on my neck and pushes me gently towards the swing. "I hope you'll like it too, Tita. Try." Yes, I think I'll like it too. And our friends. But Coralie! I don't think I've ever seen her so bouncy. She jumps down from the trapeze, slides her feet into the rings and swings high.

"Careful!" Mother says. She's not happy. The whole design of her garden is ruined. But she's not going to say anything. Too late.

Yes

Once a month monsieur Bonnafous, the chartered accountant, comes to Father's office for two days. He's a big man with side whiskers, and he always wears a brown suit, with a yellow shirt or sometimes a purple one. He shakes my hand in the morning and all through the day he treats me as if I were a normal occupant of the office. When he's around I keep especially quiet, because he needs to look at all the accounts, and at any time he might ask Berthe or Simone to get him this or find him that. It's a completely different atmosphere, very focused but pleasant too. He even makes a joke once in a while.

Today, when they stop for lunch, monsieur Bonnafous, putting his jacket back on, comes to look at what I'm typing. "What's this?" he asks.

"It's a play. Well, I hope it's going to be a play. For the time being, it's just a bunch of scenes we're working on. I'm trying to arrange them in some kind of order."

He takes the pages I've already typed. It's still the same comedy I started writing before camp, with Coralie as Diavola, but now it takes place in a boarding school where the girls try to stay alive, think, laugh, even though they're stuck inside a building all week and don't learn much from the teachers. At the moment we're rehearsing every afternoon, and after each rehearsal there's a lot I cut or try to improve.

"Who's the author?" monsieur Bonnafous asks.

"Tita wrote it all," Simone explains, enthusiastic as usual. "She writes all kinds of plays, she gives shows with her sister and her friends."

Monsieur Bonnafous is reading and reading. After a while, I stop typing. He frowns. "Where do you get all these ideas?" he asks.

I shrug. "In books, and..."

My main inspiration, apart from camp and what the girls told us about Assomption, is Colette's *Claudine à l'école*. But better keep quiet about it.

"She reads all the time," Berthe says. "She never stops."

"You write well," monsieur Bonnafous says. "Perfect spelling!"

At the end of the afternoon, when we're done rehearsing, our friends go home and Coralie jumps onto her trapeze. I walk around the house, which feels empty. Grandmother is away on her annual tour of brothers, sisters, older daughter and nieces, all around Lyon or in the Jura. Loli is back in her village for the grape harvest and Kamel, her fiancé, is spending his vacation with her family — he sleeps in her uncle's house and helps with the grapes. Like Loli's brother, he's a *porteur*: the pickers (women, children, older men) empty their buckets into the *hotte* he carries on his back, and when the *hotte* is full, he takes its contents to the truck. On Monday I went there with Father, because Loli needed her espadrilles, which she'd left at our house. I wanted to stay and pick grapes with them, but Father said, "Next year, maybe."

In the garden, I find Mother sitting in the sun. "What is it you're knitting?" I ask.

"Booties for Arlette's little boy. The baptism is next Tuesday."

"Can I go?"

"No. It's nothing special, just church and then lunch at the Bon Coin."

"But I'd like to see little Romain. I've only seen him once."

To this she doesn't respond.

"He's nearly five months old," I go on. "Isn't it better to baptize babies right away? Because if they die unbaptized, they'll go to limbo."

Mother chuckles. "This baby is not going to die."

As if she knew. "How old was I when I was baptized?" I ask.

Silence, for quite a while. "You were two or three weeks old," Mother finally says. "We went to stay with friends of your father's in Juan-les-Pins for a few days, and you got sick. Your father took you to the priest, who baptized you, but without a ceremony."

"Then what happened?"

"You kept vomiting a lot, and the doctor finally said we shouldn't give you milk, only vegetable broth."

"You could have baptized me yourself, you know. You didn't need to take me to the priest."

"Don't talk nonsense."

"It's true! Mademoiselle Pélican explains it to the new students every *rentrée*. In an emergency, sickness for instance, or accident, or if the parents don't want a child baptized, anybody is allowed to baptize. And it's a duty. You just throw some water on the baby, you say the words, "I baptize you in the name of the Father, the Son, and the Holy Spirit," and it does the trick. The baby will go to heaven directly. Better than limbo."

Once more, Mother remains silent. You'll never catch her admitting that she was mistaken. It isn't just because I'm a child: she's exactly the same with adults. She won't push her point either. She'll just press her lips together, and look aloof.

The next morning, in the office, Berthe asks if I want to race her new mechanical calculator: while she does her sums, subtractions and multiplications on the machine, I try to be faster without it. Sometimes she wins, sometimes I do. I'm careful not to make any noise; we just exchange glances, nods and smiles. Berthe is not quite used to this calculator yet. On the old one, she won most of the time.

At noon, monsieur Bonnafous puts on his scarf, which is beautiful, dark red with a silver border. Monsieur Bonnafous must be the largest man I've ever seen close up. His round cheeks, the layers around the center of his body make me feel comfortable. I can't imagine why Mother only likes slim people. When she meets someone, her first reaction is "fat bottom" or "thick legs". As if people were nothing but body parts, and the less there was of them, the better.

Monsieur Bonnafous looks at my calculations, then pulls my plaits, but nicely. "How old are you?" he says.

"I'll be eight on October third."

"I guess you skipped a few levels," he says. "You must be ready for Feris Delteil this *rentrée*."

Get into Feris Delteil? Instead of boarding school! It's never even crossed my mind. Feris Delteil is right here in Cugnac. But Sainte-Blandine girls never go to Feris Delteil. It's the public lycée. I thought it was only for children who've attended the *école laïque*.

"She's at Sainte-Blandine," Simone says, "where there's only one class for all the girls who can read. She listens to everything. That's why she's way ahead."

"Don't they have to take an exam for Feris Delteil?" Berthe asks.

"Yes, they do," he says. "In June. But I think there's another session in September for the children who couldn't make it to the first one. You know, sickness, accidents, new arrivals..."

278

Now my heart is beating so hard I have to breathe in, then out, a few times. "How old do you need to be?" I ask.

Monsieur Bonnafous smiles as he buttons up his coat. "Usually, it's eleven, and from the age of ten you can try. If you're younger, you need special permission, which my grandson Jacques obtained last year when he was nine," he says. "But you won't quite be eight, so I'm not sure. I'll inquire."

When he's left, Simone pulls me onto her lap and jiggles me up and down. She says, "Good for you, baby! He has lunch with the headmistress of Feris Delteil every Monday. He'll find out." Simone always knows everything. "Don't hold your breath," she goes on, "but maybe..."

"Do you really think..." Berthe says. "She's so young!"

"Young, but special!" Simone says, kissing me on both cheeks.

The next Tuesday, after lunch, Father takes his cup of coffee into his study and asks me to follow him. I sit on the scratched leather chair facing him, with his wide desk between us.

"I saw monsieur Bonnafous this morning," he says. "About Feris Delteil."

Again, my heart is racing. "Did he say I can take the exam?"

"Maybe," he says. "But... " He leans on his elbow, his hand under his cheek.

279

"Please! I've been at Sainte-Blandine for *ever*! And then, boarding school..."

He sighs. "I know. I worried about Assomption. Cami told me more than you did about the camp, and I... According to monsieur Bonnafous, Feris Delteil is quite decent, and much better than all those convents. The young woman who teaches French and Latin to his grandson lives around the corner from him. She comes from Bordeaux and has a young daughter. He says she's bright and competent."

Latin! I love monsieur Bonnafous. I love the headmistress he has lunch with. I love his neighbor the Latin teacher. I love Father. "And Simone told me it's free!" I say. "Why would you want to spend a lot of money to keep me prisoner?"

"Yes," Father says, sighing again. "And Justine didn't do so well... It's just that... nobody in our family has ever attended a state school, and..."

"In our family? Mother has! And Grandmother."

He hadn't thought of that. "Quite true," he says. "Not here, though. Here, it won't go down easily."

I'm thinking of something else. "What about Coralie?" I ask. "Please, please don't leave her with mademoiselle Pélican. Remember what she was like after the nuns, in Lourdes? Mademoiselle Pélican is *so* wrong for her! Can she go to the *école laïque*?"

Father strokes his forehead, up and down, with all his fingers. Then he looks up, resting his chin on his clasped hands. He shakes his head. "I can already see the *Dames de charité* lining up to foretell atheism and debauchery. But I might as well be hanged for a sheep..."

A sheep? But Father looks revived, as if he rather liked, after all, the idea of a fight.

"The exam is on the 16th, and the headmistress wants to see us first," he says. "Are you sure this is what you want?

"Yes," I say.

Marin

We drive to the sea in the late afternoon, when the sun is no longer hot. There are quite a few beaches to choose from, all about half an hour from Cugnac. Leucate is Mother's favorite because it's immaculate, she says, and there's a cliff that protects you from the Cers. The Cers is our north wind, dry and strong — so strong that, when it blows against you, downhill can feel like uphill. You push the pedals of your bike with all your strength and hardly manage to stay put. Mother abhors the Cers, especially at the beach, where it makes the sand fly into every nook and cranny of your clothes, towels, bags and body. She objects to our other wind too, the Marin from the southeast, because it often brings rain. I love the Marin, which is fresh, soft, and imbued with invigorating scents from the depths of the Mediterranean.

Today the Marin is blowing mildly, and we are at Gruissan, which is unlike any other beach because all the houses are made of wood and built on stilts. That's because sometimes the water comes up almost to the level of what would be the upper floor (actually, the only floor), and you need a rowboat to go from house to house. The sand here is dark, dense, slightly wet, so Mother unfolds her towel on the pier. "This beach never looks quite clean," she says, curling her upper lip. Justine, who is back from England, settles next to her. I think she'd like to run to the sea right away with

Father, Coralie and me, but she's no longer a child, so she's going to keep Mother company. We leave them behind, two ladies in their bikinis, lying on beds of flowered terrycloth to get a tan from the setting sun.

We swim out far beyond the pier, on and on, as if heading for the high seas. Once in a while, Father waits for us, floating on his back. He taught us how to swim when we were little. Before Coralie could quite walk, our brothers were already in the habit of throwing her into the water from the boat. Then they tossed her a rope to help her get back to the ladder. They stood ready to dive if she sank, but she always bounced up and chortled. They say that they did the same with me, and that I too enjoyed paddling with my little hands.

Now, as soon as we get near a body of water, the attraction is irresistible. What I like best is to drift underwater until I meet a school of fish. Then I follow them. I try to forget that my eyes sting, that I'm not one of them. Coralie wears a mask and snorkel, but I don't. In the water, I'd rather do without human equipment. I don't mind coming up once in a while to take a breath.

When Justine finally joins us, only a few rays of red light linger on the horizon. "Odette wanted to take advantage of the sun before it got too low," she explains. We swim back together to the rocks at the end of the pier. Justine has been to a swimming pool in England with her friends, and she shows us how to dive in pike position.

From the rocks, we see Mother slowly entering the sea with her arms crossed over her chest and her sunglasses on. Shivering. After a while she starts her usual breaststroke, where she keeps her head up, out of the water. She doesn't want to get her hair or her glasses wet. She never swims very far, so I don't think she'd need perfect vision to make her way back to shore, but she says she's totally helpless without her glasses. You never see her naked eyes, except when she's asleep or in the shower, and then it's only the lids.

While Mother and Justine walk back to change in the car, Coralie and I, our wet hair unbraided, follow Father to Marcérou's, a rambling café-restaurant close to the pier. There we meet Estelle and Bertrand Vié, who've just arrived. Estelle, as usual, is trim in a simple off-white dress, and nonchalant. Bertrand, as soon as he sees me, crouches to kiss me on both cheeks. "How's it going, my golden goby, how's it going, my beloved bookworm?" He has hundreds of bizarre names for me, of fish and vermin. Then he takes Coralie in his arms and bounces her up and down on his knee with an Occitan song about horses and ditches, which makes her giggle. Unlike most people, he remembers that she doesn't like to be kissed. "We should have brought the children," he says to his wife.

Estelle rolls her eyes, then waves at Mother, who is creating a small sensation as she enters the room in her splendid green and orange low-cut dress (suns and foliage), her wavy auburn air falling artistically to her shoulders. Her arm is around Justine's waist, and our sister, with her ponytail, green tartan shirt, jeans, and ballerina flats, looks, as usual, preternaturally Parisian.

The Viés and our parents discuss the menu and nod to passing acquaintances. Coralie has joined three little boys at another table. Bertrand pulls me up onto his lap. "Congratulations!" he says. I look up at him, wondering what he's talking about. "On your exam! I'm sure you'll do very well at Feris Delteil."

"Thank you," I say.

Estelle lays her hand on Father's. "I hope you noticed how quiet I kept. Isn't it a wonder? But you must have heard more than enough from our holy lady friends. You certainly gave them something to talk about."

"I do appreciate it, Estelle," Father says.

"Tita is Tita. " She shrugs. "I'm sure you know what's best for her."

At the beginning of September, Father and I met with the headmistress of the lycée, who said that I could take the exam. Noëlle and Anne-Claude were taking it too, it turned out. Anne-Claude said we'd better not tell anybody, in case we failed. But people were stopping me on the street to ask what was going on, and I couldn't lie. They didn't seem too worked up about Noëlle, but Anne-Claude's father is a pillar of the church, practically best friends with the priest, so her case was even more shocking than mine. Cami said, "Religion is all very well, but our daughters come first!"

On September 19th the results were displayed on the door of the lycée, and the next morning *L'Indépendant* ran an article about the three of us, with photos (mine was from the ballet show, worse luck!) because we were the first girls from Sainte-Blandine ever to enter Feris Delteil. The title was, "Three Young Pioneers".

After the bouillabaisse, when the orchestra begins a tango, Bertrand looks at Estelle, gesturing towards the middle of the room. She shakes her head, so Bertrand asks Mother, who stands up. An unknown young man in a black shirt whirls Justine away.

Estelle chuckles and turns to Father. "Your Justine will never be a wallflower! By the way, did you find a school for her?"

"Yes," Father says. "Next week she'll be in a new boarding school in Paris, not a Catholic one this time. They have psychologists as well as teachers, and they work with gifted children who are failing in the regular school system. Justine's tests were good, and her English helped. Let's hope it works out. I don't think we can afford any more mistakes."

"Oh well," Estelle says, "she's so pretty, she'll just marry early and you won't have to worry any more."

"Even if she gets married," Father says, "it doesn't mean she can do without an education."

"Of course," Estelle says, "a woman should be well read, know something about art, play an instrument if she can. But I hope you don't share these new ideas about girls going to university. Intellectual girls won't be very attractive to men."

Father shakes his head. "Nothing will stop girls from being attractive. And remember, my daughters won't have a dowry. They should be able to fend for themselves."

"Their husbands will provide for them!" Estelle says.

"What if they become widowed? Divorced? What if their husbands don't do well? These things happen."

Estelle shudders. "Come on, why must you imagine catastrophes?"

Mother and Bertrand are back, and Bertrand asks me this time. A cha-cha! I'm excited: I just learned this dance last week with Justine. But I'm so small next to him. When Father stands up with Coralie, I decide that Bertrand, who's much shorter than Father, is right for me. He's not so good at the cha-cha either, so I relax.

Mother dances again with Bertrand, Justine with Father, Coralie and I with the little boys. Not so little: my partner turns out to be exactly my age. Estelle is at the other end of the room talking to a bunch of blondish women covered with make-up and bright jewelry, who look like they're from Béziers. Then Coralie and the boys ask if I want to play hide and seek outside, but I'd rather go back to our table.

Bertrand and Mother are waltzing, Estelle settled in with her women friends. Father and Justine have been talking to some people at the other end of the room, and now Justine starts dancing with one of them. "A son of Emile and Bernadette Clady from Prades," Father says as he sits down next to me, "I hadn't seen them in ages." He orders a bottle of Boulou water. He looks tired.

"When I grow up," I say, "I want to work. I want to work all the time, even when I'm married. I'm not going to live on my husband's money."

Father smiles, and takes me into his lap. "I'm sure you'll be a wonderful worker," he says.

"But what kind of work shall I do?"

I've been thinking about this. I don't see myself as a saleswoman, a waitress, or a hairdresser — I'm too clumsy. Eléonore's mother is a wine dealer: she runs the office, and her husband takes care of the cellars. But I'm not going to be a wine dealer. I'd just bungle it, like Father. There's also Sabine's mother, who's a doctor at the hospital. Sabine's father is a doctor too, and our families have known each other for ever, but we seldom see them. Once I heard Mother say that it's no wonder those people live like hermits: a woman can't both work and entertain.

"You'll study," Father says, "and then you'll see what you like."

"What I like is to teach my dolls," I say. "Do you think I could be a teacher?"

288

"Certainly."

I think of mademoiselle Pélican. "How many students do you need, to make a good living?" I ask. I plan to have quite a few children, and I'll need to provide for them.

Father sits me on the table in front of him, pours water into two glasses and hands me one. "You won't be that kind of teacher," he says. "You'll live in a city, and you won't work in a Catholic school. In a lycée, maybe. You won't have to worry about numbers."

As we drive back to Cugnac in the moonlight, Justine dozes off on the towel bag. Coralie's head is in my lap; there are traces of chocolate cake on her cheeks and hair, a spot of *rouille* on the collar of her light-blue dress. She breathes slowly and once in a while makes a soft whistling noise. She too is saved from Pélican: she's signed up for the *école laïque*.

In the front seat, Mother says, "Estelle puts up such a good front. I don't know how she can bear it."

I know what "it" is. Father knows too, but he doesn't want to discuss it.

So Mother goes on. "Being left all alone while he..."

Estelle, all alone? Mother doesn't seem to know what goes on in the Vié house. Apart from her three children and four live-in servants, Estelle has friends staying with her most of the time. All kinds of friends. That's why I like her house. Last weekend there were two women from Montpellier, mother and daughter, who were excellent company. The daughter played the flute, and Estelle accompanied her on the piano. Over dinner, the mother said I should eat only what I like because "the body knows what it needs"!

"Estelle seems fine to me," Father says. "She and Bertrand have never spent much time together. She's in Béziers or Montpellier a lot, she's so keen on bridge. Whereas he loves sailing, hunting, riding, staying at L'Etang and discussing when to prune with his *ramonets*."

Mother would call the *ramonets* "overseers". She doesn't like our local words. "No problem with hunting," she says. "But this young woman! Taking her out in public!"

"This young woman" is a striking redhead, the undertaker's daughter, who's been the subject of much gossip in the last few months. People say Bertrand always had girlfriends, but he took this one to La Vieille Auberge on the Narbonne road, and to various seaside restaurants where people like my parents go. That, apparently, is not done.

Father doesn't react. Like me, he'll stand by his friends. And I don't think Mother spoke out of sympathy for Estelle. She is pleased that Father is not like Bertrand, that he doesn't have lovers, because it allows her to feel superior. Estelle is rich, but Mother is... What is she? Loved. Officially loved. And that's what she wants to be. Superior, and loved.

"Were you talking about Paris with Estelle?" Father asks.

"Yes, I'm driving to Paris with Justine on Saturday. I'll reserve that nice little hotel in Souillac, and we'll be in Paris Sunday afternoon."

"But you know I've already booked a couchette for Justine!"

"Can't you get a refund?"

"I don't know. And don't you think it would be a good idea to stay here for the *rentrée*, with both girls going to new schools? Just for a week or two? You could go to Paris later."

"I've already told Caroline that I'll be there on Sunday," Mother says. "She's got seats for Gilbert Bécaud at l'Olympia in the evening. Cami will be eaten up with jealousy when I tell her about this, she's so crazy about her Monsieur 100,000 Volts. She never goes to Paris, poor woman."

"But the girls..." Father says. "Loli won't be done with the grape harvest until the middle of October, your mother is away..."

"I'll ask Ginette to take Coralie to and from school," Mother says. "They'll be fine. Tomorrow afternoon I'll go to Narbonne and buy them everything they need for the *rentrée*."

But I already have everything I need. I have a Latin book, an English book, eight books in all for the *sixième*. No more worries. An auspicious wind has blown them all away.

On Monday, I'll get up at seven and bicycle, between the vineyards, to Feris Delteil.

TITA'S GLOSSARY

à demain to tomorrow = see you tomorrow. *Demain* comes from Latin *de mane*, "in the morning".

Âmes vaillantes valiant souls. A weekly Catholic magazine for girls, founded in 1938, nine years after *Coeurs vaillants*, "valiant hearts" a magazine for boys – in French *âme* is feminine, *coeur* masculine.

apéritif something that opens the appetite. From Latin aperire, "to open".

Arago, François a Catalan mathematician who became a Minister for Marine Affairs and Colonies in the Provisional Government of 1948. He abolished flogging in the French Navy.

Au ciel dans ma patrie in heaven, my fatherland. From a hymn about the Virgin Mary which starts with "I'll join her one day in heaven".

avant-propos foreword.

aventure what happens to someone unexpectedly; love affair. From Latin *advenire*, "to happen".

bac or baccalauréat the exam you take at the end of secondary education.

belle-mère beautiful-mother = mother-in-law or stepmother. The adjective *beau* or *belle* is used in French for all step and

293

in-law family relationships, probably in order to encourage good feelings that might not arise naturally.

biens paraphernaux the property of a married woman that she can use as she likes because it isn't part of her dowry (Greek *phernē*).

bigarreau large, juicy, firm-fleshed cherries, with partly white, partly bright-red skin. From *bigarrer*, "to give contrasting colors".

Bon appétit! Good appetite! It's polite to say this to people who are eating or getting ready to eat, whether you're sharing their food or not, whether you know them or not.

Bon Coin good corner; good spot. A very usual name in France for cafés and restaurants.

bons points a *bon point* is a small piece of cardboard with the school stamp on it, which stands for a good mark.

bouillabaisse a traditional fish stew from Marseille. From Occitan *bolha-baissa*, "boil and reduce".

Boum, Quand notre coeur fait Boum, tout avec lui dit Boum Boom, When our hearts go boom, everything around says boom, and love is on its way... That's the beginning of a very popular Charles Trenet song (from 1938) with a lot of onomatopeiae as well as depictions of everyday sounds: the clock goes *tic-tac-tic-tic*, the birds *pic-pac-pic-pic*, the broken dishes *cric-cric-crac*, the wet feet *flic-flic-flac*, etc.

Bourbons a family of kings who ruled over France, from Henri IV (1589), to Charles X (1830) with some revolutionary and napoleonic interruptions. Several European countries were governed by the same dynasty, and Bourbon kings are still on the thrones of Luxembourg and Spain.

bourgeoises feminine plural of *bourgeois*, which originally just meant "free town dweller", as opposed to aristocrat, clergy or peasant.

C'est le mois de Marie This is the month of Mary. So begins a hymn that continues "it's the most beautiful month, to the blessed Virgin, let's give a new song." May has long been linked with the Virgin. Special month-long ceremonies started in Rome in the 18th century and, through the Jesuits, spread all over Italy and France. The word *May* comes from Latin *Maius [mensis]*, "month of Maia". Maia was an Italic goddess of spring, warmth and fertility.

cabinet de toilette a small room with a washbasin and a mirror; it might also include a shower, but never a bathtub (in that case, it would be called a *salle de bain*).

Café de la Gare is the name of many French cafés that happen to be near a railway station (*gare*). Almost every town has one. A café or restaurant inside the station itself is usually called *Buffet de la Gare*.

caillou stone.

Caprices de Giselle (Les) Giselle's tantrums. A novel by the comtesse de Ségur, published in 1867. Giselle is an obnoxious six-year-old who manages to get her own way by throwing tantrums. Nobody can stand her, but her parents think she's perfect.

cartagène a *mistelle* from Languedoc. A *mistelle* is a drink made by adding grape spirit to grape juice that has just started to ferment. The fermentation is stopped, so the juice keeps its fruity sweetness. From Occitan *cartagena*, from the name of the Spanish city.

cassoulet a traditional dish of white beans and goose, from Castelnaudary in Languedoc. From Occitan *caçòla* "earthenware dish".

295

Catalonia a territory where the Catalan language is spoken, and which has been part of Spain and France at various times. The area that's now part of Spain became in 1979 a nationality, or autonomous province (capital: Barcelona), where Catalan (with Spanish and Aranese) is one of the official languages; most of the French area, also called northern Catalonia, is now part of the département of Pyrénées-Orientales.

Cers our northwestern wind. From Latin *cersium* or *cirsium*. The way Cato describes it in the 2nd century BC is beautifully accurate: *Ventus Cercius, cum loquare, buccam implet; armatum hominem, plaustrum oneratum percellit,* "When you speak, it rushes into your mouth; it knocks over an armed man, or a loaded wagon" (Origines, quoted by Aulus Gellius). In the 1st century AD, Pliny (*Natural History*) calls it "the most famous wind in the province of Narbonne, and as violent as any."

Champs-Elysées I wondered how Jean Santeuil could go and *play* on the Champs-Elysées, which is an avenue with luxury stores, crowds and cars. But Justine told me that there's another part of the avenue that has beautiful gardens. Then I remembered that *Jean Santeuil* takes place in the nineteenth century: at the time there were only horse carriages.

chou cabbage; puff pastry in the shape of a cabbage; sweet person. From Latin *caulis,* "stem".

Coeurs vaillants a French magazine for boys. Cf *Âmes Vaillantes.*

cogitatione in thought; ablative case of Latin cogitatio, from *cogito* (cum + agito), "to intend, mull over".

Confiteor A prayer starting with the words *confiteor,* "I confess".

Conti short for *Continental.* The name of many cafés and hotels in France. I have no idea why. At least in England it could mean that the place evokes mainland Europe. But in France?

coudre to sew.

Crédit Lyonnais A French bank started in Lyon in 1863.

culture physique physical exercise.

dames de charité ladies of charity. Their organization was founded in 1617 by Louise de Marillac and Vincent de Paul to help the poor and the sick.

De Profundis a prayer for the dead starting with *De profundis*, "out of the depths"; from Psalm 130.

dentelle rebrodée de ruche ruffle-embroidered lace.

département The territory of France is divided into *départements*: 96 of them. There are five more French *départements* in the West Indies, South America, and the Indian Ocean. Father and his friends all learned the alphabetical list of *départements* by heart in elementary school. At the time, there were only 89.

des enfants du commun ordinary children. Le *commun* means "the common people" as opposed to the elite.
Domus aurea, house of gold.

école laïque non-religious school, state school. In France, practically all private schools are Catholic. *Laïc* (feminine: *laïque)* means "not a priest" and also "independent from all religions".

école libre free school, a French expression for "private school", i.e., most of the time, "Catholic school". In France, before the Revolution, all schools were Catholic. Then there were various visions and projects of a totally secular education system. This never quite happened but, at various times, religious orders were forbidden to teach, or even exiled. At other times, like now, the state chose to help Catholic schools financially and control the quality of the teaching.

Ecole Polytechnique one of the most prestigious higher-education schools in France and even in the world, founded in 1794 by mathematician Gaspard Monge. It specializes in science and technology.

faillir almost do; as in *j'ai failli m'évanouir quand on m'a servi du foie de veau*, "I almost fainted when I was served calf's liver".

falloir need; must, should. Defective verb, which (like, for instance, *bruire, concerner, découler, échoir, pulluler, résulter*) can only be conjugated in the third person singular.

félicitations congratulations. From low Latin *felicitare*, "make happy".

Fillette little girl, young girl. The magazine *Fillette* was founded in 1909 by Publications Offenstadt. It features the comic series *L'Espiège Lili*, "mischievous Lili," about a girl whose parents have to go into exile; they leave her in the care of an absent-minded philosophy teacher, monsieur Minet.

Filochard one of the three cartoon characters in *Les Pieds Nickelés*, the quarrelsome one with a black patch over his right eye. Slang *filocher*, "to shirk".

Galeries Modernes a typical name for a store. Galerie comes from medieval Latin *galilaea*, "church porch".

Gallimard a publishing house founded in 1911 by André Gide, Jean Schlumberger and Gaston Gallimard under the name "Editions de la Nouvelle Revue française".
genou knee.

georgette de laine wool georgette. A sheer, lightweight woolen fabric. From a French dressmaker whose first name was Georgette.

gésir to be lying. A defective verb, used only in the present and imperfect indicative, and the present participle. On tombstones, you often see the expression *ci-gît*, "here lies".

Gilbert Bécaud French singer, composer and pianist born in 1927. Famous for "La Corrida" (1956), with lyrics by Louis Amade, "Mes Mains", "Quand tu danses" (1954), and "Le jour où la pluie viendra" (1957), with lyrics by Pierre Delanoë.

goûter a French meal taken between four and five in the afternoon. Also called *quatre-heures,* "four o'clock", it is compulsory for children, and optional for adults, who tend to call it *thé*, "tea". It usually consists in a slice of bread and a few squares of chocolate, or two slices with jam in the middle. For a birthday *goûter*, there's a cake with candles, fruit salad, and juice. From *goûter*, "to taste".

grande dame a woman admired for her moral, intellectual or artistic qualities, or her elegance.

gros pain large, long, thick bread, weighing 1 kg. It's the most usual kind of bread, especially for tartines; as opposed to more expensive varieties: *flûte* (thinner) and *baguette* (still thinner).

Henri IV a public secondary school for boys, in the Latin Quarter of Paris. Its building used to be the abbey of St Geneviève, founded in 506. Henri IV was a king of France (1553-1610), famous for saying "Paris is well worth a mass" when he converted from Protestantism to Catholicism. Also for wanting his subjects to have, on Sundays, "a chicken in every pot".

illustrés that's what we call magazines with pictures in them, and comic strips.

299

infiniment extremely. A word you mostly see after *merci*, "thank you". More pompous than *merci beaucoup*, "a lot", and seldom used by children.

innumerabilibus peccatis, et offensionibus, et negligentiis numberless sins, offenses and negligences.

Jardin des Modes garden of fashions. A monthly fashion magazine founded by Lucien Vogel in 1923.

Jean Santeuil the protagonist's name in a novel (or essay) Marcel Proust began in 1895 and didn't finish. The drafts were published in 1952, thirty years after Proust's death.

jeune fille a girl, but one who looks grown up, or nearly; my sister Justine, at 14, can be called a *jeune fille* (just) because she has shapely legs, and breasts. Two years ago, she was definitely still a *petite fille*.

jour de garde day of guard duty. Each Sainte-Blandine pupil engages to attend mass every week on a certain day in order to keep guard – over the holy tabernacle, I guess.

kermesse charity fair, bazaar. From Flemish *kerkmisse*, "church festival".

L'Indépendant a daily newspapers founded in 1846 by François Arago. It is distributed in two *départements*: Aude and Pyrénées-orientales.

La Belle de Cadix (1946) the beauty of Cadix. A popular operetta by Francis Lopez, then a film by Raymond Bernard (1953), both starring Luis Mariano.

La Petite Illustration a weekly literary journal created in 1913, which published plays, novels, stories, and some poetry. It included illustrations. All the issues in our attic are from before the war.

La Revue nautique the nautical magazine, founded in 1944.

La Semaine de Suzette, Suzette's week, a weekly magazine for girls founded in 1905. It featured *Bécassine*, the first French comic strip with a female protagonist – a young mouthless Breton housemaid in traditional costume. *Bécasse* means "woodcock"; also, "silly woman". There are quite a few feminine bird names in French with the same kind of derogatory denotation: *buse* (buzzard), *perruche* (budgerigar), *poule* (hen), *grue* (crane), *dinde* (turkey hen), *oie* (goose). Not so many for men.

Le Bon Usage the proper usage. Also called *Le Grevisse*. A unique descriptive grammar of the French language by Maurice Grevisse, first published in 1936. Grevisse, a Belgian, gives many examples and counter-examples illustrating the life of the language: evolution, regional differences, complications and inconsistencies. According to André Gide (in *Le Figaro*, February 8, 1947) "he doesn't legislate; he observes".

Le Chanteur de Mexico (1951) the singer of Mexico City. An operetta by Francis Lopez, then a film by Richard Pottier (1956), both starring Luis Mariano.

Le Midi Libre free south. A daily newspaper founded in 1944 in Montpellier. Its motto: "From the Alps to the Pyrenees, from the Auvergne to the sea".

le mois le plus beau the most beautiful month. Cf *C'est le mois de Marie*

Léonie veut aller à la fête Léonie wants to go to the party.

Les femmes sont charmantes women are charming.
Les Petites Filles modèles (1858) perfect little girls. A novel by the comtesse de Ségur.

Les Quatre Filles du docteur March (1880) Dr March's four daughters. The French title of Louisa May Alcott's *Little Women*.

Les rois qui se sont succédé sur le trône the kings who succeeded each other on the throne.

librairie Honoré Champion a bookstore (on the quai Malaquais in Paris) and publishing house founded in 1874.

Lisette an illustrated weekly magazine for girls, dedicated to stories and serialized novels. It was founded by Editions de Montsouris in 1921. *Lisette* is a girl's name, short for Elisabeth.

Luis Mariano French singer of Spanish Basque origin, born in Irun in 1914, famous for his parts in many Francis Lopez operettas and films based on them.

maman what little children usually call their mothers in France. It's okay for children (other than Coralie and me) but the trouble is, some adults go on calling their parents *maman* and *papa*. As a term of address, I'll bear with it: if someone wants to remain a baby, who am I to object? But you have to cringe when people use these words when talking to and about someone who's no longer a child. As in "poor man, his *papa* just died", or "her *maman* will come from Brittany to attend her wedding".

Marcus Aurelius (AD 121-180) was a Roman emperor and a Stoic philosopher. He wrote his thoughts in Greek while leading a long campaign against Germanic tribes. His book was later titled *Meditations*, but what he called it was *To Myself*. And he did write for himself, trying to be "free from passion" and not to busy himself "about trifling things". He died in Vienna, which at the time was called Vindobona. From Gaulish *vindo*, "white", and *bona*, "bottom".

Marin (short for *vent marin*) a southeast wind blowing on the Mediterranean coast from Perpignan to Toulon. Mild and moist, it is more frequent in autumn and in spring.

Maxence & Fils Maxence & Sons. In France, *Maxence* is a masculine first name as well as a family name.

Mickey (full name: *Le Journal de Mickey*) a French weekly magazine for children, founded in 1934 by Paul Winkler, of the Press Agency Opera Mundi. It introduced American comic strips into France.

Monsieur 100 000 Volts a nickname for singer Gilbert Bécaud, who created an electric atmosphere in French music-halls, smashing his piano to pieces while enthusiastic fans tore up their seats.

monsieur le curé the priest (term of reference); Father (term of address).

mourir to die.

mousseline de soie silk muslin. The word *mousseline*, like *muslin*, seems to derive from Mosul, a city in Iraq.

Nous Deux the two of us. A romantic magazine for women with a lot of photo-romances and some housekeeping advice. It's published by Cino del Duca (also a film producer), who launched many other magazines of the same kind, like *Intimité*, and comic strips for children.

Nous n'irons plus au bois we'll go to the woods no more. A circle game song, going on with *les lauriers sont coupés*, "the laurels have been cut".

Occitan a Romance language spoken in southern France and parts of Spain, Monaco and Italy since the Middle Ages. Its literature, starting with the troubadours, was the first to be written in a Romance language. The language is also called *provençal, languedocien*, or *langue d'oc*. Most of us, in the south, can speak it, and in villages it's the main language.

Occitania a region of southwestern Europe where Occitan was the main language until World War I. It includes the southern half of France, Monaco, and small parts of Italy and Spain.

Occupation The period of German Military Administration in France, from the armistice of June 22, 1940, (which resulted in a division of the country into an occupied zone and one administered by the Vichy government) to the liberation after the Allied landing of June 1944. From November 1942, the "Free Zone" was also occupied.

omissione by omission.

opere by action.

ouf an onomatopoeic interjection, of relief after effort, fear or discomfort. A bit like phew, except it's never about disgust; or like whew, except it can't express surprise.

Parce que c'est comme ça Because that's the way it is.

pâtisserie pastry shop. From Latin *pasta*, "paste".

patronage, or patro, youth club. From Latin *patronus*, "patron, protector", derived from *pater*, "father".

patronne feminine of *patron*. From Latin *patrona*, "women protector".

Péguy, Charles (1873-1914) French poet and essayist. His mother was a widow and a chair mender. He edited a literary magazine, *Les Cahiers de la Quinzaine*. He was a socialist. He loved the Virgin, Joan of Arc, the Beauce region, and

Orléans, where he was born. He despised money and the modern world. He died in battle in World War I.

pétanque a game where you throw hollow metal balls as close as possible to a small wooden ball called *cochonnet*, "piglet". It's played mostly in the south of France, and there are many complicated rules. From Occitan *pè tancat*, "foot rooted".

petit suisse little Swiss. A cylinder of fresh cheese about the size of a bobbin. It came from the idea of a Swiss cowherd working on a farm in Picardie.

Pétrole Hahn a petroleum-based lotion that's supposed to make your hair irresistibly shiny, and get rid of dandruff. It was invented by Charles Hahn in 1885.

Pieds Nickelés nickel-plated-feet. A comic series started by Louis Forton in the magazine *L'Épatant*. The three protagonists' feet are too heavy, or too precious, for work, so the the poor men have to become crooks.
place du marché market square.

plate Beauce flat Beauce. The Beauce is a region between Paris and Orléans, with a lot of wheat fields and the cathedral city of Chartres in the middle. Probably from pre-Latin *belsa*, "plateau".

pou louse.

promenoir standing room area in a theater, for which you can get cheap tickets. From *promener*, "walk" – originally the area was for all spectators to stretch their legs during intermission.

propriétaire owner; landowner.

propriété property; estate.

Quel amour d'enfant what a dear little child.

ramonet in parts of southern France, an overseer or foreman who looks after workers on an estate. His wife, the *ramonette*, organizes the women workers and cooks for everybody. The *ramonet* receives a yearly wage from the estate owner.

religieuse a nun; a cake consisting in a small cream puff above a larger one, with chocolate or mocha inside and on top, that's supposed to look like a nun in a habit.

rentrée return from summer vacation; beginning of the school year. It always takes place on the first of October.

Requiem aeternam eternal rest.

Ribouldingue one of the cartoon characters in *Les Pieds Nickelés*, the friendly fat one with a beard. From *ribouldinguer*, "to party", probably from franco-provençal *riboule*, "harvest festival".

roman-photo (or photo-roman) romantic story that looks like a comic strip, except it uses photos instead of drawings. From Italian *photoromanzo*. The genre was invented in Italy in 1947 and soon became very popular in France. It's part of the *presse du coeur*, "press of the heart", a derogatory expression for romance magazines.

Rosa mystica mystical rose. From Greek *mystos*, "mysterious, hidden". One of the names in the Litany of the Blessed Virgin Mary.

rossignol de mes amours nightingale of my loves.

rouille a sauce made of garlic, chili peppers, bread crumb and olive oil, eaten with bouillabaisse.

Sabaoth a Hebrew word meaning "armies". So, *Deus Sabaoth* is the God of Armies, but nobody seems quite sure whether these are the armies of Israel, the angels, the stars, or the whole universe.

saint-honoré a cake consisting of creampuffs with a lot of cream and caramel around and on top of them.

Sainte-Trinité Holy Trinity. A mystery: three persons (Father, Son, Spirit), one essence. No women or girls.

Sans Famille without family. A French novel published in 1878 by Hector Malot. Translated into English as *Nobody's Boy* by Florence Crewe-Jones in 1916.

sardana the traditional circle dance of Catalonia; the music written for the *cobla* that accompanies it. The word (probably from *Cerdà*, "inhabitant of Cerdanya") dates from the 16th century; the dance was codified in the 19th century during the Catalan Renaissance. From the beginning it was linked to republicanism, and it was repressed during the dictatorships of Primo de Rivera and Franco. Most Catalan composers have dedicated part or most of their work to the sardana. It is popular throughout Catalonia and beyond, with hundreds of groups organizing each year thousands of gatherings, festivals and competitions.

Sciences Po shortened name for *Institut d'études politiques de Paris*, "Paris Institute of Political Studies", a French school specializing in social science and international relations.

Ségur, comtesse de (1799-1874) a celebrated writer of children's fiction. On the cover of her books, she made sure that "née Rostopchine" was always added under her married name. Sophie Rostopchine was born in St Petersburg and grew up in Russia. Her family went into exile in Paris, where she married Eugène, comte de Ségur, when she was twenty. They had eight children. Sophie started writing in her fifties, for her grandchildren. Her novels are mostly dialogue, and the most interesting parts are about bad, inventive children as opposed to their nice, sensible friends. The author doesn't openly encourage bad behavior, but she describes it with gusto.

Série Noire an imprint founded in 1945 by publisher Gallimard for non-conformist crime novels and directed by translator Marcel Duhamel. It started with Peter Cheyney and James Hadley Chase, going on to Raymond Chandler, Horace McCoy, David Goodis. The first French title was Albert Simonin's *Touchez pas au grisbi*.

sixième sixth. It's the name of the first year of secondary education. In France, the last year of secondary education is called *terminale*, the last but one is *première*, and so on. Yes, we start from the end.

Soir de Paris Evening in Paris, a perfume created by Ernest Beaux in 1928 for the Bourjois brand.

sou a currency unit no longer current in France since 1947 but still remembered: older people call one franc *vingt sous*, "twenty sous" and five francs *cent sous*, "a hundred sous". From Latin *solidus*, "solid".

Stella matutina morning star.

surexcitation overexcitement.

tabernaculum tabernacle; Latin tabernaculum, "tent", from *taberna*, "hut, shop".

tartine a slice of bread covered with butter, honey, jam or another spreadable ingredient.

Touchez pas au grisbi (1953) *Don't Touch the Loot*, a novel by Albert Simonin, who also wrote the screenplay for the Jacques Becker film (1954). *Grisbi* is a slang word for "money", from the name of a coin, the *griset*, from gris, "grey", from Frankish, a Germanic language.

Trénet, Charles An extraordinary singer and songwriter, born in Narbonne in 1913. His father was a lawyer and a composer of sardanas. Trenet is sometimes called le *fou chantant*, "The singing madman", perhaps because he always sounds so happy. He tells stories about a man who's left his horse at a nightclub's cloakroom, about Canadian pharmacies where you can buy toys and ice-cream but you can't see any medications, about a garden where ducks speak English, about a missed appointment between the sun and the moon.

Turris eburnea ivory tower.

une diablesse a she-devil. From Christian Latin *diabolus*, "devil".

Vaillant: le journal the plus captivant Valiant: the most captivating magazine. A comic weekly published by the French Communist Party. From medieval Latin *valens*, "strong, energetic".

verbo in word. Ablative case of Latin *verbum*, "word, expression"

Violettes impériales (1953) Imperial Violets. A Franco-Spanish film by Richard Pottier, music by Francis Lopez, with Luis Mariano, Carmen Sevilla, and Simone Valère. It includes the song *L'Amour est un bouquet de violettes*, "Love is a bouquet of violets", where we learn that we'd better hurry to pick these little flowers before they wilt.

voiture French word for "automobile" and "horse-drawn carriage". From Latin *vectura*, "transportation".

zibeline sable. From Middle French *sabelin*.

Acknowledgements

For their generous help with various chapters and drafts of this novel, many thanks to Nicola Keegan and Laurel Zuckerman; to Reine Arcache Melvin, Laure Millet, Hannah Davis Taieb, and especially to Georgia Smith; to Mary Ellen Gallagher, Gwyneth Hughes, Dimitri Keramitas, Barry Kirwan and Christopher Vanier; to Janet Skeslien Charles; and to Linda Healey, who turned copy editing into an adventure and, for me, an education.

For encouragement and inspiration, thanks also to Pansy Maurer-Alvarez, Rose Burke, Dylan Brie Ducey, Florent Faguer, Manolita Farolan, Mathilde Fleury, Alystyre Julian, Anne Korkeakivi, Claire Lecoeur; to Julie, Boris, Léonie and Samuel Lojkine; to Alassane Ly, Ken MacKenzie, Lori Soderlind, Lesley Valdes, Evelyn Walsh, and Katharine Weber.

About the author

Marie Houzelle grew up in the south of France. Her work has appeared in the collection *Best Paris Stories* (Summertime Publications), in *Narrative Magazine, Pharos, Orbis, Serre-Feuilles, Van Gogh's Ear*, and in the chapbook *No Sex Last Noon*. "Hortense on Tuesday Night" was chosen by *Narrative Magazine* as one of the five top stories of 2011. "Belle-famille", a story in French, came out in Kindle Single in July 2013.

After Toulouse, Liverpool and Berlin, she now lives in Ivry, near Paris.

CPSIA information can be obtained at www.ICGtesting.com
Printed in the USA
LVOW11s1702040914

402457LV00007B/1082/P

9 781940 333014